**"What d[...]
about?"**

James hesitated a moment before answering, "He wants me to marry you."

She blinked a moment, as if she hadn't heard him correctly. "He what?"

"He believes I should marry you and offer the protection of my title." He took the remainder of the brandy and finished it in one swallow. "It would be quite difficult to arrest a countess."

Evangeline's disbelief transformed into dismay. "That's a terrible idea. You and I are not suited at all." But there was a faint undertone in her voice, as if she were trying to convince herself.

"I agree." Though he hated the idea of hurting her feelings, he couldn't let her build him up into the man she wanted him to be. "We both know I'll never be the right man for you."

Her eyes grew luminous with unshed tears, and she nodded. "You made that clear enough when you sailed half a world away."

"You could have any man you desire, Evangeline," he murmured. "Just choose one of them instead." He wanted her to find her own happiness with someone who could give her the life she deserved.

The very thought made his hands curl into fists. And that was the problem. Every time he tried to do the right thing and let Evie go, he kept imagining her in someone else's arms. And the idea only provoked jealousy he had no right to feel.

Author Note

When I was a teenager, I was terrified of school dances. As an introvert, I felt awkward and uneasy, and because of that, I've always rooted for the shy wallflowers in historical romances. I love transformation stories of shy young women who find their courage. Evangeline Sinclair, the heroine of *The Taming of the Countess*, becomes exactly that sort of woman. She's been in love with James Thornton, the Earl of Penford, for most of her life, and when he turns her down, it becomes the catalyst for her to stop pining and become the strong woman she was meant to be.

James has his own reasons for avoiding marriage, but when he returns from his world travels, he finds that Evie Sinclair has a reputation as the worst shrew in London—and it's his fault. He's intrigued by her spirit, and although she avoids him at every turn, he is falling hard for the woman who pushes back the shadows of his past and makes him come alive again.

To discover more of my books, subscribe to my author newsletter at: www.michellewillingham.com/contact.

THE TAMING
OF THE COUNTESS

MICHELLE WILLINGHAM

Harlequin

HISTORICAL

Harlequin®
HISTORICAL

ISBN-13: 978-1-335-54008-9

The Taming of the Countess

Copyright © 2025 by Michelle Willingham

Recycling programs for this product may not exist in your area.

 Harlequin Enterprises ULC
22 Adelaide St. West, 41st Floor
Toronto, Ontario M5H 4E3, Canada
www.Harlequin.com

Printed in U.S.A.

RITA® Award finalist and Kindle bestselling author **Michelle Willingham** has written over forty historical romances, novellas and short stories. Currently she lives in southeastern Virginia with her family and her beloved pets. When she's not writing, Michelle enjoys reading, baking and avoiding exercise at all costs. Visit her website at michellewillingham.com.

Books by Michelle Willingham

Harlequin Historical

The Legendary Warriors

Untamed Highlanders

Sons of Sigurd

Warriors of the Night

Warriors of Ireland

Visit the Author Profile page
at Harlequin.com for more titles.

To all the shy wallflowers of the world
who only want to stay home with their cats.

Chapter One

Spring, 1844

Evangeline Sinclair hated being the centre of attention. She would have much preferred staying at home with her cat instead of attending the Duchess of Worthingstone's ball. Or reading some of her favourite books on the settee. But sadly, she had no choice in the matter since the duchess was her aunt. Her mother had insisted upon a Season for her, and tonight the most eligible gentlemen in London would attend the gathering.

An anxious twist caught her stomach, even though she tried to tell herself that dozens of other young ladies would be there, including her dearest friends. It would be all right.

With any luck, *he* might be there—James Thornton, the current Viscount Melville and the future Earl of Penford.

Hopefully her future husband, if she could somehow capture his attention.

He'd certainly captured hers, for as long as she could remember. She'd known his sisters for years, and James had always been there. He was handsome and quiet, and she'd dreamed that one day, he would fall madly in love with her.

Sometimes he'd teased her when she'd been visiting Lily and Rose, which had made her adolescent heart flare. It meant he had *noticed her*. But unfortunately, James had never treated her with anything but brotherly affection.

Which was a problem. He simply didn't see her. She could only hope that it would be different tonight when she made her début.

Her mother sat across from her in the coach and squeezed her hand. 'It will be all right, Evie. Just smile and keep your shoulders straight. It's not an execution.'

'It feels like one.' Her stomach was tied up in knots, as if she were about to walk towards her impending demise. She'd never been very good in large crowds, and she couldn't imagine being anything but a wallflower. The thought of men flirting with her really did make her feel as if she were about to attend her own hanging.

'You will be fine.' Margaret continued holding her hand. 'You are a lovely young lady, and I am confident you will find dozens of suitors.'

Not the right one, Evangeline thought to herself.

She wanted so badly for this evening to go well, for Lord Melville to ask her to dance and perhaps see her as a woman.

More likely, he would treat her the same way he had during the past ten years—like his sister's best friend.

She also imagined that everyone would stare at her and probably not for the right reasons. Her heart started pounding, and her palms grew sweaty inside her gloves. More than once, she wished she didn't have to do this. She didn't want to be a débutante or follow the thousands of society rules. All she wanted was to be happily married to the viscount and have a large family with lots of babies. But she desperately feared that Lord Melville would never care for her the way she did for him.

Deep inside, Evangeline had the bone-deep fear that no one would ever see her for who she was. Whenever they looked at her, they saw only a young woman surrounded by a scandalous family and a generous dowry that couldn't quite make up for it. She was slightly plump because she had a tendency to eat cake when she was upset. Which was a bit too often for her mother's tastes. Then, too, Evangeline didn't consider herself a beauty. Her hair was entirely too dark, almost the colour of a raven. Her eyes were nice enough, a clear blue. But her pale skin made her look wretched, as if she were sickly.

Tonight, her mother had made her wear a white gown, which only made her ghostly complexion appear worse. She'd tried to make Evangeline wear diamonds, too, but at that, Evie drew the line. It was bad enough that her family was ridiculously wealthy—she didn't have to flaunt it.

'Are you all right?' Margaret asked gently. 'You look as if you're about to be sick.'

'I feel like a sacrificial virgin,' Evangeline sighed. 'I despise this dress. I look wretched in white.'

Her mother reached out to take her hand. 'You look like every young girl who is about to make her debut. You're going to be fine. Just…try not to speak your mind. For two hours at least.'

'Must I be silent?' She gripped her palms together and regarded her mother.

'Of course not. But… Evie, you tend to say whatever you are thinking. And sometimes it's not, well, quite what others want to hear.'

A hint of a smile caught her mouth. 'Are you saying I'm rude?'

'Precocious,' her mother corrected. 'If you would simply think before you speak, it would be so much easier.'

Easier for the men, her mother meant. Margaret wanted her to hide who she was and pretend to be like the rest of the sweet lambs on the marital auction block. Truthfully, Evangeline *wanted* to behave herself and be like all the others. But sometimes the words just blurted right out of her mouth like a runaway horse before she could stop them.

'I'll try.' It was the best she could do, and her mother reached out to squeeze her hand in support.

The carriage pulled to a stop in front of the ducal residence. Evangeline paused to watch the guests arriving in silks and satins. In many ways, she was grateful to have her debut at her aunt's ball. She would be among family during the most terrifying moment of her life. And although she wasn't the blue-blooded daughter of a nobleman, her aunt would never let anyone speak a word against her. Evangeline had visited the house so many times, she knew every room. Which meant there were many places to hide if this night turned out to be as miserable as she thought it might be.

'Are you ready?' her mother asked. 'You do look lovely, Evie.'

'No, I'm not ready,' she answered. 'But I don't suppose I'll ever be.' Her stomach was still lurching, and she clenched her skirts, hoping she could somehow find her confidence.

'You might find the husband of your dreams,' Margaret murmured. 'I believe you will.'

She thought it more likely that she'd find a fortune hunter but didn't say so. Her mother was so hopeful on her behalf, but Evie didn't want to ruin Margaret's wishes.

They entered her aunt's house, where they were announced by a footman. Though Evangeline had visited Aunt Victoria during balls in the past, this was her first time as a true guest. She knew her mother and aunt had undoubtedly concocted a list of suitors for her, but she didn't want their help. At least, not tonight. She'd never told them about her feelings for James Thornton out of fear of their meddling.

As she passed a group of people, she saw the familiar, knowing smirks. Margaret's posture stiffened, and she raised her chin and smiled. 'Ignore them, Evangeline.'

Although her mother and father had built an empire of wealth, most of society looked down on them because her father was a Highlander who possessed no title. Her mother helped him manage a business, and most regarded them as being of the merchant class. It didn't seem to matter that Evie's grandfather had been a baron or that her aunts had married well. She and her parents weren't invited to most of the gatherings except those hosted by family.

But Evie firmly believed that if a man avoided her because of her father's lack of a title or because of their family's business, then he wasn't the sort of husband she wanted.

She brightened when she saw that the husband she *did* want was standing on the other side of the room.

'Excuse me, Mother. I see Lily.' She hurried towards her best friend, and her heartbeat quickened at the sight of Viscount Melville, who stood beside his sister. Dear Lord, the man was magnificent. His brown hair had a hint of red, and his green eyes were the colour of spring leaves. He was tall, strong, and there was a restless spirit about him, as if he were caged in society. He reminded her of a wild animal, pacing behind invisible bars.

She understood that feeling all too well, even if her prison was formed of silks and ribbons.

'Evie! I'm so glad you're here.' Lily smiled at the sight of her and beamed. Her best friend wore a light blue gown trimmed with cream lace, while her older sister, Rose, wore a mauve gown.

Though Rose had made her debut earlier, she had not yet settled on a husband. Lily, on the other hand, was deeply in love with the Earl of Arnsbury. Evie was quite confident that Lily would marry the man someday. They made a striking pair, and it warmed her heart to see them together.

'James, don't be rude. Say something to Miss Sinclair,' Lily urged her brother.

The earl sent Evangeline an amused, knowing smile that made her face flush. 'Something.' The single word was a taunting act of rebellion against his sister. Evangeline hid her smile, trying not to reveal her secret adoration.

At that, Lily elbowed him in the ribs. 'Be polite. You're acting like a beast.'

'But I'm always polite.' With that, he gave Evangeline a slight nod and a wicked smile that made her go breathless. Lord Melville was a man who broke all the rules, and his eyes held an insolent stare that provoked her own desire to defy her mother's expectations.

If she'd had a choice, she would wear sapphire blue, not white. She would dance with Lord Melville and say exactly what was on her mind. She'd known him for so many years, it was easy enough to talk with him.

'Hello, Lord Melville.' Before she could stop herself, her mouth ran away with her again. 'Are you hoping to find a bride at the ball tonight?' The moment the words broke free, she wanted to curse herself.

Idiot. Why had she ever voiced such an idea? She couldn't have said anything worse.

'God forbid,' Melville answered cheerfully. 'I intend to remain a bachelor, free from marital chains for as long as possible.'

Oh. She should have expected this, but his response felt like a kick in the stomach. She braced herself and took another breath. 'Marriage isn't imprisonment, Lord Melville.'

'Yes, it is,' he countered. 'The moment I marry, I'll be trapped for the rest of my life. I'll never be able to see the world or go exploring.'

She'd never realised that he wanted to travel. Rose and Lily quietly stepped back to let them talk. 'You're serious, then?'

His expression shifted, and in his eyes, she saw his longing. Though she wished he would look at her in that way, somehow, she knew it wouldn't happen. Not yet.

'All my life, I've wanted to leave England,' he admitted. He glanced around him. 'Don't you ever feel like all this is an illusion? It's not the real world.' His gaze turned distant, as if his mind had wandered half a world away.

'And what do you consider the real world?' She kept her voice quiet so as not to let anyone else overhear them.

'It's difficult to say, since I've never been farther than Scotland or Wales.' He saw a few matrons approaching him with their daughters, so he offered Evie his arm. 'Walk with me so I don't have to speak to them.'

She rested her gloved hand on his sleeve, feeling as if they were conspiring together. He led her around the edge of the room, and her heartbeat quickened.

'Where would you travel if you could?' she asked.

'India, I think. My father has shipping investments

there. It would be a good excuse to see another part of the world.'

'So far away,' she murmured. The idea of travelling so long was unimaginable. And from the way he spoke of it, she feared he intended to go soon.

He slowed his pace. 'Yes. I've a need to stretch my wings, to escape this place.'

'Why? What's so terrible about England?'

'All the women are here, searching for a husband.' His hands closed atop hers, and she tried to suppress the thrill of his touch. 'The bachelors are searching for a dowry to pay off their debts. The marriages mean nothing at all.'

She shouldn't have been surprised by his words, but they did make her pause. 'Not everyone sees marriage as you do,' she countered. 'I, for one, intend to find someone who is kind and someone I can love. My own parents have been quite happy together. Marriage can be wonderful.'

'I wish you luck, then,' he said. 'Even if I don't share your views.'

With a slight bow, he departed, leaving her to stand alone. Though she should have expected his reluctance to wed, she couldn't help but feel a twinge of regret. Her brain warned that she ought to look elsewhere for love. He'd made his position clear enough. And yet, her heart had savoured the few moments she'd spent with him.

With a sigh, she walked towards a group of unmarried young women. There were several bachelors speaking to them, and she decided to try her luck there.

It might not be so bad, she told herself.

Surely there had to be at least one gentleman who would not judge her by her family's business.

She braved a smile and crossed the room. Once she reached the group of young women, she smiled at Miss

Everett, a lady she had met before. But the young woman said nothing and turned back to the others. It was as if Evie were invisible.

Her instincts sharpened, and she tried to shield herself from the rising embarrassment. It was happening again—the silent cut direct. But before she could decide what to do, one of the gentlemen spoke. 'Ah. Miss Sinclair, isn't it?'

She hesitated, not knowing what to say. It wasn't entirely proper to be speaking to this man when they hadn't been formally introduced, and she wondered exactly how she should respond. With a quick glance behind her, she saw that her mother was standing on the opposite side of the room beside her sister, the duchess.

'What a perfect evening, wouldn't you agree?' His tone rang out with false courtesy. There was something about the smug expression on his face that put her on her guard, and he gave an exaggerated bow. 'Would you care to dance? Surely you have plenty of empty spaces on your dance card.'

He was mocking her; she could see it in his eyes. His pompous demeanour was meant to put her down. But she would not play any part in it.

She offered him her sunniest smile and gave a slight curtsy. 'No, thank you, sir.'

I don't dance with men who make fun of me.

'Oh, come, now. Who else will ask you to dance if you don't dance with me?'

The men standing around broke into laughter, and several of the young ladies tittered behind their fans.

Evangeline felt her face burning, but she kept her shoulders square and walked past all of them. No doubt her mother would be appalled at her behaviour, but she simply couldn't stand the man.

Part of her worried that she'd been overreacting, but her instincts warned that she was right because of the way the other ladies had laughed. She had been the subject of a joke, and it bothered her deeply.

Not all men are that way, she reminded herself, thinking of the viscount.

Lord Melville was a good man, even if he did intend to abandon his responsibilities and travel. She braved a smile and told herself that it would be all right. Lily and Rose were dancing, and so she took a moment to slip away from the rest of the guests, keeping her back to the wall.

Her dance card *was* empty and would likely remain that way until her mother or aunt intervened. Evie tried to force a smile on her face, but it grew strained when she saw the couples turning and promenading during a country dance.

You're being a coward again, she told herself.

She needed to stop worrying about what others thought and simply try to get through the evening.

She took a deep breath and then moved into her wall-flower position at the back of the room. Her friend Lily was dancing with the Earl of Arnsbury. Lily appeared besotted with the man, and it made a softness bloom within Evangeline. Perhaps one day a man would look at her like that. She didn't want to accept anything less.

Evangeline heard a slight cough nearby, and when she turned, she saw another man venturing a smile at her. 'Forgive me that we've not had a formal introduction yet. But perhaps we can arrange one. I am Sir Lionel Norwood.'

Evangeline glanced around, but no, he really was talking to her. A tendril of hope bloomed inside, though she knew it wasn't exactly proper. Neither her mother nor any other matrons were nearby—only other unmarried young ladies, like herself.

Still, it would be rude not to listen to him, so she waited.

His expression appeared hopeful. 'I wondered if you, that is, if you might be willing to—that is, if you're not already spoken for—perhaps you might…wish to dance?'

His nerves were as terrible as her own had been. And perhaps that was why she took pity on the man. At least he hadn't attempted to mock her or smirk at her. She set aside her own feelings of awkwardness and nodded. 'Perhaps. But first, if you would follow me?'

He appeared somewhat intrigued, and Evangeline led him through the throng of people until she found her aunt Victoria. The duchess wore a rose gown, her shoulders bare, with a silver and pearl necklace around her throat. Her blond hair was coiled atop her head, and there were threads of silver mingled within the strands. She smiled warmly at Evangeline and said, 'It's so good to see you here, my dear. Are you enjoying yourself?'

Evangeline managed a nod because it wouldn't be polite to tell her aunt that it had been quite embarrassing so far. 'Of course,' she said softly.

Then she shifted her glance back to the gentleman in a silent request. Her aunt understood immediately and inclined her head in understanding. 'Sir Lionel, have you met my niece, Miss Evangeline Sinclair?'

He returned the smile. 'I have not had the formal honour, Your Grace.'

'Then allow me to present her to you. Miss Sinclair, this is Sir Lionel Norwood, Baronet Townson.'

Evangeline gave a nod. 'I am pleased to meet you, Sir Lionel.'

'Would you care to dance, Miss Sinclair?' he asked again, for the benefit of the duchess.

'Certainly.' In many ways, the very introduction ceremony felt like a formal dance. But she knew how important it was to maintain the rules, for the sake of her mother and herself. She followed Sir Lionel to the dance floor and realised with dismay that it was a quadrille. Though it was an older dance and she knew the steps, it involved switching partners with three other couples.

Sir Lionel bowed while she curtsied. Then Evangeline turned and curtsied to the next gentleman, who seemed to leer at her. Though she tried to keep the smile pasted on her face, it felt deeply uncomfortable.

You're letting the fear take control, she warned herself. *Try to enjoy the dance.*

For honestly, she did like dancing. There was something magical about the turning, the curtsies, and the way movement made her skirts swing. For a moment, she allowed herself to forget that she was wearing a ghastly shade of white. Instead, she concentrated on the music, and in time, her smile grew genuine.

Then she passed by Miss Smythe, another young lady. 'I must admit, you did surprise me, Miss Sinclair.'

They moved forward to turn in the circle, and Evangeline asked, 'Why is that?'

'I'm surprised that you know this dance, considering how barbaric your father is. Didn't he spend time in prison?' With a sugary smile, Miss Smythe returned to her partner.

Evangeline's cheeks burned, and she nearly choked her retort back. The young woman would never understand the honour her father possessed—his brief time spent in prison was only to save his younger brother's life before

Jonah's name was cleared. But all anyone else could see was the scandal.

She returned to Sir Lionel, who grasped her hand and led her into the circle. 'Are you all right, Miss Sinclair?'

'I'm fine,' she lied. 'It's simply warm in the ballroom.' She switched partners again, and this time, she was paired with the man who had mocked her earlier. Oh, dear. She'd hoped to avoid seeing him again.

'I thought you didn't want to dance with me,' he teased.

She saw no reason to be polite. 'I don't.'

'And why is that? I'm a very charming fellow.'

'Not to me. You aren't sincere.' If anything, his arrogance was quite clear, and he probably believed she should be grateful for his attentions.

'Oh, come, now.' His smirk deepened. 'I'm certain if you grew better acquainted with me, you might change your mind. We could go for a walk in the gardens. It's a beautiful night.'

'You're asking me to walk with you alone, and I don't even know your name,' she said. 'My answer is a resounding no.'

'I am Hubert Buchanan, Viscount Dunwood,' he answered.

'Again, my answer is no, Lord Dunwood.'

She was about to switch partners, but then he pretended to bump into her, sending her flying into Sir Lionel, who staggered backwards. Several women gasped, and Miss Smythe openly tittered. 'So clumsy.'

Humiliation washed over Evangeline, and for a moment, she wanted to disappear into the floor. She'd made a terrible spectacle of herself, and several people came forward to help. Sir Lionel tried to take her hand, apologising. 'Are you all right, Miss Sinclair?' he asked.

'Excuse me,' she said, hurrying away from the others. Her face was burning with embarrassment, and she nearly bumped into her mother.

'Evangeline, I—'

'Just leave me alone,' she pleaded. 'I'll be fine. But I need some time to myself.'

Her mother's pity made her feel even worse. 'Try the library. No one will bother you there.'

Evangeline's emotions were strung so tightly, she refused to blink for fear that she'd start crying. She stopped by the refreshment table and snatched a plate of cake on her way to the library. Behind her, she thought she could hear more laughter, but perhaps it was just her imagination.

Once she shut herself inside the library, she sat down on the floor behind the desk, not caring that it wrinkled her skirts. Then she let the tears stream down her cheeks, even while she took a bite of the cake, indulging in the sweet jam and custard filling.

She couldn't have had a worse debut, she decided. Not only had the young men and women gossiped about her father's shadowed past, but Lord Dunwood had ruined everything.

Evangeline withdrew a handkerchief and blew her nose, letting out the tears. Perhaps if she hid in the library for the next hour or two, no one would be the wiser.

A knock sounded at the library door. 'Miss Sinclair?' a familiar male voice asked.

Evangeline remained silent. She had no desire to be found, but unfortunately, the library door swung open, and the man's footsteps drew nearer.

Chapter Two

James had seen Evangeline fleeing the ballroom, taking the plate of cake with her before she disappeared into the library. He felt badly for the young woman, especially after seeing the snide expression of Lord Dunwood. He fully believed the man had caused her to stumble, for Evangeline had always loved dancing.

James knew he shouldn't follow her—but he'd seen the stricken look on her face as she'd fled the others and the laughter that had followed. No young lady deserved to have her debut ruined. He wasn't about to stand by and allow it.

From behind the desk in the library, he could see the white fabric of her gown spread out on the floor. He wanted to help her, but he had no idea what to say. She was a brave young woman, and she was far too spirited to let her feelings be trampled.

'Are you hurt, Miss Sinclair?' he asked softly.

'Yes,' she sighed. 'My pride is utterly ruined.'

He walked closer and saw her with her knees drawn up, an empty plate beside her. 'Should I call him out on your behalf?'

'I'm a better shot than you,' she said, wiping her eyes with a handkerchief. He hid a smile and leaned against the desk. She wasn't wrong about that.

'But sadly, it wouldn't do any good,' she continued. 'I refused to dance with Lord Dunwood, and he got his revenge by pushing me.'

'You're not going to let him get away with it, are you? Surely, you're planning your own vengeance.' If he'd done something like that to her, she'd have taken him to task. Evangeline wasn't the sort of woman to stand by and become a victim.

'I need more time to think of something diabolical,' she said. 'So, I'll just stay here. You can go back and join the rest of them.' Her stubborn tone made her defiance quite clear.

He sighed and tried another tack. 'If you stay, they'll have won. I know you're not afraid of them. You're better than that.'

'This has nothing to do with fear,' she insisted. 'I just… don't want to be mocked because of my family's past. I'm not a true lady, and there's nothing I can do about it. It doesn't matter how I dress or how I behave. Without a title, I'm nothing to them.'

For a moment, he thought about leaving her alone. When his sisters were in bad moods, there was little he could say to lift their spirits. But he sensed that there was something more behind her disappointment.

And so, he sat down on the floor beside her.

'What are you doing, Lord Melville?' Evangeline asked. 'You should go back to the ballroom.'

'As should you. But here we are.' He glanced around. 'I suppose, as hiding places go, it's not bad.' He leaned back against the wall, behaving as if it were an ordinary thing to escape society in such a way. 'Have you heard any good gossip lately?'

Her discomfort seemed to grow. 'Mother says it's not ladylike to gossip.'

'That wasn't what I asked. If we're to remain in hiding, surely you must have an entertaining story to share.' He rested his wrists upon his knees and waited. 'Well?'

She bit her lip, as if making a decision. 'If I share the story I've heard, then you must tell me one in return.'

'I don't have any stories.' It wasn't at all true, but the gossip he'd heard among the men was nothing a lady needed to hear.

'Then I'll tell you one,' she said. 'And you can think of yours.'

He shrugged, and then she leaned closer. He caught the faint scent of rose water, and her blue eyes gleamed with wickedness.

Not for you, he warned himself.

Although she was a close friend of both his sisters, and he shouldn't allow himself to be attracted, he couldn't deny that Evangeline Sinclair had caught his interest.

Her dark hair framed a lovely face, and generous curves strained at the seams of her gown. He could imagine sliding his hand against the thin fabric, stroking her breast until her nipple hardened against his fingers. But it was her bright spirit that held his interest the most. He liked the fact that he could freely speak his mind without worrying about whether she would take offence.

She leaned in closer to whisper into his ear. Her warm breath against his skin only deepened an unexpected physical reaction of desire. 'Do you know Miss Primrose?'

'Yes,' he answered. 'What of it?' He was rather distracted by the lock of hair that had fallen from her chignon and was resting against her throat.

'Well, she intends to be married next month,' she whispered. 'To Lord Hafton.'

He waited to see if she would add anything else, but when she didn't, he asked, 'Are we supposed to offer felicitations?'

She shook her head. 'The viscount has no desire to marry her, but he…um…that is, they *have* to wed.'

James fully understood what she'd implied. 'He compromised her.'

'Yes. And while he seems quite eager for the match, she has been weeping every day, according to her sister. She wants nothing to do with the man.' Evangeline lowered her voice. 'She thought becoming lovers would be terribly romantic, but it wasn't at all what she'd expected.'

It took a great deal of control to say nothing. Likely the lady had been dreaming of passion and had experienced an ordinary coupling. 'She doesn't have a choice now,' he pointed out. 'If she's carrying his child, then they have to wed.'

'Oh, I know, but I do pity her. She should have known that it wouldn't be very good.'

James blinked at that. Though he knew it wasn't wise to say anything, he couldn't help himself. 'And what do you mean by that?'

'Anyone could see that Lord Hafton has no imagination. He might have money, but he's got the romantic sensibilities of a block of wood. He couldn't seduce a lady if his life depended on it.'

'And…you have knowledge of this how?'

Evangeline's face did blush at that. 'Well, my parents *did* build their fortune upon the sale of ladies' undergarments. I'm not completely ignorant about lace and silk.'

This conversation had taken a turn he wasn't certain he wanted to pursue.

Her expression turned thoughtful. 'I believe that a man who is excellent at seduction has a certain way about him,' she continued. 'There's an invisible power, a way that he looks at a woman. As if he would die if he couldn't have her.' She tucked the fallen lock into her hair, and she closed her eyes. 'That's the sort of man I want. Someone who looks at me as if I'm his reason for being alive.'

Her smile grew wistful, and he realised that, as fascinating as this conversation was, they were both in danger of gossip turning against them.

'Eventually, you'll find the right person, Miss Sinclair.' James stood from the floor and helped her stand. 'We should probably return to the ballroom. Otherwise, someone might believe that *I* compromised you.'

Evangeline gave a wry smile. 'And that would be your worst nightmare.'

'It would be, because I'm not going to be married,' he repeated. 'Not for a very long time.'

For the past year, he'd been trapped in a life he didn't want. Each day, his father demanded that he spend hours learning about the estates and burying himself in ledgers from dawn until dusk. If he made a single mistake, George's tone grew even sharper, demanding that he memorise every detail.

The very thought of inheriting the earldom was a nightmare. He wanted time to live, time to become the man he wanted to be…instead of the man everyone thought he should be. And marriage would bring another set of expectations and responsibilities that he simply didn't want to face right now. He needed a chance to breathe before the suffocating responsibilities drowned him in misery.

He would face it eventually. Just not now.

When he glanced over at Evie, he saw the hopes and dreams of a young woman who wanted the same fairy tale as every marriageable miss in the ballroom. And while there was no doubt in his mind that Evangeline would indeed make some man a good wife, she deserved better than a man like him. He would only disappoint her, the way his father saw him as not quite good enough.

'Is it because you want to travel or because you're trying to escape your father?' she asked.

The question pressed too close to the truth. 'Perhaps both,' he said. 'I just need a chance to see distant shores. To look upon new faces and discover a different way of life. I want to feel the desert sand against my face. Perhaps sail to an island no one has glimpsed before.'

But the true reason was because James sensed, deep in his bones, that his time was running out. If he didn't leave now, he might never have the chance to travel.

He suspected his father might be ill, though George scoffed at the idea. There were days when his father hardly left his chair, and when he did, his balance appeared unsteady. It made him question whether the earl was losing his ability to walk. He didn't want to believe it, but his father's mood had darkened as of late, holding the desperate air of a man who hated to admit any weakness.

Though it might be selfish, James hungered for another life so different from the one waiting for him. He wanted to escape—even if it was only for a year or two. Then he would return, take up the yoke of responsibility, and those memories would sustain him through an uncertain future.

'It sounds like a wonderful journey,' Evangeline said. 'Though I—I mean your sisters—would miss you very much.'

'They would understand.' He could already feel the prison doors of responsibility closing all around him. He knew it was selfish—down deep, he knew it was wrong to leave. But there was still time. His father wasn't dying—not yet. And if he left now, he had time to see the world before he had to face an uncertain future.

Perhaps then, he would be ready to look after his family and say farewell to his freedom.

Evangeline allowed the viscount to return to the ballroom first, and she waited a few moments in the corridor to avoid gossip. Though really, no one would believe that she had spent a quarter of an hour alone with him. Lord Melville had an air of unattainability, which made women only long for him more. A pang caught her stomach at the realisation that he had been telling the truth. He truly didn't want to be married. Although she didn't understand why he wanted to travel so far away, she fully understood his need to escape.

She remained with her back against the wall, trying to repair the broken pieces of her pride while watching her friends dance.

Her mother returned to her side and asked, 'Are you feeling better, Evangeline?'

'Yes,' she lied. 'But I wouldn't be disappointed if we returned home early.'

Margaret paused a moment, as if she questioned the idea. Then she gave a nod and said, 'I'll speak to my sister.'

Evangeline continued watching the dancers, and across the room, she glimpsed Lord Melville with another young lady. The sight brought a pang to her heart. The more time she spent near him, the more her heart faltered. It made her want things she couldn't have, dreaming of a man like James.

His green eyes held warmth, and as she watched him move, she remembered how he had sat beside her in the library. She'd wanted to rest her head against his shoulder. No, more than that. She wanted to be kissed, for she sensed that a man like Lord Melville knew exactly how to seduce a woman. He would know how to lean in and capture her lips, his hungry mouth tempting her towards ruin.

She blinked a moment, reminding her brain to stop its idle fantasies. The viscount didn't want her, and he didn't want to be married. The only way Lord Melville could be snared into a marital union was if he were trapped into it.

Her heartbeat quickened at the thought. No, she could never do such a thing. He would despise any woman who dared to try something so foolish. But the thought had taken root, making her wonder. There was a masculine power about him, a sense that he would take command. A man like Lord Melville would take her breath away if he were ever to become her lover.

Don't, her brain warned.

It was a terrible idea, imagining a seduction. Though she had never been touched by any man, she'd overheard her mother and her aunts gossiping when they thought she wasn't there. She wondered what it would be like to experience James's strong hands unlacing her corset, his palms caressing her bare skin. Beneath her gown, she grew more flushed, and her breasts seemed to tighten with her own imagination. She knew it was wicked, but she didn't care. Instead, she savoured the vision, simply dreaming of what would never be.

Three days later

'Ah, there you are, James.' His father, the Earl of Penford, entered the breakfast room with a ledger tucked beneath one arm. Despite the earl's smile, shadows lined his eyes, as if he hadn't slept well in days. His pallor was grey, and he continued, 'Will you join me in my study? There are some matters we need to discuss.'

'As soon as I've finished eating,' James answered. 'Won't you join me for breakfast?'

'No, thank you. I'm going to wait until luncheon. Food isn't settling too well this morning, I'm afraid.'

Though his father smiled, James didn't miss the underlying air of illness. 'I'm sorry to hear it.'

'No matter. It will pass, as it always does.' His father was about to leave when his wife entered the breakfast room.

Iris smiled warmly at her husband. 'Are you feeling better, my love?'

'How can I not, when you are here?' He leaned in to kiss her, and James turned away to grant them privacy.

'I shall have Cook prepare something special for this evening,' Iris promised. 'Perhaps she can tempt your appetite.'

'Perhaps.' His father touched her cheek and then said to him, 'Come to the study when you're ready, James.'

His mother joined him at the table, and only after his father was out of earshot did he ask, 'How is he really?'

Iris's smile grew strained. 'Oh, he'll be all right. Sometimes he doesn't sleep well. It's probably gout, I'm sure, but he never complains. If I give him laudanum in a cup of tea, that often helps. But…' She shook her head and stared at her plate as if trying to maintain her composure.

'What has the doctor said?'

'Only that he needs to eat plain foods and rest. If he does that, he'll be fine.' She braved a smile, but her voice had gone brittle. He noticed that her fingers were shaking when she poured her tea.

'It will be all right,' he said gently.

'I just—don't know what I would do without him,' she whispered, and she seemed to be holding back tears. 'The very thought of losing him terrifies me.'

He reached over to embrace her, and she held on tightly. After a time, she seemed to grow calmer, and then she pulled back. 'You'd better go and help him with the estate matters. I'll be fine.'

James dropped a kiss on her cheek and then left the breakfast room. In all likelihood, he would be trapped in the study for the rest of the day. He suppressed a groan, knowing he had no choice.

He opened the door and found his father seated at the desk. Several books lay open, and the earl dipped his pen into an ink-well and was writing something in one of the ledgers.

James crossed the room, and his father brightened when he saw him. 'Close the door. There's something I want to show you.' There was an air of excitement in his father's voice. James hadn't heard that in a long time, and he wondered what this was about.

'I have something for you,' the earl said. 'Something that I think will bring you a great deal of joy.' He beckoned for him to come closer.

There, on the desk, James saw a ticket for passage from London to India. He picked it up and stared at it in disbelief.

'Your ship leaves in three days,' his father said. 'I've

made all the arrangements. You'll make some investments for me, travel, see everything you've always wanted, and then return to England by the end of next year.'

James couldn't bring himself to speak. Finally, at long last, he could experience the searing heat of India, taste exotic spices, and see the world. He was torn by a wave of excitement, but now that he'd been handed such a gift, it made him question whether it was right to leave his father.

'I don't know if I should,' he hedged. Not when he wasn't certain how ill his father was.

'Listen to me,' his father said. He crossed from behind the desk and gripped James's hands. 'I know I've been hard on you, the past few years. Let me make it up to you in this way. This is your best chance to travel, the way I know you've always wanted to. And I want to give you that gift.'

His father drew him into a hard embrace, and James could hardly command the emotions that rose up from deep inside. He'd never imagined George would give him such a gift.

'I want you to go,' his father reassured him. 'But don't tell your mother I've done this. She will find every reason in the world to coerce you to stay, and I won't have it. Instead, you're going to pretend that you've purchased the ticket without my permission. We're going to have a terrible argument, and you're going to leave.'

'But why?' If he did such a thing, his mother and sisters would be appalled, believing him to be selfish.

'It's the only way they'll let you go. And because I want their sympathy,' his father admitted. 'While you're gone, I'll find husbands for Rose and Lily. And I'll hire a secretary to help me. If I told them the truth, they would only try to talk us both out of it.' With a sigh, he added, 'And you'd probably listen to them.'

He stared at his father, wondering if the earl understood how grateful he was. This was everything he'd ever wanted, and the gift overwhelmed him. 'Thank you, Father. I cannot tell you how much it means to me.'

'I look forward to hearing about your adventures after you return,' George said. 'And I'll expect letters.'

'Are you truly certain about this?' James asked. 'I could stay.'

His father gripped his shoulder. 'Let me give you this journey, James. I know how much it means to you. And it will make me feel better if you accept it.' He pressed the ticket into his hand, and James took it. 'But promise me—we'll have a terrible fight. Make it a good one.'

'I promise.' He smiled at his father, suddenly realising that he had to begin packing at once. 'And thank you.'

After his son left, George sank down in his chair. Exhaustion flooded through him, mingled with satisfaction. James would be burdened with the earldom soon enough, but it gave him comfort to know that he could offer his son this dream.

Now all that was left was to see that his daughters married well and that Iris had everything she needed.

Today was the day they'd agreed to break the news. Last night, his father had guided him on what to say. Although James didn't want to start a fight, he'd made a promise.

He entered the drawing room and saw his father seated with his bad leg propped up. George gave him a faint nod, and his sister Lily had a troubled expression on her face. It seemed as if they'd already been arguing.

James straightened and addressed them both. 'I came to tell you that I am leaving in a few days.'

Lily stared at him in shock and discreetly shook her head in a silent plea. He could already read his sister's thoughts. And she was going to be even more upset, soon enough.

His father's expression turned stunned, and he shook his head. 'You cannot leave, James. There is too much to be done here.' Even his tone held pain, but James suspected he saw a twinkle in the man's eyes.

'I intend to sail to India,' he informed them. 'I expect to be gone for the next year, at the very least. Perhaps longer.'

The silence within the room was tempered only by his sister's expression of horror. George gave quite a convincing performance of being torn between disbelief and fury, while Lily was in shock. 'But why?'

His father struggled to rise from his chair, his complexion purple with feigned rage. 'Absolutely not.'

That man was truly enjoying his play-acting, James realised. But he continued, 'We have business dealings there. I believe now would be a good time to expand our interests.'

'You have responsibilities here,' George insisted. 'You are my heir, and you cannot go traipsing off on a fool's errand in India. I forbid it.' There was a slight gleam in his eye, though the words should have been ruthless.

James gave a faint smile. 'Of course, you do. But I intend to go, nonetheless. And you cannot stop me.'

His father's face turned thunderous. 'If you try, I will cut off your funds.'

Oh, George truly was enjoying this fight. It was difficult to hold back a smile and pretend to be defiant.

'I have my own wealth, Father,' James said quietly.

'And I am quite certain that you can continue ruling Penford in my absence, just as you've done for the past twenty-five years.'

His sister's expression begged him to stop. 'James, please,' Lily pleaded. 'India is so far away. I don't want to imagine you alone for an entire year. It may not be safe.'

Her concerns were valid, but he'd already confided his plans to his best friend Matthew, who had asked to join him. It was far safer if they travelled together, and Matthew was just as eager to see the world. But his sister would be devastated when she learned of it.

'Oh, I'm not going alone,' he said gently. 'Arnsbury is accompanying me. It will be an adventure, and we will seek our fortunes before the chains of marriage are clapped upon us.'

He tried to keep his tone light, but he didn't miss Lily's dismay. 'Lord Arnsbury is going with you?' Her face had gone so pale, she looked as if she might faint.

'Yes. Matthew is going to keep me out of trouble.' James winked at her. 'He can try anyway.'

And with one last conspiratorial look at his father, he turned and left.

'He what?' Evangeline stared at Lily in disbelief.

Her friend had arrived late in the afternoon, her eyes still red from crying. 'James is leaving for India. He's already booked his passage. Mother is beside herself with worry, and I don't blame her,' Lily said. 'But worse than that, Matthew—I mean, Lord Arnsbury—has decided to go with him!'

Evangeline sank into a chair, barely aware of what was happening. If the men left now, it would be more than a year before they returned. Lord Melville would never know how she truly felt about him, and the thought brought a wave of melancholy. 'So, he just…bought a ticket and he's leaving? Why would he go?'

Lily clenched her hands together. 'I don't know. It might be something to do with his cousin Adrian. I know they've been fighting, but I'm not sure what it's about.'

Evangeline let out a heavy sigh. Both men were distant cousins of hers—Matthew on her great-aunt's side, whereas Adrian was a cousin on her great-uncle's. She'd heard enough family gossip to have an idea of what this was about.

'Adrian has a lot of debts,' she told Lily. 'I've heard Papa talking about him. He gambles a great deal.' Wincing, she added, 'He probably wishes *he* were the earl instead.'

'Well, he's not,' Lily said. 'If anyone should leave England, Mr Monroe should.'

She agreed with that, but she guessed that her cousin Matthew had the same idea as Lord Melville—to travel the world and do as he pleased. Which made her wonder if he was trying to avoid his own responsibilities.

Lily's face turned crestfallen. 'I wish I could stop them, but I don't think we can.' She wrung her hands and said, 'I need your help, Evie. I want you to tell my mother that I'm spending the night with you.'

'I suppose you can, but aren't you supposed to attend Lady Callista's ball tonight?' She kept her tone bright, even though she hadn't been invited to the gathering. 'You could come over afterwards, certainly. But don't you want to say goodbye to Lord Arnsbury?' She regarded her friend, and then with a jolt of realisation, she understood that this was exactly what Lily intended. Her cheeks warmed with embarrassment. 'Forgive me, I wasn't thinking. You weren't planning to attend the ball, were you?'

Lily blushed. 'I would attend for a short while. Then, I would make an excuse to leave and pretend I'm planning to spend the night at your home.'

Light dawned upon her when Evie understood her friend's plan. Because she and her family hadn't been invited to Lady Callista's ball, no one would know any differently. 'But you're not actually coming to my house, are you? You're going to see Matthew instead,' she predicted, keeping her voice low.

Her friend blushed but nodded. 'He's asked me to come, and I've given my promise. It will be some time before he returns home to England.'

Evangeline wanted to caution her best friend not to do anything rash. Although it was terribly romantic, it was also dangerous to be alone with Matthew. 'I worry about you, Lily. What if…there are consequences? If anyone finds out that you were alone with him…'

Lily shook her head, her blush deepening. 'Please, Evie. I just want to see him before he leaves. I need to.'

Evangeline didn't dare to ask what exactly Lily was plotting, for it would cause a scandal if anyone found out. She would never dream of betraying her friend. 'All right. I will help you,' she promised.

Yet, the thought turned over and over in her mind, like a spinning coin. If Lily spent the night with Lord Arnsbury, he would undoubtedly marry her. Although she knew Lily loved the earl, and he returned her feelings, this might force his hand.

It made her think of Lord Melville and whether there was even a shred of a chance for herself and James. Logically, there wasn't. He didn't want to wed, and even if he did, the man was so sinfully handsome, he could marry any heiress he wanted. He would never want someone like her.

He did sit with you in the library, her heart reminded her.

But he probably regarded her as an acquaintance, nothing more. He'd never made a single overture, nothing beyond friendship. And Evie was afraid to reach for more, for fear that she might shatter the tenuous acquaintance they had.

'I will attend the ball with Mother and Rose this evening,' Lily said. 'Then, I will tell them I'm going to spend the night with you since you weren't—'

'—invited,' Evie finished.

Lily appeared dismayed, but she continued, 'The carriage will take me to meet Lord Arnsbury, and everyone will believe I'm with you. I'll return early in the morning to your house, and no one will be the wiser.'

There were a hundred things that could go wrong. Matthew's servants could easily learn the truth and spread gossip. Lily's parents might discover their plans and intervene. But in her heart, Evie was a hopeless romantic and only wanted her friend's happiness. 'What about your brother? Won't he be making plans with Arnsbury?'

'No, James will be at home tonight. He's still packing his belongings.'

Which meant the viscount would be alone. A reckless side of her rejoiced at the thought, even knowing that it was a terrible risk to pay a call on him tonight while his mother and sisters were at the ball. But that would give *her* the chance to say goodbye. If she felt particularly daring, she might even tell him the secret feelings hidden in her heart.

Was there any chance that Lord Melville *did* see something in her? Should she try to find out? Even if it was humiliating, perhaps she should simply bare her feelings and see what he said. If nothing else, at least he would know the truth.

'Good luck, Lily,' she said, embracing her friend. And inwardly, she wondered if she had the courage to reach for the man she wanted.

Chapter Three

James stared at the brass-bound trunk, feeling as if it belonged to someone else...as if another man were about to travel half a world away. Both his parents had gone to Lady Callista's ball this evening, along with his sisters. In their absence, the silence of the house seemed to embrace him in one last farewell.

He walked outside, breathing in the night air. A few months from now, it would no longer be the cool spring air of London but instead, the sweltering heat of India. A part of him still questioned whether it was right to go, but his father had been insistent upon it, claiming that he was perfectly fine. And during the past few days, there had been a spark of interest in George, as if he were excited about the gift of this journey.

He would stay a year and a half...two years at the very most, James decided. That would be enough time to make the investments on his father's behalf, see the world, and then travel home to shoulder the responsibilities that awaited him.

From the far side of the garden, he heard the gate closing and then the rustle of skirts. Had Lily returned home early? He started towards the opposite side and then saw

Miss Sinclair approaching. Her gaze was upon the ground, and her steps slowed.

'Miss Sinclair?' he called out. 'Is everything all right?' It couldn't be, or else why would she be here?

Her expression turned panicked as if she'd not expected to find him here. 'Oh. You're here.' She paused a moment. 'I thought you would be inside. But um…yes. I suppose everything is fine. Mostly.'

He waited for her to elaborate, but she seemed even more uncomfortable in his presence. 'Were you looking for Lily? I thought she was already at Lady Callista's ball with my parents.'

'Yes, she is. And I've asked her to come stay the night with me later so she can tell me all about it.' James remembered, then, that the Sinclairs were rarely invited to balls. But he found it strange that Miss Sinclair had made such an effort tonight with her own appearance. Her dark hair gleamed in the moonlight, and white rosebuds were pinned behind one ear. She wore a white gown that wasn't quite a ball gown, but it was entirely too fine for paying an unexpected call.

'Why are you here?' he finally asked.

Her cheeks flamed, and she managed, 'I—that is… I was hoping to talk to you. Before you leave for India.'

Her confession surprised him, but his wariness went on alert as well. 'Do you want to come inside? I could ring for tea and refreshments.'

'That wouldn't be wise. I'm really not supposed to be here, and servants do talk. I wouldn't want anyone to get the wrong idea.' She spoke rapidly, revealing her nervousness.

Whatever was bothering Evangeline was eating away at her like misery. James had no idea what to say to make her feel better, so he offered his arm. 'What if we walk through the garden, and you can tell me everything? No one will see us.'

In the moonlight, she lifted her gaze to his. Such innocence in those blue eyes. And yet, Evangeline Sinclair had a rebellious side, just like her Highlander father. He had a feeling that she'd learned something about Lily or Rose.

'Is this about my sisters?'

Surprisingly, she shook her head. 'No, actually, it's about me.'

At that, she released his arm and went to stand by the fountain. She stared into the water as if trying to find her courage. Then she admitted, 'By the time you return from India, I suppose I'll be married.'

'You might,' he acknowledged. But strangely enough, he felt an odd twinge at her statement. He'd known Evangeline for years, and he couldn't quite imagine her as a married woman.

'I'll probably be wedded to some poor gentleman with a title and a mountain of debts,' she continued. 'And the more I think of it, the more it frightens me.'

'Why would you be afraid of marriage?' he enquired. 'I thought *I* was the one who should be afraid.' He'd meant it in teasing, but her face had turned serious.

She bit her lower lip, deep in thought. Then she blurted out, 'I'm afraid because you'll leave for India, never knowing how I feel about you.'

For a moment, her words washed over him in a wave of disbelief. He should have guessed what she was about to say. And although he supposed he ought to be uncomfortable at her confession, the startled surprise shifted into a very different response. Her words seemed to reach behind his invisible armour to a chink he'd never known

was there. He ought to say something kind, for she was
his sister's closest friend. But all James could do was stare
at her, as if he were seeing her for the first time.

He couldn't seem to form an answer. He couldn't tell
her that she was too young at the age of nineteen or that
they didn't know each other well enough. He was barely
thirty himself, and his mother had been chiding him for
years to take a wife.

No, he'd always liked Evangeline. But in this moment,
he held the power to destroy her heart. And that wasn't
something he wanted to do.

She was watching him, those blue eyes filled with vul-
nerability. She had laid her soul bare before him, and
damned if he knew the right answer.

A kiss, perhaps. He could kiss her farewell on the
cheek, and that would be enough. She would hold a good
memory, and his conscience would be relieved, knowing
that he'd answered her confession with kindness.

'Evangeline,' he began, but she cut him off.

'Don't say it.' She closed her eyes, steeling herself. 'I
know you don't feel anything for me, and that's all right.
I just…wanted you to know before you left, that's all.'
She started to turn away, but he caught her by the hand.

'Wait,' he said.

She went motionless, and he brought her close enough,
intending to kiss her cheek and say goodbye. Instead, he
found himself drawn by the softness of her lips, the aching hunger in her gaze. And he knew he needed one taste
of that mouth. Just enough to satisfy his curiosity, but not
enough to make her believe there could be more. He released her hand and cupped her face.

Beneath his fingers, he could feel the pulse at her throat
pounding wildly. He bent to take the kiss he wanted—

but the moment his mouth claimed hers, she gained the upper hand.

Her lips were warm, sweetly yielding beneath him. And when he kissed her, she utterly disarmed him. He tasted her innocence, but more than that, there was a glimpse of more.

She kissed him back slowly, savouring his mouth in a way that drove him wild. There was nothing at all coquettish or insincere about Evie, and damn him, she got under his skin. He craved her even more with every breath in his body.

He'd kissed women before, experienced women who knew how to give pleasure. But there was something about the sweetness of Evangeline Sinclair that took him apart.

He didn't want anyone to find them together, so he led her deeper into the garden by a stone bench at the furthest end. Here, they were shielded from any onlookers, but more than that, he could take his time, kissing her longer.

For he didn't want to stop.

Evangeline could scarcely catch her breath. Never in her wildest dreams had she imagined that Lord Melville would kiss her. She'd expected James to smile with sympathy, thank her for the words, and send her on her way. Instead, he'd leaned in, giving her the most precious gift. Her body had come alive, tingling at the intoxicating flood of sensations pouring through her. She clung to his hand as he led her to a more private area of the garden.

Her brain was warning her to stop, to leave right now. But she couldn't have moved if her life depended on it.

This wasn't proper at all. She ought to be fighting against him, telling him no. But all she could think of was—this was what she'd yearned for over the years. She wanted passion and love in a marriage. With a man like the viscount, she didn't feel awkward or lonely. Instead, he made her feel beautiful.

And although it was wrong, wanting to experience such a moment with him, she couldn't bring herself to push him away.

In the darkness, his mouth moved to her throat. She gasped, gripping his hair as more heat burned through her. She'd never understood why women surrendered to ruin, but now she did. If James wanted her…and if that resulted in a future for them, she wouldn't hesitate to take his offering.

All her life, he'd been the handsome rake who had stolen her heart. He'd never treated her as inferior because of her family's business or let her feel somehow less than a woman. And now, he was kissing her as if he couldn't help himself. It wasn't a farewell kiss any longer…instead, it was an awakening.

Against the curve of her hip, she could feel the hard ridge of his arousal, and a secret part of herself grew damp and restless. It was hard to catch her breath, and when his hands moved to the back of her gown, he paused, waiting for permission.

Or perhaps he was trying to stop the madness.

It didn't matter. She wanted him, and she had no desire to end what was happening between them. Part of her sensed that if she gave him time to stop and think, he would stop touching her. And God help her, she didn't want that.

'Please,' she whispered. No longer did she feel the chill of the spring night. Instead, she was only aware of this man and the forbidden feelings rising within. She had never imagined this moment, but there was nothing wrong about it. If anything, it might result in the engagement she'd always dreamed of.

'This is wrong, Evie,' he murmured.

'I don't care,' she whispered. It was the first time he'd ever called her by her nickname. And it warmed her blood, dropping the invisible boundaries between them. He was the only man she'd ever desired, and she wasn't about to let him go now. Not when she needed him so much.

His expression grew pained, but he sat down on the stone bench and drew her to his lap. She reached up to touch his face and brought him back down into another kiss. This time, it turned more desperate, and she grew aware of his hard length pressed against her. Instead of being afraid, it evoked a sensual thrill, and she revelled in the sensation until she could only imagine what it would be like to make love to this man. She was aching for him, wanting something she could not name.

'Are you certain about this?' he asked.

'Stop talking and kiss me.'

He obeyed, his mouth hungry upon hers while his hands moved against the back of her gown. This time, he didn't stop until her gown was fully unbuttoned.

For a moment, he struggled with the laces of her corset, even while he kissed her again. She could feel his hands fumbling in the darkness, and at one moment, she murmured, 'Do you need a knife to cut them?'

He choked back a laugh, but finally, she felt the easing of the ties. Then, he reached beneath the neckline of her gown and chemise to cup her breast. A searing heat blazed through her when his thumb caressed her nipple. She let out a soft groan, and instinctively, she pressed herself against his erection. The motion brought a delicious ache between her legs, and she grew restless upon him.

The thought disappeared when James's mouth closed over her nipple. She nearly cried out at the devastating pleasure that washed over her, and she bit her lip to keep anyone from hearing her. His tongue swirled over the erect tip, and a wild storm of need took her prisoner. She lost every thought of common sense until there was only the mindless pleasure of his touch.

James reached beneath her skirts and petticoats. 'Will you allow me to touch you?' His voice was a husky whisper. She didn't know what she was agreeing to, but when she murmured her assent, he pushed aside her undergarments cupping her intimately. She barely had time to grasp what was happening before he slid one finger inside her moist depths. The pleasure exploded within her, and she dug her fingers into his shoulders.

Words utterly failed her, and she could only cling to him as he stroked her from inside. He added a second finger and began a rhythm of entering and withdrawing from her body. Evie arched her back, unable to grasp a clear thought. The rest of the world seemed to fall away, and she surrendered to him, giving everything of herself.

He kissed her breast again, and the sensation only heightened the intense pleasure. She was crying out now, unable to bear the fierce tension rising higher.

'Let go, Evangeline,' he commanded.

She didn't understand what he meant until his thumb found a sensitive place, sending her over the edge. She shuddered as the pleasure ignited every inch of her skin, and she spasmed against him. He seized her hips and rubbed himself against her centre until he groaned and collapsed with his mouth upon her throat.

Her heart was pounding, her body spent. She knew he'd never intended to touch her like this. It had spiralled out of control, but she held no regrets. She wanted to marry James, and she had no doubt that it would happen now. No man would ever touch her the way he had, and she was glad of it.

He helped her to dress and buttoned her gown again, though she suspected her hair was an utter mess. 'We'd better get you home before my family returns.'

At that, she realised she had to remind him about his sister. 'You're right. And Lily is coming to spend the night with me. I should go home...before she arrives.' He helped her to stand, though her knees still felt weak. 'Will you want to speak with my father in the morning?'

It was a risk, but she needed to know what their future would be. James was an honourable man, and surely, he would do what was right.

For a moment, he paused. Then he took her face between his hands and kissed her mouth gently. 'We'll talk of it later.'

Her heart swelled up with the unspoken promises, and she nodded. 'All right.' Evie paused at the gate and turned back to him. 'I don't regret what we did.' She refused to feel guilty for the stolen moment she'd seized. If it meant he would stay in London and marry her, it was all worth it. Even now, her body felt as if it had awakened to what love was supposed to be.

He said nothing but squeezed her hand. And when he arranged for his driver to bring her home, her heart soared with dreams of what the future would bring.

He was a cold-hearted bastard. There was no other term for it. James had known that Evangeline wanted marriage. She'd come to confess her girlish infatuation, and like a blackguard, he'd taken advantage.

He couldn't even say why he'd done it. He'd never imagined that he would behave so badly, but there was something about her sweetness that had silenced his good sense. Her lips had ignited a madness within him. He couldn't have stopped the storm any more than he could stop ocean waves from crashing against a cliff.

Never had he imagined she would enslave him to such desire. He'd always liked Evie, but he'd had no idea that she had such a sensual nature. He had fallen beneath her spell gladly, and he couldn't stop thinking of her.

She deserves better, his conscience admitted.

There was no doubt of it. Evangeline wanted what every woman wanted—a home, a family, and a husband who loved her. And after he'd pleasured her last night, she would expect him to ask for her hand in marriage. If he were a true gentleman, that's exactly what he'd do.

The weight of guilt burdened him, for he couldn't be that man. Not yet. This was his last and only chance to see the world, and he simply had to go. It was bad enough that he'd touched Evangeline so intimately, but at least he'd left her a virgin. If she did marry while he was away, no one would know what they had done.

But a darkness curled within him at the thought of another man touching her.

He tried to tell himself that it was for the best if he let her go, to be loved by someone else. But he would never forget the sweet taste of her lips, the soft curve of her breasts, and the way she had responded to his touch. Even now, the memory of Evie evoked an arousal he wanted to deny.

He never should have touched her, never should have tasted that forbidden fruit. He'd considered writing a letter to Evangeline, but there was no apology that would atone for what he'd done.

She would despise him, as she should. And perhaps that was what needed to happen. If she hated him, it would be easier to let her go.

He'd already packed his trunk and intended to leave at dawn, disappearing without saying goodbye. It was easier that way. Otherwise, he might change his mind and stay.

The weather was grey and overcast, which suited his dark mood. He reminded himself that he'd promised his father that he would go and explore India. He ought to drink in every last adventure before returning home.

But his heart grew heavy as he left everything else behind.

'Evie, you need to eat something.' Margaret set down a plate of cake in front of her, but the thought of eating made Evangeline's stomach twist.

James was gone, and he wasn't coming back. He wasn't going to talk to her father or ask for her hand in marriage. No, he'd taken advantage of her and had disappeared to the other side of the world. She'd practically given herself to him in the garden, and in return, she'd been left with nothing.

Her initial shock had faded, and now, it was replaced by rage. How could he do this? How could he listen to her naive confession and then treat her like a courtesan? If the man she loved had behaved like this, how could she ever trust anyone else?

'Evie?' her mother prompted again.

'Just leave it there,' she murmured. Under any other circumstances, she would have consoled herself with cake.

But now, it seemed to make a mockery of her, reminding her of the time she'd spent in the library with Lord Melville.

She'd let her heart lead her down the path of temptation, and it was only through good fortune that she hadn't been caught. The thought of ever letting any man close to her again was unthinkable.

'You cannot hide away forever,' her mother continued. 'I want you to come with your father and I to your aunt Juliette's musicale. It will be a small gathering. Lily and Rose will be there.' It was a veiled attempt at consolation.

'And will there be other eligible bachelors there as well?' she prompted.

Her mother shrugged. 'Of course. But I know it's too soon for you, Evie.' She moved closer, and Evangeline felt the weight of her mother's palm upon her shoulder. 'I never realised you had feelings for Lord Melville.'

'It's my own fault,' she admitted. 'He told me from the beginning that he had no interest in marriage.'

'It still hurts,' her mother acknowledged. 'But all I ask is that you don't hide yourself away.'

She couldn't confess her reasons or her secret shame. Guilt brought a flush to her cheeks, and she realised that she'd centred her life around one man. But there was far more to living. She'd never searched inside herself to find out who she truly was or what she wanted.

Maybe it was time to do some soul-searching and find out. But in the meantime, she intended to avoid marriage. She would wear the most unflattering gowns she could find and chase away any man who dared to court her.

Instead of becoming the most desirable heiress, she intended to become the least likely to marry. She would say whatever she wanted—especially against men like

Lord Dunwood. A smile caught at her lips as she imagined becoming a veritable shrew.

'Will you come with us?' her mother asked.

Evangeline nodded, imagining a dreadful hairstyle and the worst gown she had in her wardrobe. 'Only if I can wear whatever I choose.'

Her mother expelled a sigh. 'So be it.'

Chapter Four

Summer, 1846

James stared outside the window at the London streets, feeling like a stranger in his own homeland. It was strange to see the fog slipping around the townhouses and even stranger to feel the cool weather. He'd grown accustomed to the blazing sun of India.

It seemed nearly impossible to slip back into the privileged life he'd known before. He'd glimpsed a part of the world he'd never imagined. He'd witnessed unspeakable poverty…and the greed of shipping companies who had built their fortunes upon the backs of those who could not defend themselves.

Never again would he invest his family's fortunes in such a way.

He'd once believed that India would change him, giving him a taste of adventure in a new land. He and Matthew had travelled for months, half a world away, with a footman who was half-Indian and spoke the language. But Javas had betrayed them.

A knot tightened in James's stomach. He'd believed Javas when the man had claimed that a sailor had spoken of rubies in the north. The footman had suggested that they travel there and invest in mining.

Instead, they'd been caught up in a military conflict between the Sikh and the British.

Only now did he understand that Javas had deliberately separated them from the others. Their wealth had made them a target, and the man had robbed and abandoned them to a group of rebels. He and Matthew had been captured and imprisoned for months before they'd barely escaped with their lives.

And although they'd made it home again, he wasn't the same person any more. Not only from the wounds he'd received in prison, but also from the crushing guilt of his own failures. Matthew had suffered so badly, the man could barely even speak. James blamed himself for everything that had happened. But most of all, he shouldered the blame for what had happened to his family while he'd been away.

His father had died over a year ago. Never again would he see George's face or the hint of pride in the man's smile. Although James had once dreaded the endless hours of learning estate matters, now the ledgers filled up the emptiness left behind by his father's legacy. Seeing George's handwriting left a bittersweet ache of grief within him.

God above, he wished he'd never left. Even though George had insisted that he go, James knew he shouldn't have listened. His sisters and mother had needed him, and he hadn't been there for them.

Footsteps approached, and out of instinct, James reached for a weapon that wasn't there. It took a moment to calm his heartbeat, and then he realised it was his sister Lily approaching.

You're safe, he told himself. *It's nothing.*

He took a slow, deep breath and tried to behave as if everything was normal.

'James, I was hoping we could talk.'

He glanced back at the window, trying to steady his own frustration. He knew why his sister was here—but he struggled to keep his emotions under rein. She was gripping her hands together with nerves, but he already knew why.

Yesterday, their mother had dressed in her favourite ball gown, rhapsodising about how romantic it was that Lily would be married to Arnsbury, but thankfully there was no child.

'You seem angry,' she started to say. 'Did—did Mother tell you—'

'Tell me that Arnsbury ruined you before he left for India? She did.' His words were brittle and sharp. Although he'd known that his sister had been in love with Matthew before they'd left England, he'd never imagined that his best friend would dishonour Lily in such a way. It felt like a betrayal he'd never imagined.

There were no words to describe the fury that permeated every part of him. It enraged him beyond rational thought.

You're a hypocrite, his conscience warned. *Because you did the same thing when you couldn't resist Evangeline's kiss.*

His sister was staring back at him, her face scarlet with humiliation. Silence descended between them, but he couldn't bring himself to fill the space with meaningless conversation. He wanted Lily to stay away from Matthew, for the earl could no longer be the man she wanted. Arnsbury had suffered in captivity, just as he had. They'd been questioned and tortured for information they didn't have, and neither of them was fit for marriage. Not any more.

But James had silently vowed to himself that he would

reveal nothing about India to his family. It was better to suppress the nightmares, and eventually they would disappear.

At last, Lily broke the silence between them. 'Matthew didn't ruin me, James. I married him in secret before he left. We spoke wedding vows to one another.' She reached for the silver chain around her throat and revealed a gold signet ring.

Her words were an invisible blow. Not once, in two years, had Matthew mentioned this to him. It felt as if his friend had tricked his sister into believing it was real. And James felt compelled to point out, 'The marriage wasn't legal. Not without a licence or my permission.'

He turned and saw Lily's stricken face. Her hands were clenched together, but she faced him with her chin raised. 'Matthew nearly died in India. I've been waiting two years for *my husband* to return.'

'Arnsbury was never your husband.' And part of him was glad of it. Lily didn't know, *couldn't* know, how far his friend had descended into madness.

But Lily only raised her chin. 'If our marriage was illegal, then I will simply marry him again.'

Of course, his sister was as stubborn as she'd always been. She wasn't about to listen to reason. In her heart, she probably believed that Arnsbury was eager to reunite with her.

James tried to keep his voice gentle. 'Matthew is not the same man you knew, Lily. His mind was…damaged after what we endured.'

The months in captivity had stolen pieces of their lives. Although their outer wounds had healed, the scars—both seen and unseen—remained. The man Lily had fallen in love with was gone, unfit to be anyone's husband.

And James knew he was the same. Duty be damned. He couldn't imagine taking a wife now or siring an heir.

'What did you endure?' Lily asked. 'You never said what happened in India.'

'I won't speak of it,' he told her. 'It's better left in the past.'

There were some memories he refused to relive. It seemed like a lifetime ago since he'd departed. If he'd only known how much his life would change in two years, he'd have reconsidered his plans. Sometimes he longed to go back and tell his younger self not to be such an arrogant fool.

He only wished he could follow his own advice. He certainly didn't want anyone to know that he'd suffered nearly as much as Matthew. His dream of seeing the world had become filled with nightmares, being caught in the midst of war. Even after he and Arnsbury had escaped, it had been another endless journey from India back to England while avoiding the battlegrounds.

Although they'd made it out alive, it still made little sense to him why he and Matthew had been captured in the first place. There was no ransom demand from the group of rebels—only endless questions about the British Army's movements. Perhaps it truly had been a situation where they'd been in the wrong place at the wrong time, and the rebels had believed they were spies. He still didn't know.

It didn't matter now. He was home again, and he had to somehow pick up the shattered pieces of his family's life and mend them—even though the nightmares haunted him still.

'Are *you* all right, James?' his sister asked.

No, he wasn't. So many nights, he'd awakened with a

gasp of fear, his body drenched in sweat, his heart racing. His obligation to marry and sire an heir seemed impossible. He was broken, just as Matthew was. And no wife deserved that.

With reluctance, he faced the grim truth of his own hypocrisy. He blamed Lily for succumbing to seduction, but the truth was, he'd nearly done the same to Evie.

God above, he'd tried to shut her out of his mind. Yet, for the past two years, those forbidden memories had haunted him. He remembered the sweetness of her innocent mouth and the way she'd tempted him to abandon his own honour. Never had he imagined that such a shy wallflower held such a passionate heart. He couldn't deny that he wanted to see her again.

Was she still hiding in the shadows, or had she found someone else to love? Was she all right? But then, he didn't deserve those answers.

'I'm fine,' he lied. It was better to wear the mask of normalcy, letting his family believe that he had escaped without any trouble. 'But Arnsbury isn't.' He met his sister's gaze and said, 'Matthew will never be the same again, Lily. It would be best if you let him go.'

'I can't let him go, James. I love him, and I intend to stand by him.' Her voice was calm and determined as her gaze narrowed upon him. 'I also don't believe you're fine. Not if you endured the same captivity Matthew did.'

He shook his head in dismissal. 'It doesn't matter about me. I'm not the one who wants to be married.'

At that, her expression turned discerning. 'Don't you think it's time you found a wife of your own? Rose will be married in a few weeks. And after you finally set your stubbornness aside, I'll marry Matthew. Neither of us wants you to be alone.'

He hadn't missed the way she'd tossed in her own rebellious intentions amid their sister's betrothal. But he wasn't about to rise to her bait.

'I don't need a wife, Lily.' But he was happy that their sister Rose had fallen in love with an Irish earl. At least one of them had found happiness in the future that lay ahead.

She paused a moment. 'What about Evangeline?'

He tried to behave as if he had little interest in her. 'Surely she's married by now, isn't she?'

'No. After you left, she wasn't the same. She's…very different now.'

He couldn't stop himself from asking, 'Different in what way?'

His sister's cheeks reddened. 'She is quite independent. And wealthy beyond anyone's imagination.'

'Then she likely has no shortage of suitors,' he guessed.

Her expression turned pained. 'I fear that Evangeline has gained a rather dreadful reputation. They call her a shrew. Rose and I have tried to help her, but she seems to be enjoying chasing the men away. I don't understand it at all.'

His curiosity was piqued at the idea. The Evangeline he remembered was a lovely young woman with a large heart and a friendly warmth. He couldn't imagine her becoming shrewish at all.

'I think you ought to pay a call upon her again,' Lily predicted. 'She hasn't seen you since you left.'

He did owe her an apology—there was no denying that. Although he wasn't so certain it was a good idea to show up on her doorstep. Her overprotective father might greet him with a pistol in his hand.

'When you do see her, at least consider her as a bride,'

Lily suggested. 'I always thought the pair of you might suit.'

'Are our finances that dire?' he mused. 'You're suggesting that I wed Miss Sinclair for her dowry?'

'They're not dire, no. But you meant the world to Evie once.' She paused a moment and added, 'Honestly, I have no idea what Mother did with the estates while you were away.'

As if in response to her question, their mother wandered into the drawing room. She was wearing a black dress, a dark cloak, and her hands were tucked inside a fur muff.

'Are you going somewhere, Mother?' Lily asked.

'I am going to Spain tomorrow,' Iris answered. 'Do be a darling and make sure my trunks are packed. My George will be meeting me there. He's been gone for so long, you see.'

James met Lily's gaze. It seemed that Matthew wasn't the only one who had fallen into madness.

He'd known that their mother had grieved deeply for the loss of her husband. But he hadn't realised how lost she was in a world of her own making. His own mood grew sombre, 'Mother, Father is—'

'—missing you very much,' Lily finished. 'As I know you miss him.'

She shot James a warning look not to reveal the truth of George's death. He met her gaze, not understanding why she was shielding Iris from reality.

Tears gleamed in their mother's eyes. 'I want to see him again very soon.'

'I know you do,' Lily murmured. 'Perhaps you could go and write him a letter?'

Iris brightened at that. 'Oh, that is a wonderful idea. I shall go now.'

After she wandered out of the room, Lily turned to him. 'Our mother has changed a great deal while you were gone. She is not herself any more.'

He'd gathered as much from her attire yesterday and the way Iris had been delighted about another impending wedding.

'She believes Father is alive?'

Lily nodded. 'Among other things. Some might call her mad, but I still love her. Just as I still love Matthew and want to be his wife.' She reached for a chain around her neck and fingered it. 'Dreams are worth holding on to, James. Even if they aren't what they used to be.'

He wasn't so certain he had any dreams left at all. More like nightmares that would never go away.

Evangeline stood outside her mother's shop, staring at the glass front window. She was considering changing the display. Colourful bolts of silk and satin caught the morning sunlight, drawing the eye—but she was starting to wonder if there might be other ways to show off the fabric.

For most of her childhood, she'd been embarrassed by the idea of her family selling ladies' undergarments, even if it was a lucrative venture. But whether she liked it or not, Aphrodite's Unmentionables had become her legacy, and she intended to make the most of it. She'd discovered that she was quite good at making money.

During the past two years, she had begun helping with the business. There had been a time when they hadn't owned a store at all—they had simply taken exclusive orders and had hired the best seamstresses for the designs. But now, there was value in having a place where customers could choose the fabrics, laces, and designs.

Evie's latest venture was selling cotton drawers, pantalettes, and chemises that were ready to wear in several sizes. She had arranged for a dozen to be dyed in various colours, ranging from soft pink and lavender to a deep green. Some had embroidery, and others were slightly daring in the way they clung to a woman's body.

After they had sold out everything within days, she realised there was a true opportunity to continue offering certain garments in common sizes. And of course, after being measured, the ladies could also order the unmentionables in any size, style, or colour.

Last summer, Evangeline had travelled with her father to Scotland and Ireland where they had expanded the manufacturing, selling their garments in Edinburgh and Dublin. There were no factories, but all the undergarments were sewn by hand, giving women an opportunity to earn their own money. They could work at home and were paid by the quality of their efforts.

Although her family was incredibly wealthy, Evie enjoyed the money for a different reason. There was something empowering about being able to change people's lives for the better, whether it was paying bills anonymously, sending food to a needy family, or donating to orphanages. Her father was happy to fulfil her requests, for he had been raised in poverty himself. He knew what it was to be hungry, and unlike the rest of the London *ton*, he hadn't sheltered her from that side of life. He'd taken her to the poor houses, showing her the people who needed help.

For that reason, she was glad to continue selling unmentionables. If it made her family a laughingstock, so be it. No one else needed to know the greater purpose—of helping the poor and downtrodden. *She* knew what the power of money meant, and that was enough.

Even so, Evie often felt the loneliness as she'd watched other young women her age marry and have children. She, herself, had given up on the idea, two years ago. No man deserved to win her heart, and she refused to ever consider falling in love again.

Evie fully intended to remain a spinster with her animals to keep her company. Her enormously fat dog, Annabelle, and her cat, Dasher, gave her all the love and affection she needed. And neither of them would ever consider abandoning her. Now she only attended a few balls, mostly those hosted by family and friends, merely to be polite.

She lifted her chin and was about to enter the shop when a male voice said, 'Miss Sinclair?'

When she turned to see who it was, a coldness encircled her heart. James Thornton, the new Earl of Penford was standing a short distance away. His brown hair had lightened from months in the sunlight, but his eyes were still that vivid shade of green. Only this time, they held bleak shadows instead of rakish mischief. No longer was he the carefree viscount who had left for India—instead, it seemed that Fate had punished him.

Which was just as he deserved, she supposed.

Evangeline was torn between wanting to ignore him and enter her shop—or telling him exactly what she thought of him. And yet, something made her pause.

'What do you want, Lord Penford?' she asked calmly.

'I…honestly didn't expect to see you here. But since our paths have crossed, I suppose I owe you an apology.' Lord Penford took a step closer, and Evangeline shook her head, putting her gloved hands up.

You suppose? She could hardly believe the words coming out of his mouth. Did he expect her to fawn all over him and accept his apology?

'I would sooner eat rats than accept your apology,' she said, lifting her chin. 'Good day.'

Lord Penford raised an eyebrow. 'I deserve that, I know.' He glanced around and suggested, 'Would you care to have tea with me? I know an establishment that has a wonderful selection of cakes,' he suggested. 'Perhaps we could go there and talk.'

There was nothing whatsoever to talk about. Did he honestly believe she was still so enamoured of cake that she would set aside her pride and behave as if nothing had gone wrong?

'No, thank you,' she said airily. 'I have no intention of accepting your apology, so you can be on your way.'

Although her words were calm, inwardly, her emotions were churning. The sight of the earl evoked a blend of fury and anguish. He didn't know, nor could he understand how she'd grieved. He hadn't stolen her virginity, but he'd stolen her trust in men. With his abrupt departure, he'd shattered the fairy tale she had held so close to her heart.

And stomped on the pieces.

And burned them into ashes.

Evie turned her back on him and entered her shop, fully expecting him to leave. But the earl doggedly followed her inside.

'I was wrong to leave,' he said. 'And I behaved abominably.'

'Stop following me,' she insisted. 'I might have once been a young, starry-eyed girl with dreams of loving you,' she continued, 'but you can rest assured that I am no longer that person.'

He studied her face but remained a slight distance away.

'You startled me that night when you came to call. I got caught up in something I never imagined. And... I knew I couldn't be the suitor you wanted me to be. Not then.'

His eyes stared into hers in a way that seemed to unravel her senses. She'd mistakenly thought she was over him, but her heart warned that it would take very little to fall back into his arms. She had to push him away, to guard herself from being hurt again.

'You're right,' she said. 'You let me dream of marriage and a family with you when that was never your intention. I think you should leave, Lord Penford. I don't want to see you again.'

He gave a single nod. 'I understand. But I did want to apologise, even if the words are never enough. I hope you found a gentleman worthy of you. And perhaps I'll see you again at Rose's wedding in a few weeks.' He tipped his hat and turned to leave.

Evangeline suppressed a curse and walked to the opposite side of the store, pretending to concentrate on the design sketches. It only made her feel worse. Seeing the images of undergarments and corsets only reminded her of how James had unlaced hers in the garden. Her face burned at the memory, and she closed her eyes, willing back the scandalous vision.

A sudden flare of liquid heat flooded through her. She remembered everything, his hands unlacing her, his hot mouth on her...

Evie shoved the thought away. She never wanted to feel that sort of passion again, only to be abandoned. Being a spinster would suit her better. At least then, she would have her freedom and could live as she chose. She would inherit her family's business and that would become her purpose.

Somehow, it had to be enough.

Ireland,
Three weeks later

James had been careful to keep his distance from Evangeline, but he couldn't stop staring at her during Rose's wedding. He couldn't even say why—perhaps it was the grey dress she wore that contrasted with the bright colours of the other wedding guests. Perhaps she was trying to remain unnoticed, but with her dark black hair and deep blue eyes, the grey gown seemed almost silver. She carried herself like a queen, unlike the shy wallflower she'd once been. It seemed as if she simply didn't care what anyone else thought of her.

A wistful expression came over her face when the ceremony ended, and the newly wedded couple kissed. James clapped for his sister, who was beaming. Bagpipes resounded with a joyful tune, and Lord Ashton picked up his new wife, turning her in a slow circle. Rose laughed, her long Irish veil getting tangled.

But it was Evangeline's face that he kept glancing back at. She dabbed her eyes with a handkerchief her mother gave her, and the smile on her face reminded him of the way she had once smiled at him. It made him realise that, if he had simply asked for her hand in marriage two years ago, she might have become his wife.

Then, too, if he'd decided to stay in London, he would have had another year with his father. The familiar grief and guilt washed over him at the thought of all the mistakes he'd made. Yet, he couldn't go back and change the past. There was little point to it now.

'James,' Lily murmured. 'We have to see to the wedding feast.'

At that, he shook himself out of his reverie. 'Of course.'

His sister's face narrowed. 'Were you just staring at Evangeline?'

'No,' he lied. 'I was watching the wedding. Rose seems very happy.'

'You *were* watching her, weren't you?' Lily appeared fascinated at the prospect. 'After all this time, you still care for Evie, don't you?' Her expression turned scheming, and he felt the need to stop her from making plans.

'You should be more concerned about your own future, Lily,' he warned. 'And it won't be with Matthew, I can tell you that.'

Her face turned soft. 'You're wrong. Lord Arnsbury will heal, and we will start again. You should do the same.'

He didn't argue with Lily, not wanting to spoil the day. But it infuriated him that his best friend had seduced and ruined Lily under the pretence of marriage vows that weren't real.

Why she still held out hope, he didn't know. Had it been any other man, he'd have demanded that the blackguard marry her. But he didn't want his sister wedded to someone who could not give her the happiness she deserved.

James couldn't say anything more, for Rose and her new husband were approaching. He embraced his sister and murmured. 'You look beautiful, Rose.' When he drew back, he shook the earl's hand. 'I wish you both happiness.' It was a sincere wish, but unnecessary, for he could already see the love and joy between them.

'It's glad I am, to call you Brother,' the earl answered. 'I will cherish Rose each and every day.'

The newly wedded couple joined the guests, walking towards the tables set out for feasting. James stepped back while the Irish villagers lined up for the food. The delicious scent made his stomach rumble, but the local wedding guests were far hungrier after the recent famine had taken their crops. He wanted to be certain that they had their fill first.

Evangeline and her family had discreetly brought a great deal of food with them, to ensure that there would be too much for the wedding feast. At first, James hadn't wanted to accept the gift, but her father insisted that the leftover food would have to be given away to the people. Which was exactly the intent.

Now that he'd seen the gaunt faces of the Irish children, James understood why the food was so necessary. The wedding gave the people a celebration and also a sense of hope.

Only after the others had taken helpings of the roasted chicken, potatoes, and bread, did he join the line after Evangeline. She stiffened the moment he did, as if she couldn't stand to be in his presence. He deserved that, he supposed.

She didn't say anything to him, nor did he speak to her. But he took a moment to study her closely. Her dark hair was as beautiful as ever, tightly coiled up with pearls adorning the strands. She held her posture erect, and he noticed the curves of her body, as if the grey gown had been melted upon her. And God help him, he remembered the sweet softness of her bare skin.

He turned his attention away, for he'd made that mistake once before. She despised him, and rightfully so. It was better if he focused his attentions on his family and estate, not Evangeline Sinclair.

One of the Irishmen handed her a tin cup and then gave another one to him. James smelled the whiskey inside, but Evangeline took a drink and coughed a moment before she seemed to recognise what it was.

'Are you all right?' he asked, after they stepped away from the table.

'I'm fine.' But her wrinkled expression revealed her inexperience with drinking spirits. He eyed her more closely, and she added, 'I'm certain you have other people you would rather speak with, Lord Penford.'

Her dismissal was quite evident. And he truly ought to leave her alone, he knew. But something about her haughty tone challenged him.

'Thank you for coming to my sister's wedding,' he said. 'It meant a lot to Rose and Lily.' He kept his voice entirely polite, but he fully knew he was annoying her.

'Your sisters are my dearest friends,' she said coolly. 'Of course I would attend. Now, if you'll excuse me...'

'Does it bother you so much to be in the same room with me?' He took a step closer, but she held her ground. 'You don't have to avoid me, you know.'

'I am *trying* to avoid you.' She lifted her chin in open disdain.

'I deserve that, I know. But would like to make peace between us,' he added. Then he remarked, 'I'm surprised that you didn't marry while I was away.'

From the stricken look on her face, he regretted the words as soon as he'd spoken them. He'd meant them as a compliment, but clearly, she didn't see it that way. Her blue eyes were stormy, her mouth tight with anger.

'I have no intention of being married,' she said, lifting her chin. 'I prefer having my freedom, thank you.' She gave a slight nod and turned her back on him.

But not before he caught her hand. 'Forgive me. It wasn't my intention to make you uncomfortable. I actually came to ask for your help—'

Miss Sinclair wrenched her hand away and glared at

him. 'I don't think so. I'm terribly busy.' She drained her whiskey cup, and the fierce burn made her start coughing.

'—with the wedding guests,' he finished. In a low voice, he added, 'Your father and I are distributing the extra food you brought. But I want to do more for them.'

Her expression grew sombre when she seemed to re-alise that this wasn't about the rift between them. 'What did you have in mind?'

'Let's go and discuss this somewhere the others don't overhear us.' He led her past several men and women who were already dancing, the ladies' skirts swinging while the pipers played a lively tune.

'I thought of games with money as prizes,' he contin-ued. 'The Irish people are too proud to accept charity. What do you think? Would they join in?'

She glanced back at the guests, and her gaze stopped upon the children and elderly guests. 'I think those who need money the most are the weakest,' she admitted. 'The games should not be based on skill.' She thought a mo-ment and said, 'You should involve the children.'

'Should we hide coins for them to find, do you think?'

'No. They would fight over them.' Her brow furrowed, and she said, 'Games might be too much of a distrac-tion from the wedding. Perhaps you could hide the coins with the leftover food baskets. Tie them up with a hand-kerchief and be discreet. Let them find the money when they are alone.'

Her suggestion held merit. 'All right. I'll see to it.' He offered a friendly smile, but Evangeline didn't return it. Instead, he saw traces of hurt and frustration in her eyes that she quickly veiled. Although she tried to behave as if she were indifferent to him, he saw more beneath the surface—and it was *his* fault.

He didn't deserve her forgiveness, but he'd meant what he said. He did want peace between them, even if friendship was impossible.

And yet, a part of him wished he could go back to the way things had once been between them.

With a light smile, James turned to depart. For a moment, Evangeline felt a slight twinge of disappointment. He'd spoken to her with friendliness and not a trace of interest. Which was exactly as it should be. She didn't want him, and he didn't want her.

But Lord Penford was as handsome as he'd always been. He wore a black cloth jacket and a white shirt and cravat, as well as buff-coloured trousers. His skin still held the tan of India, and during their conversation, she'd found herself thoroughly distracted by his quiet stare. He had gazed at her as if he'd remembered every stolen moment in the garden. God help her, she'd certainly never forgotten it. Her defences rose up and tightened at the thought.

Memory brought back the coaxing kiss, the way his hands had slid over her skin, teaching her what temptation was. Although it had been forbidden, she couldn't quite bring herself to be sorry. For one forbidden moment, she'd lost sight of the world, and it had stolen the breath from her lungs.

Not to mention, her innocence.

Her face flamed with the memories of their passionate interlude, but worst of all was his rejection. She'd given herself to him wholeheartedly, dreaming that he felt the same way about her. Instead, he'd walked away without a trace of honour, leaving her heart shredded.

The Earl of Penford was a wicked rake, and she simply had to stay away from him from now on.

From behind her, Evangeline heard the cry of a baby. She turned back and saw a young mother patting the infant's back, speaking soothing words. The sight of them brought an unexpected clench to her heart.

The only problem with never marrying was that she'd always wanted a baby of her own. Lots of children, actually. She imagined holding a child, pressing a kiss against a downy head. The invisible ache deepened, and she turned away, trying to distract herself.

As she passed by the young mother, she said, 'You have a beautiful baby.'

'Oh, you're very kind,' the woman smiled. 'The wee one is tired, that's all.'

An older man stumbled forward, laughing as he did. Though he appeared close to eighty, there was a spring in his step and a strong scent of whiskey on his breath. Evangeline took a step backwards, then another. The man was harmless, but she was more afraid of him falling over.

He beamed at her. ''Twas a bonny wedding, I must say.'

'It was,' she agreed. And she truly was happy for Rose.

'And will the two of you be the next to wed?' he asked, his voice slurred.

The two of who? Evangeline turned around and saw Lord Penford standing behind her. The earl didn't appear amused, and for a moment, it seemed as if he had approached with the intent of protecting her.

'I think he means us,' Penford answered.

'Absolutely not,' Evangeline said to the old man.

'No, not at all,' James agreed. He took a step closer, placing himself between her and the Irishman.

Though she knew the man was only drunk, James was making his intent to protect her quite clear. She didn't know what to think about that.

'And why would you not marry such a beautiful *cailín* as this?' the old man asked, still smiling.

An impulsive reply blurted from her lips. 'Because I was holding out hopes for you.'

At that, the man howled with laughter and slapped his knee. 'Well, now, I'll find the priest, and we'll get on with it.'

Evangeline couldn't stop her own smile, but Lord Penford didn't appear amused. She nodded her head to him and said, 'I should return to my family. It's getting late.'

Before she could leave, he touched her spine gently. 'I'll escort you back.'

From the pressure at her waist, he wasn't about to be deterred by arguments. She waited until they were out of earshot of the other guests before she stepped away. 'Thank you, but I can find my family on my own, Lord Penford.'

'It's a courtesy,' he said softly. 'I don't want anyone to hurt you.'

'You already did that two years ago,' she reminded him. Did he honestly think that time had healed her embarrassment?

'And I'm sorry for it.'

'Your apology doesn't change what happened.' She crossed her arms and stared at him. In a low voice, she added, 'I want you to stay far away from me.'

'I was hoping we could be friends once again,' he offered.

His words were a blade slicing through her wounded heart. 'No.' Her face burned red, and she added, 'I can't be your friend, Penford. Not ever.'

'I deserve that,' he admitted, 'but it's not what I want.'

'You lost the right to be my friend that night,' she continued. 'And every time I'm around you, I think of how naive and foolish I was. It consumes me.' She shook her head. 'I need distance from you. Please don't talk to me again.'

For even after all this time, she had feelings for him. He'd destroyed her trust when he'd left her behind, but her foolish heart still pined.

It was far better if she never saw him again. Or better yet, if she was so unspeakably rude, he would never again look at her with interest.

Chapter Five

For the first time in years, Evangeline was looking forward to a ball. Not for the possibility of marriage—quite the contrary. Instead, she had decided to dress as the most unmarriable young lady in London. Her mother appeared pained by the idea, while her father thought it was great fun.

Hubert Buchanan, Viscount Dunwood, had renewed his courtship, and Evie wanted to deter the man in every way possible. He still treated her as if she should be honoured at his attentions, when she found him to be condescending and horrible.

He'd married a sickly young woman a year and a half ago and was already a widower. Despite the requisite mourning period, he'd begun sending Evie notes and flowers. He had set his sights upon her dowry again, and she was determined to push him away and convince him to leave her alone.

Tonight, she'd chosen the ugliest gown she could find. She had lied to the modiste and claimed that it was for a masquerade. The greyish-brown silk made her appear sallow, and the neckline rested at her throat, covering every inch of skin. A large bustle formed behind her, making her backside appear enormous. Last, she'd asked her maid to arrange her hair in a style befitting a spinster, tightly drawn back.

Instead of behaving like a well-bred lady, she intended to behave in the opposite manner. She would express every opinion and say whatever was on her mind. She didn't care if it ruined all future marriage prospects. Men like Lord Dunwood were only interested in her dowry, so it probably wouldn't make a difference. But tonight, she intended to be entirely herself. If that was unappealing to a gentleman, so be it.

Lily appeared confused by her attire, though she said nothing. In contrast, her best friend wore a lilac-coloured ball gown and had tucked violets into her hair.

'You look lovely tonight, Lily,' Evangeline said. 'Especially in that colour.' For so long, her friend had been a wallflower beside her because she had given her heart to Lord Arnsbury. Evie had thought the two of them still planned to be together, but Lily's eyes appeared shadowed, as if she no longer knew what would happen between them.

'Have you…changed your mind about finding a husband?' Evie ventured.

'Not at all. Thank you.' Her friend's voice was cool and disinterested, which made her wonder what had happened.

An awkwardness settled between them, and Evie wished she hadn't asked. Even a few weeks ago, Lily had seemed eager to wed Lord Arnsbury. But now—something had changed. What was it?

Lily paused a moment and finally asked, 'I do not mean to offend, but was this truly a gown of your choosing?'

A smile broke over her face. 'It's perfectly dreadful, isn't it?' Evie remarked. 'I asked the modiste to find silk the colour of mouse fur. Now I can safely remain a wall-flower, and no man would dare ask me to dance.'

Especially Lord Dunwood. With any luck, the man would stay far away from her.

'It is…certainly a different colour than any I've seen before.'

Which was precisely why she'd chosen it. 'My mother was horrified. She thinks I should make a greater effort to find a husband, but why would I want a man to govern my life with his own rules? I am perfectly happy with my books. And my father seems content to let me remain a spinster.'

Lily managed a nod, but they both knew it was the truth. Cain Sinclair considered no man worthy of his daughter. And Evie knew if her father had the slightest idea of what had happened between her and Lord Penford two years ago, Cain would have shot him.

At that moment, the earl crossed the room and joined his sister. Evangeline pretended as if he wasn't there, and Penford did not acknowledge her presence. But there was still an invisible tension between them. She was entirely aware of the way his jacket outlined his muscular form and the faint sandalwood scent of his skin. She remembered, too well, the taste of his mouth against hers.

'Lily, would you care to dance?' the earl asked his sister.

'Not just now, thank you,' Lily answered. A smile of mischief lifted her mouth. 'But I am certain Evangeline would be happy to take my place.'

Oh, no. Not that.

She wanted to throttle her friend for even suggesting such a thing. The thought of being in James's arms again was unthinkable.

She turned to the earl and answered cheerfully, 'I would sooner stand in a corner and peel wallpaper. But thank you for the offer.'

James's posture stiffened, and he coughed as if he were trying not to laugh. His eyes suddenly gleamed with mischief of his own. And strangely, she felt as if she'd just thrown down an invisible gauntlet. 'I see your manners have not improved, Evangeline.'

Oh, he had no idea just how rude she could be. She fully intended to accept that challenge.

'Forgive me,' James apologised to his sister, 'but I am trying to avoid being matched up by the meddling mamas.'

'Matchmaking meddling mamas,' Evangeline repeated. 'Now there's a phrase I'd wager you couldn't say three times without twisting up your tongue.'

'I don't recall that you are part of this conversation.' James gave her a teasing sidelong glance, as if daring her to fire back at him. It was an open dare, and one that she accepted willingly.

'I don't know that I want to be part of a conversation with *you*.' Without another word, she spun and strode away, disappearing into the crowd.

Was it terrible that she had enjoyed their verbal sparring?

You shouldn't, she warned herself. *You're only trying to destroy any wayward feelings you still have.*

But even as she turned down another man's invitation to dance, she caught Penford watching her from across the room. Whether he'd admit it or not, there was a slight smile on his face, as if he'd enjoyed himself as much as she. And somehow, he'd talked Lily into dancing with him, to avoid the matchmakers.

Evangeline accepted a glass of lemonade from a footman serving at the refreshment table and watched as the pair of them danced together. Once, she would have gladly taken Lily's place. Her brain warned that it wasn't a good idea.

No, her decision to stay away from Penford was the right one. And perhaps someday, she would be able to look at him and not remember the searing heat she'd felt in his arms.

She finished her lemonade and took another stroll to the opposite side of the room. Unfortunately, Lord Dunwood was waiting and greeted her with a sardonic smile. 'You look lovely this evening, Miss Sinclair.'

Why, oh, why had she allowed herself to be distracted by James instead of paying attention to who was waiting for her?

Evangeline suppressed a groan. She honestly didn't want to talk to him. And though it was terribly rude, perhaps that was the best way to handle the situation.

She hadn't forgotten the way the viscount had mocked her during their first meeting, and it irritated her that he still seemed to think she should be flattered by his interest. Although she supposed he was passably handsome, it was his arrogance that made him hideous.

'Miss Sinclair?' he prompted. 'Did you hear what I said to you?'

Unfortunately. She weighed her options, wondering if she should simply mutter a thank you and continue walking. But no. Why should she be polite to a man she was trying to get rid of?

Instead, her good sense went out the window, and she blurted out, 'It seems that my attempts at deterring your interest have failed. Or you may need to see a doctor about your eyesight, Lord Dunwood.'

He ignored her remark and asked, 'Would you care to dance, Miss Sinclair?'

'Not in a thousand years, thank you. But I believe Miss Brown might be delighted.' She nodded towards a young, giggling maiden who lacked the sense God gave a goose. Only she might be able to endure his company.

'I would prefer to dance with you.' His smooth smile was as empty as his compliments.

Evangeline highly doubted that. 'No, sir, I imagine you would prefer that I entertain the idea of a future with you. But I would have to be completely desperate to wed a fortune hunter, such as yourself. And I assure you that I would rather be a spinster for the rest of my life.'

A darkness slid over his expression, though he masked it with another smile. 'It's been two years, Miss Sinclair. Have you had a single offer of marriage other than mine?'

She'd had plenty of courting gifts from gentlemen. She'd even had a poem from one suitor who had praised her hair, comparing it to sunlight…though her hair was so dark, it was nearly black. Evangeline guessed that he had probably sent the same poem to every unmarried lady.

'There has been no shortage of offers from impoverished gentlemen who want my dowry.' Sadly, it was the truth. 'And you, yourself, were married for several months.'

'I am out of mourning now,' he said. 'And I need an heir.'

Not from me, Evie thought.

She dismissed Lord Dunwood by saying, 'I think it's time for you to turn your charms upon someone else.'

She had nearly escaped him when he suddenly reached out for her wrist. He squeezed it tightly and drew her back.

Without thinking, she slapped him with her fan. 'Do *not* touch me, sir.'

'One of these days, you'll come to regret your rudeness, Miss Sinclair.' He did release her hand, but she suspected the skin would bruise.

'I highly doubt it.' But she did regret speaking to him. And what did he mean she'd come to regret being rude? It sounded like a threat, and that was something new from him. She was beginning to wish she'd walked away the moment she'd seen him.

Evangeline strode past Lord Dunwood, keeping her head held high, so as not to appear afraid. She looked for Lily and then saw Lord Penford dancing with Miss Brown. She was smiling prettily, laughing in delicate little trills that made her curls bounce. Although the earl retained his own smile, she suspected that Miss Brown's giggling was beginning to wear upon his mood.

The earl's gaze caught hers, and she wondered if he'd seen her strike Lord Dunwood with her fan. There was a look in James's eyes as if he wanted to approach her.

The dance ended, and he bowed to the young woman before making a hasty retreat. Evangeline tried in vain to move out of his path, but he moved towards her and said, 'Are you all right, Miss Sinclair?'

'I am, thank you.' She tried to behave as if nothing were wrong, but he appeared doubtful.

'Good. Then you can dance with me.'

Dance? Why would he want to do that? The very thought flustered her. 'I believe we've already discussed this. The answer is no.'

He smiled warmly at her. 'Oh, you needn't worry that it means anything. I need to escape the matchmakers.'

'And what if I don't want to be used like that?' She was indignant that he was once again treating her like a sister. 'I ought to take you over to the matchmaking mamas and introduce you. I could tell them how much you are looking forward to meeting their daughters and finding a wife.'

'You'd feed me to the tigers?'

'Without hesitation.' She smiled at him, but there was a dangerous glint in his eyes.

He took her hand and placed it on his arm as they strolled through the ballroom.

'Why did you hit Lord Dunwood with your fan,' he remarked. 'What did he do?'

'He made the mistake of trying to grab my wrist.'

Lord Penford's expression darkened with annoyance. 'He should know better. Do you want me to speak to him?'

'I already did,' she said. 'And you're not responsible for me.'

He gave a slight nod of agreement. 'As you say.'

'But if he asks me to marry him again, I might borrow Lady Allston's ear trumpet to ensure that he actually hears me when I refuse.'

'So, you've no wish to indulge in matrimonial bliss?'

'Not with a fortune hunter like Viscount Dunwood.' She began fanning herself, for it was becoming rather hot. 'What of you? Are you still avoiding marriage?'

'With every bone in my body.'

His words relaxed the tension she didn't know she was carrying. 'You do realise that your avoidance will only make the matrons even more determined to wear you down? You're far too desirable to remain a bachelor.'

'Let them try. I'm less suited for marriage now than I ever was.' Though his tone was light, she suspected there was a shadow beneath the words.

For that reason, she tried to keep her own questions conversational. 'Because you still wish to travel the world?'

'No. I'm happy to remain in England for the rest of my life. But let us simply say that our travels in India left their own scars.'

His honesty surprised her, for she'd not expected him to reveal that truth to her. Though she wanted to probe deeper, to ask him what he meant by that, his expression appeared haggard. And the James she knew would never reveal any weakness. If she asked what had happened, undoubtedly, he would refuse to speak of it. Even Lily and Rose had revealed nothing; they'd been intensely private about their brother's return.

Although she understood that they were protecting Penford, she couldn't help but be curious about his travels. And what were the scars he spoke of? She sensed that they were not physical scars, but something else entirely.

And yet, she reminded herself that this was not the time or place for such a revelation. Not during a wedding celebration.

'I suppose we both have the same goal, then. To avoid marriage.' Evie fluttered her fan, averting her gaze.

'I thought there was a time when you wanted to find a husband.'

Once, that had been true…when she'd hoped to marry *him*. But instead, she answered, 'Not any more.'

His expression grew concerned. 'It's my fault that you changed your mind, isn't it?' He let out a harsh sigh. 'I'm sorry.'

For a moment, she didn't quite know what to say. It had begun that way, but then she had found a different purpose during their two years apart. She'd found a hidden part of herself, and she refused to give up that independence in exchange for marriage vows.

'You did break my heart,' she agreed. 'But no, my decision not to marry is for another reason. A husband would never allow me to continue managing Aphrodite's Unmentionables. It's my family's legacy, and I've enjoyed the challenges of maintaining a business. It's entirely inappropriate for a lady…but I was surprised to find how much I've enjoyed it.'

'And you think a husband would make you give it up?'

'I know he would. A titled lord would likely be ashamed of me and insist that I have nothing to do with it—but only after he's spent my entire dowry, of course.'

He eyed her with interest but merely nodded in agreement. They both knew it was true. 'Then I'll bid you luck in your quest to avoid matrimony. The dress was a good choice. I've never seen anything uglier.'

'It's perfectly hideous,' Evangeline agreed. 'I asked the modiste to give me fabric the colour of mouse fur. I would say she succeeded.'

'Indeed.'

After spending several days in his father's study, trying to make sense of the family accounts, James was left with one inevitable conclusion. He was going to have to pay a call upon Evangeline's father, Cain Sinclair.

He'd read through the ledgers half a dozen times, and he kept finding the same answers. His mother had given over a huge sum of money to the man to invest a few months ago, and God only knew why or what had happened.

Although he trusted Evangeline, he knew very little about her father. And why Iris had given an acquaintance their money was a mystery he intended to unravel.

His driver brought him across town to the Sinclair residence. When James disembarked, he was surprised to find gentlemen waiting outside the townhouse. Most were carrying bouquets of flowers, while others held gifts of different sorts. They were all here to court Evangeline, so it seemed. Was this an everyday occurrence to have such a queue outside her house?

He started to walk past the men when one called out, 'And just where do you think you're going? You'll have to wait like the rest of us.'

'I am here to pay a call upon Mr Sinclair.' James ignored the men and crossed to the front of the group. But when he was nearly there, he saw Viscount Dunwood among them. The man sent him an irritated look, and it was clear that he was frustrated at having to wait.

It seemed that Evie's refusal had indeed fallen upon deaf ears.

When the footman opened the door again, James repeated his request. 'I am the Earl of Penford, here to see Mr Sinclair.'

The footman raised an eyebrow but led him to the hallway, along with the next suitor in line. 'You can both wait here.'

James cast a sidelong glance at the suitor, who appeared to be twenty years older than Evangeline. In his hands, the man held a brown paper parcel.

'What did you bring her?' James asked.

'That's none of your affair,' the suitor answered. He lifted his chin and stared at the drawing room.

'How long have you been waiting to speak with Miss Sinclair?' he prompted.

'An hour,' the man answered. 'And I promise you, she will not see us both at the same time.'

'As I said before, I am not here to see Miss Sinclair. I am here to speak with her father.'

But just then, Evangeline arrived, along with her mother. Margaret Sinclair's eyes gleamed when she saw him. 'Lord Penford. It is good to see you again.'

'And you, Mrs Sinclair,' he agreed. He turned to Evangeline, who was wearing a gown the colour of dead leaves. Her hair was severely drawn back into a tight arrangement, and she appeared ready to do battle against the suitor.

He couldn't stop himself from smiling at her. 'Is that your latest gown, Miss Sinclair?'

She sent him a murderous glare. 'It is.'

'And you look absolutely breathtaking,' the suitor interrupted. 'I have never seen a more lovely lady than yourself.'

'Lies,' James countered. 'I have never seen an uglier gown in all my life. Aside from the one you wore at the ball the other night. What was it? The colour of mouse fur? And what would you call this one? The colour of horse dung?'

Margaret Sinclair appeared horrified at his words, but Evangeline broke into a laugh. 'I believe you're right.'

The merriment in her eyes accentuated her features, and he couldn't help but return the smile.

Margaret nudged her daughter sharply, and Evangeline muttered to the suitor, 'Thank you.' To James, she said, 'I thought we had agreed not to see one another again.'

'True enough. I didn't come to see you. I came to speak with your father.'

Her face turned curious. 'And why would you do that?'

'To find out why my mother gave him over half our family assets,' he said. 'And, I suppose, to thank him for ensuring that her investment turned a profit.'

'Ah, I see.' Evangeline gave a nod.

'Evie, I think we should go into the drawing room,' Margaret said. 'There are many gentlemen waiting.'

'I wish you great fortune in achieving your goal,' he said to Evangeline with a wink. She rolled her eyes, though he meant her goal of avoiding marriage.

'Good day, Lord Penford,' Mrs Sinclair said politely.

He gave a slight bow, and Evangeline sighed as she followed her mother inside. But not before she sent him one last look. It almost appeared as if she wanted to be rescued.

After a quarter of an hour, her father strode down the hallway. Cain Sinclair still had hair that was longer than was fashionable, tied in a queue down his back. The dark strands were shot with grey, but there was no denying the physical strength of the Highlander. His broad shoulders strained the seams of his jacket, and he crossed his arms.

'And just why have you come to see me, Penford? It's no' about my daughter, is it?'

'Indeed, no. I am unworthy of your daughter, and we both know it.'

At that, the Highlander cracked a smile. 'We agree on something, then. Come, and we'll talk outside in the garden.'

James followed the man down the hallway, and it was then that he noticed the subtle touches of wealth. The stairway was carved with leaves and finials, and the polished floors gleamed with exotic woods he'd not seen before.

It surprised him that Mr Sinclair wanted to speak outside when it was November. But then he saw targets set up in the garden along a stone wall. The winter air was clear and crisp, and he saw a row of pistols upon a table.

'Do you shoot?' Sinclair asked.

'Only while hunting.' It had been some time since he'd fired a weapon.

'If you're wanting to practise, be my guest,' Sinclair invited.

'After you,' he offered. While the man chose a weapon, James began, 'I wanted to ask you about the investments my mother made with your help.'

Cain's expression sobered. 'Lady Penford did no' take your father's death well. It...shattered her mind in her grief.'

He'd seen glimpses of that already. His mother still seemed lost and lonely, as if she were barely hanging on to her place in the world. 'Unfortunately, you're right. I don't know why she came to you.'

'She was grieving and needed help. Your sister Rose fell ill, and your sister Lily was pining for Lord Arnsbury,' Sinclair admitted. 'Lady Penford was worried about your father's debts and asked me to invest on their behalf.'

'And you agreed to this?' He kept his voice calm and deliberate, but if Sinclair had dared to take advantage of their family, he wouldn't hesitate to set things right.

The Highlander loaded his pistol, took aim at the target, and fired. There was a clean hole in the centre of the target. 'Your mother was kind to my family when so many others were not. Even now, we are no' welcome in many ballrooms.' He glanced around at their house. 'My Margaret is the finest lady I've ever known. And your mother, Lady Penford, stood up for my wife and daughter against those who wanted to spread lies about them. When she came and asked for help, I was only too glad to give it.'

He reloaded the pistol and took aim again, blowing a second hole through the centre of the target. 'I used the investment money she gave to help expand our fam-

ily's business. And I doubled her profits within a year.'
The Highlander's voice softened. 'We also helped many
women find work so they could feed their families.'

He finished by saying, 'I returned everything to Lady
Penford, along with the profits. Your sisters now have
generous dowries.'

There was a subtle censure to his tone, as if James ought
to be more grateful.

And he was, in truth. 'Thank you for your assistance,
Mr Sinclair,' he said. 'I know things were difficult for my
family after my father passed and I was away.'

'Your mother is no' well,' he said. 'I suppose she's
wanting to live in a world where your father is still alive.'

James nodded. 'We all miss him.' He paused a moment and offered, 'If we were to…invest again in your
family's business—'

'You'd have to speak with Evie,' Cain answered. 'She
is the reason why you earned such a profit. Never seen
anyone with such a head for numbers as my lass.' A sly
look crossed his face. 'Should I go and ask her to join us?'

'I wouldn't want to intrude upon her suitors,' he answered. 'You can simply tell her that I'll speak with her
later.'

'Speak to me about what?' came Evangeline's voice
from the doorway. Her gaze narrowed upon him, and she
let out a sigh. 'Please don't tell me that *I* was the subject
of your discussion with my father.'

'Indirectly,' he answered. 'Rest assured, I am not here
to request your hand in marriage.'

'Thank goodness.' Evangeline hurried down the stairs.
'I've had enough of gentlemen for one day. Especially
after Lord Dunwood, who still cannot seem to grasp that
I despise him and would never consider him as a hus-

band. I told Mother to send them all away.' Her expression turned interested when she saw her father's pistol. 'Are you practising your shooting? May I join? I feel the need to shoot something right now.'

'Go on then, lass,' her father answered. 'Lord Penford is considering investing more money in Aphrodite's Unmentionables. If you're willing to allow it.' He leaned down and kissed the top of his daughter's head. 'I'll leave the pair of you to discuss it.'

'Without a chaperone?' James pointed out. 'Is that wise?'

The Highlander cracked a smile. 'I've given my daughter a pistol. I'd say that's chaperone enough.' He placed a few bullets in Evangeline's palm, and his eyes gleamed. 'Make good use of it, lass.'

Her face brightened, and she loaded the weapon. Her father retreated to the house, leaving James to wonder what sort of discussion this was going to be.

'Were the suitors that terrible?' he ventured as she loaded the pistol.

'No, they were the same as always.' She took aim at the target. 'Empty compliments, along with their mistaken belief that I am unmarried because I had no offers.' Slowly, she squeezed the trigger and struck the centre of the target. 'If anything, I have too many. But I tell them what I think of them, and they usually go away. Except Lord Dunwood.'

He wasn't at all surprised. Although Evangeline Sinclair might have been a shy wallflower at one time, that young woman had disappeared. 'And what did you say to him today?'

'I told him that he ought to try listening to a woman, instead of telling me all the reasons why I should be grateful for his proposal.' She set down her pistol and winced. 'Do you know, the first suitor tried to sing to me.'

He tried to suppress his smile. 'That sounds like torture.'

'It was. And he simply wouldn't stop.' A look of mischief crossed her face. 'That is, until I joined him in singing. I sang loudly and very, very off-key.'

'It sounds as if he deserved it,' James said. 'But why do you take their calls if you don't plan to marry?'

'My mother holds out hope that one day I might change my mind.' She reloaded the pistol and studied the target a second time. 'But I won't.' She offered him the pistol. 'Your turn.'

He aimed and took his shot, but although it struck the target, it was not quite in the centre. Evangeline sent him a slight smile.

'You're still a better shot than me,' he admitted.

'My father and Uncle Jonathan taught me everything I know.' There was pride in her voice, and he couldn't help but feel the same way. 'They both wanted to ensure that I could always protect myself.' Her mouth twisted in a wry smile. 'Honestly, Papa would be happier if I carried a loaded pistol in my reticule.'

'Thank goodness it's not large enough,' James said. Then he turned back to his true reason for paying a call. 'I'd like to hear more about your family business. Your father thought I should speak to you about investing. It sounds as if this is about far more than earning a profit, isn't it?'

She nodded. 'It's a way for women to earn money with their needle. They can feed their children.' Her tone softened, and she added. 'It may be a scandalous business, but I've seen the good it can do.' She turned to face him. 'And I won't allow anyone to take that away from me. Or them.'

He saw the sincerity on her face, and it did seem that the investment was not only a sound one, but a charitable one. 'Then I am interested in investing once again.'

Chapter Six

E<small>VANGELINE</small> knew she was in trouble. She'd forgotten how easy it was to talk to Lord Penford. Around him, she'd always been able to be herself. But what good was it? He didn't want a wife, and she didn't want a husband.

Or, at least, she didn't want any of the men who had offered for her.

Even after the earl had left and she'd spent the rest of the day with Dasher curled up and purring on her lap, it was difficult to stop thinking of Penford. When he'd stood beside her while she was trying to shoot her pistol, she'd been entirely aware of how wonderful he smelled. She could easily have buried her face in his neck while she imagined him holding her close.

And worse, last night, she'd dreamed of him. She'd remembered the devastatingly arousing sensation of his mouth upon hers, his tongue sliding inside. She awakened in the morning, her body aching with need for something she didn't understand.

Nothing had changed between them. James still didn't want a wife, and she wasn't about to let herself fall in love again. Not with a man who didn't want her. Inwardly, she steeled her defences and decided she needed a distraction.

Her head was in a muddle, so she'd sent a note to Lily

this morning, asking her if she could come over. Perhaps, they could walk their dogs in Rotten Row. Annabelle was getting entirely too fat. At first, she'd wondered if her cocker spaniel had somehow got pregnant. But how? The dog usually went outside into their garden, and every time she'd gone for a walk, she had been on a lead. No, it was probably Annabelle just eating too much and lying around. It might do them both good to get some exercise.

Evangeline led Lily inside their townhouse and thanked her for coming over. Lily had adopted a stray dog not long ago, and she'd named him Sebastian. The dog appeared delighted to visit, and he sniffed at the carpet, his tail wagging as if it were the best day of his entire life.

From the moment they entered the sitting room, Sebastian grew excited. He pulled hard on the lead, struggling to reach Annabelle. But the cocker spaniel eyed him with suspicion, and Sebastian crouched low with his tail in the air, desperate to play.

'I think we should take them both for a walk now, don't you?' Evangeline suggested. She fastened a collar and leash around her dog's head and teased, 'Annabelle is quite fat, and I've no doubt it was caused by sitting and eating all day long.'

But the truth was, she longed to get out of the house to clear her head. She was starting to feel those same feelings again for James. Whenever he was around, something inside her went soft. And that had to stop.

Before they could go, her father blocked the doorway. 'And just where d'ye think you're going, Evangeline?'

Of course, she thought. *Overprotective, as always.*

She ventured a smile. 'Lily and I are taking Sebastian and Annabelle for a walk.'

And then I'm going to decide how to rid myself of these useless feelings for Lord Penford.

Sebastian sniffed at Annabelle's backside before he trotted over to Evangeline's father and rolled to his back, exposing his belly.

A smile creased Cain's mouth. 'You're a braw lad, aren't you, dog? A fine animal indeed.' Then he turned back to Evangeline. 'Your mother told me that Thomas Kingford, Viscount Burkham, intends to pay a call on you this afternoon. She's wanting you to stay.'

No. Not another one. Evie grimaced as she fumbled for an excuse. 'Lord Burkham was once betrothed to Rose. Have you forgotten? He abandoned her when she was ill.' How could they even consider asking her to consider marriage to the man who spurned one of her dearest friends? It was better to send him away, like all the others.

'Aye,' her father acknowledged. 'But your mother said he isn't so bad.'

'He's a fortune hunter, and I will not let him court me,' Evangeline insisted. 'Not to mention, Mrs Everett has sunk her claws into him. She intends for him to wed her daughter. Good riddance, I say.'

From the nod on her father's face, it seemed he agreed. 'If you wish to never marry, that's all right with me, lass.' Then he added, 'What of you, Lily? Have you decided upon a husband as of yet?'

'I've had an offer from Lord Arnsbury,' Lily confessed with a smile. 'I am thinking about it.'

She what? Evangeline's mouth dropped open. 'Do you mean to say that Matthew asked you to wed, and you didn't tell me? You let me go on about dogs when your life is about to change?' Although she knew Lily had been in love with the Earl of Arnsbury for years, she hadn't realised the man had offered for her. It seemed that the earl was ready to try again, despite all the years they'd been apart. Her heart warmed at the thought of their reunion.

But Lily didn't look as overjoyed as she'd imagined. 'I haven't said yes, Evangeline.'

'Oh, but you will.' It didn't matter what her own thoughts were about marriage; Lily loved Arnsbury, and Evangeline only wanted happiness for her. She looped her arm in Lily's and smiled at her father. 'Please give Mother my excuses. Lily and I must be off now so I can learn everything and talk her into the marriage.' She tugged upon the leash, but her dog planted herself firmly upon the floor and refused to budge. In exasperation, Evangeline picked Annabelle up.

'Take a footman with you,' Cain warned. 'And be back within two hours, or I will come to collect you.'

'So, we shall.' Evangeline kissed him on the cheek. 'Though we both know you will send three men to guard us. Goodbye, Father.'

Lily gave a slight tug on the leash for Sebastian to join them, and the dog trotted behind, his tail wagging.

'Thank you so much for coming to call,' Evangeline breathed. 'I know Mother means well, but I have no desire to let Lord Burkham court me. The man is empty-headed and not at all suited to me.' She waited for Lily to step inside the carriage before she placed Annabelle at her feet. 'Now tell me everything about Lord Arnsbury. Leave nothing out.'

She genuinely wanted her friend to find joy. It had warmed her heart to see Rose married, and she wanted the same for Lily. But as she listened to Lily talking about her marriage proposal, a sudden loneliness slipped beneath Evangeline's skin.

I won't ever have that same happiness, she thought.

There was a part of her that envied her friends for falling in love. It was easy to be enthusiastic for them and share in their happiness. But her own heart remained empty. It didn't matter that she had been enamoured with James and had wanted to marry him—he had never felt the same way. She refused to humiliate herself again by daring to risk her heart with him. They could be friendly to one another, but there was an invisible wall of iron that she'd built around her heart when it came to the earl.

No, she wouldn't have the babies she wanted or a loving marriage. But she could create her own contentment by helping others. That would fill up the loneliness inside, and it would have to be enough.

When they reached Rotten Row, the carriage slowed to a stop, and Evangeline kept a bright smile on her face that she didn't truly feel. But she wasn't about to spoil Lily's moment.

She disembarked with the help of a footman, but when she set Annabelle down upon the pathway, the dog lay down on the ground and did nothing. Evie let out a heavy sigh. This was going to be a terrible walk. She was going to have to carry her dog, it seemed. Sebastian, in contrast, was eager to be off, after being confined indoors for so long.

More than anything, Evie wanted to walk swiftly, to feel a breeze against her cheeks. Lily's dog might give her that chance. 'Would you care to trade your dog for mine?' she suggested. 'Mine has become terribly lazy.'

In answer, Lily held out her leash. Evie took it from her, while Lily picked up the cocker spaniel for a closer look. 'Evangeline, I believe Annabelle—'

Before Lily could finish her sentence, Sebastian jerked to attention and began sniffing the ground. Evangeline struggled with the leash while the dog pulled hard on the lead towards a gentleman. 'Oh, dear!' She tried to settle him down, but he moved sideways and tore his way free of her grasp.

Evie seized her skirts and hurried to retrieve Sebastian. The dog had already jumped up with his paws on the gentleman's waist.

Lily kept Annabelle in her arms and joined her, calling out, 'Stop it, Sebastian!'

But the dog was already licking the hands of a tall blond gentleman. A very handsome gentleman, if Evangeline were honest with herself. He looked familiar, and she was certain she remembered him from somewhere.

'My goodness,' she breathed, as she stopped running and touched her heart. How embarrassing. She should have kept a firmer grip upon the leash, and now the dog's paws were getting the gentleman's coat dirty.

When she took a closer look, she still couldn't quite place where she had seen the man before. Yes, he was quite attractive—but she kept comparing him to Lord Penford, which wasn't really fair. The gentleman laughed and petted Sebastian's head, rubbing his ears.

He gave the dog something from his pocket and then turned to them. 'Now there's a good boy.'

Evangeline took a step back while Lily was apologising for Sebastian's behaviour. She didn't appear pleased to see the man, as if something had made her uncomfortable. Now why would that be? Had they met before?

The gentleman tipped his hat. 'Lady Lily.'

So, he *did* know her. Interesting. The awkwardness between them seemed to worsen, and Evangeline questioned whether she should say or do anything. She took Annabelle from Lily but didn't say anything to the gentleman.

And Lily made no effort to introduce her, which made it even more uncomfortable.

Evie rather felt like an unwanted chaperone. Maybe it was better if she let them talk without interfering. The dog seemed quite happy around the gentleman, his tail wagging furiously.

Evangeline took another step backwards, letting them have their conversation. She glanced behind her for the footmen, and it was then that she saw Lord Dunwood strolling towards them. Oh, no. This was *not* what she needed right now—especially when Lily was preoccupied with the gentleman.

Evie decided she had two choices—she could either stand with Lily and pretend to be part of the conversation—which would be terribly intrusive. Or she could hide. The viscount was walking closer, and she couldn't bear the thought of seeing him again. It didn't appear that he'd seen her yet, thank goodness.

Evie glanced behind her, and her footmen were approaching with a curious expression. She shook her head at them and waved them back. The last thing she wanted was for them to draw attention, which would only gain Lord Dunwood's notice.

In desperation, she kept Annabelle in her arms and ducked inside a large weeping willow tree. She remained surrounded by the long branches, fully hiding herself.

No, it wasn't dignified. And probably she was behaving like a coward. But the last few times she'd been around Lord Dunwood, she'd felt threatened. It seemed as if every time she attended a family ball, he was there. Whenever she went out shopping with her mother or her friends, he was nearby. Perhaps it was only a coincidence, but it was starting to feel as if he was always watching her, which she didn't like at all.

She was truly going to have to do something about the viscount. He wasn't taking no for an answer. It seemed that James was right—she might need her father's help in dissuading him.

Lord Dunwood passed by Lily and the gentleman but didn't stop to speak with them, thankfully. In the meantime, Annabelle was perfectly content to relax upon Evie's skirts. She petted her dog, still wondering if the rolls of fat were somehow puppies. It was possible, though she still didn't understand how Annabelle could have escaped.

She waited a few more moments until Lord Dunwood was gone before she extricated herself from the willow tree and joined Lily again.

'I will miss him desperately,' she heard her friend say. 'I can't bear the thought of going home without him.'

Wait a moment. She remembered that Lily had found the stray dog only a few weeks ago. Was this the dog's true owner? How was that possible?

Evangeline hung back and heard the gentleman continue, 'Lady Lily, I am most thankful for your good care of my Louis. If I may pay a call upon you from time to time, perhaps I might bring him to visit?'

'Yes, of course.'

But Evie didn't miss the tears in Lily's voice. Was she truly planning to just let her dog go off with the stranger? Lily leaned down and hugged the dog, unable to stop her tears when he licked her face. She ruffled his furry ears and stood. 'I would like to see him to know that he is well.'

The gentleman took her gloved hand and held it for a moment. 'And I would like to know that *you* are well.' With a slight smile, he added, 'Our fathers were such good friends, after all.'

Evangeline couldn't stop the gasp that came out of her.

What was this? What was happening? *Why* was Lily even having this conversation? She was supposed to marry the love of her life, the Earl of Arnsbury. He'd offered for her, and Lily simply had to say yes.

It took an effort to close her mouth from the shock.

'Until we meet again.' The gentleman released her fingers and turned back on the pathway with Sebastian trotting at his side.

Evangeline returned to her side, and it was then that she saw the silent tears running down her friend's face. A bit of relief filled her when she realised Lily was crying over her dog—not the gentleman. 'I'm so sorry, Lily.'

Her friend blinked back her tears. 'So am I.'

'Who was that?' Evangeline asked. 'I suppose he *is* handsome, but how do you know him?'

Lily shook her head. 'He is Lord Davonshire. And he just took my dog.'

Evangeline put her arm around her friend. 'Then we'll have to find a way to get him back.' She picked up Annabelle and was about to return to her carriage when she turned and saw that Lord Dunwood had turned back and was staring at her. It seemed that he hadn't left, after all. And the possessive look in his eyes made her worry about his intentions.

She had to take stronger actions to dissuade him. And whether that meant feigning interest in another suitor or asking help from Lord Penford—the outcome was the same. She wanted Lord Dunwood to leave her alone, once and for all.

The moment James entered the ballroom with his sister, his gaze was drawn to Evangeline. She had changed her appearance once again, and this time, he couldn't take his eyes off her.

Instead of wearing a ball gown the colour of mouse fur or horse dung, she had chosen a deep rose silk. Around her throat she wore a chain of diamonds, and two tiny pink roses were tucked into her black hair. She looked exquisite, and it made him wonder why she had transformed herself from a shrew into a debutante. What had made her change? He escorted Lily to her side but said nothing beyond a quiet greeting. Then he gave a slight bow before he stepped back to let the two women converse.

Evangeline glanced at him before her expression turned calculating. 'How do I look?' she asked Lily. 'Will Lord Davonshire notice me, do you think?'

Davonshire? James vaguely recalled that his father had once tried to set up a match between the man and Lily. But why did Evangeline want to be noticed by him?

He knew the two women had walked their dogs yesterday, and Lily had learned that the stray dog she'd rescued had belonged to another gentleman. Was Davonshire the owner? James frowned, uncertain about what was going on.

'You look beautiful,' Lily told her.

He had to agree with his sister. Evangeline's cheeks were flushed, her eyes bright. But it was more than beauty—this time, he felt the sense of mischief, as if she were up to something. And for whatever reason, she hadn't told him what it was about.

'Will he be here this evening, do you think? Lord Delicious, I mean.'

Delicious? Really? Evie glanced over at him, and her smile was indeed taunting. So, she *was* doing this on purpose.

He responded with his own look of disapproval. Evangeline Sinclair was most definitely plotting something, and he couldn't tell what this was about. She wasn't behaving like herself at all. He left the pair of them alone while he overheard her gushing about Lord Davonshire. He had no desire to listen to Evie fawning over another man.

A strange thought occurred to him. Was she trying to make him jealous? It wasn't hard to imagine that most gentlemen would be fascinated with Evangeline Sinclair tonight, as beautiful as she looked. But when he met her gaze with his own, he remembered kissing the line of that delicate throat, tasting her skin. And he couldn't stop thinking of the way she had responded to him when he'd run his hands through that dark hair as he lowered his mouth to her flesh.

Even now, he couldn't deny that he was drawn to her, wanting her. It was a good thing she understood that he didn't intend to marry. And yet, he wondered if she had changed her mind. The gown she wore accentuated her curves, and the soft rose made her dark hair stand out. She was bound to attract a great deal of notice, and an inner instinct warned him to protect her.

But when he turned around, he saw Lord Dunwood standing behind him, a look of fury on the man's face.

So that's what this was about. Evangeline's conversation with Lily was meant for the viscount to overhear, probably to deter him from courtship. James walked past the man, noting the possessive look on his face when he eyed Evangeline. It seemed that the man still didn't understand the word no.

He paused a moment and glanced back at Dunwood. The man irritated him and not just because he refused to accept Evangeline's rejection. Evie deserved someone who respected the brilliant young woman she was, not a man who saw her as a wealthy dowry to acquire.

And damned if he'd stand aside and let Dunwood bother her.

It didn't matter that it wasn't his place to interfere with her life—he simply refused to stand back and let anyone hurt Evie. She was too important to him.

Lord Dunwood moved closer to the women, and James instinctively shadowed him. He kept a slight distance, but he watched as the man approached Evie. Before the viscount reached her side, James saw Adrian Monroe, asking her to dance. For a moment, Evie seemed startled by the invitation. He vaguely recalled that she didn't get along well with the man, even though they were distantly related. It was clear that she intended to refuse, but Lily interrupted. 'Of course, she would. Enjoy yourself, Evangeline.'

The bewildered expression on Miss Sinclair's face suddenly relaxed when she seemed to realise that dancing with Mr Monroe removed her from Lord Dunwood's presence.

The viscount appeared frustrated, but when he turned around, he was facing James. 'Penford.' The greeting was muttered as a courtesy, but it was clear he didn't like being in his company.

James felt the instinctive need to give the man a warning. 'I understand that you're courting Evangeline Sinclair,' he said smoothly.

There was no reaction upon Dunwood's face. It was as if James had spoken of the weather. 'What of it?'

'She has made it quite clear that she does not intend to marry. You would be better off courting a young lady who wishes to wed.'

The viscount laughed softly. 'Miss Sinclair does not know what she wants. She is a spoiled, indulgent heiress who has been insufferably rude.'

James considered whether to drag the man outside to beat him senseless or strike him right now. But before he could act, Dunwood continued. 'She is high-spirited, a woman in need of taming. Wouldn't you agree?'

'Not at all.' He let his voice go low and dark. He took a step closer and warned, 'Stay away from her, Dunwood. Miss Sinclair has refused you many times. Her no is final.'

The viscount smiled, but before he could walk away, James seized his jacket and gripped it hard. 'I know you heard me.'

'Take your hands off me, Penford.'

'Stay away from Evangeline Sinclair.' He released the man but kept his face rigid. If they hadn't been in a ballroom, he would gladly have bloodied the man's face.

Dunwood's expression was murderous as he walked away. James never took his eyes off the man, and he intended to have words with Evie's father. Between the two of them, they would keep her safe.

She's not your concern, his conscience warned.

And yet, he didn't care. Dunwood needed to get the message.

Finally, Mr Monroe escorted Evangeline back, and James wanted her to know what had happened. 'Miss Sinclair, might I have a word?'

She thanked Mr Monroe for the dance and then turned to him. 'About what?'

Just then, he spied a matron walking towards him with her three daughters. It was clear that she intended to introduce them to him. 'Dance with me a moment, and I'll tell you.'

'Now, why would I want to rescue you from the approaching matchmaking mama?' she teased.

'It's about Lord Dunwood,' he said, and her smile faded. Though she didn't at all seem enthused about dancing, she did take his arm and let him lead her into a waltz.

The moment he pressed his hand to her waist, James was taken aback by memories. The scent of Evie's skin allured him, and he wanted to lean in and inhale the soft floral perfume of her. Or was that the roses she'd tucked in her hair? It didn't matter, he decided. But he was starting to realise that he needed to put distance between them. Evangeline was far too tempting.

'So, what is this about?' she asked. 'Lord Dunwood knows I will never wed him. I've said it many times.'

'He's quite motivated by your dowry,' James said.

'And so are all the others. What of it? I've told them no.'

'Have you?' he mused. 'What of Lord Delicious? Wasn't that what you called him? Do you intend to tell *him* no?' He'd never heard her speak of any gentleman that way—and he wanted to know if there was any truth to it. Had she changed her mind? 'Has Lord Davonshire caught your eye?'

A slight blush coloured her cheeks. 'I was only teasing Lily,' she confessed. 'A man like Davonshire wouldn't even notice someone like me.'

'You're wrong,' he answered. 'Every gentleman in this ballroom notices you.'

She stared at him as if she couldn't believe what he'd said. 'Not for the right reasons.'

But it was the truth. There was a different quality about her, a quiet confidence that drew him closer. He liked the fact that she spoke her mind.

For a moment, she fell silent while he danced with her.

He kept his gaze fixed upon hers, even though it wasn't a good idea. But he studied those deep blue eyes, the soft lips he'd tasted, and that dark hair he wanted to unravel. Any man would be fortunate to win Evie's heart.

But they wouldn't deserve her.

'The right one will.' Before she could respond, James forced himself to turn their conversation back to the true reason why he'd asked her to dance.

'I need you to stay away from Lord Dunwood.' He leaned in closer to her face. 'Do not ever let yourself be alone with him, for I suspect he may try to ruin you or force you into marriage. He's dangerous.' His hand moved to her spine and pressed it gently. 'Don't let him call on you again.'

Evangeline's face paled as she met his gaze. For a moment, he glimpsed her fear before she stiffened in his arms. The dance ended, and she seemed to gather her courage. 'Thank you, Lord Penford, but you needn't trouble yourself on my account. I can take care of myself.'

With that, she curtsied and stepped away from him, turning her back on him.

She was right. If he tried to protect her from Dunwood, the gossip would spread. It was best if he warned her father; no doubt Cain Sinclair would guard his daughter fiercely.

He walked towards the opposite side of the room and was startled to see Lily and Matthew standing together. His friend had slowly begun to attend gatherings during the past few weeks, though mostly he remained on the outskirts while Lily remained steadfast and faithful to him.

His sister really did love him. And James supposed he was starting to forgive Matthew for ruining her. The earl *had* offered for Lily, and it was possible that she might be able to heal his wounds—even those unseen—in time.

James couldn't say the same for himself. He didn't deserve forgiveness, for he bore the guilt for all of it. Had it not been for him, Matthew never would have come to India—more likely, he'd have married Lily. They might have even had a child by now.

He was starting to set aside his anger and accept that his sister and Arnsbury were indeed a match. He could see the way Matthew watched over her, guarding her in silence. They deserved his blessing, even if he wasn't happy about the way his friend had ruined her.

James studied the pair of them, noticing the way his sister looked at his friend as if he had created the moon and stars. There had been a time when Evie had looked at him in that way. But not any more.

He deserved to be alone, as his own self-imposed punishment. He would help his sisters, be there for his family as best he could, and endure his penance. If his sisters had sons, one of them could inherit. He simply couldn't see himself as a husband or a father. A dark memory caught him in his gut, of all his failures when he'd been a captive. He'd failed his friend, and he'd unknowingly abandoned his mother and sisters during their time of need. What right did he have to be happy with a family of his own? It seemed impossible. He could never be the sort of man a child would look up to. Not after all that had happened.

He was about to cross the room towards Lily and Matthew when suddenly, he saw his mother. He hadn't known she would be here tonight. But as soon as he looked closer, he realised Iris was having one of her spells again. She was visibly upset and wore a necklace of daisies around her neck to adorn her mourning gown. But before he could go and help, Lily and Matthew were already at her side, gently speaking to her.

So much had changed in the two years he'd been away. He'd wanted to believe that time would heal the wounds of his mother's mind. But it seemed she was as broken as he was.

With a sigh, James turned back to the ball, wondering whether to leave. But even now, he couldn't quite turn his attention away from Evangeline. With every ball he attended, James found himself searching for a glimpse of her. He'd wanted to see what outrageous gown she would wear or what she would say to people.

And he was afraid that curiosity would only lead towards expectations he could never fulfil.

He was beginning to think he should return to Penford for a time, to give their mother a chance to grieve and so he could keep his distance from Evangeline. The last thing James wanted was to break her heart again.

Evie deserved love and marriage, even if he couldn't be the man to give those to her. A tightness caught within his gut at the thought of leaving London. But he knew it was time to stop thinking about her and let her go.

One month later

Evangeline set down her embroidery, let out a sigh, and glanced over at the hearth where Annabelle slept contentedly beside her puppies. It seemed that even her dog had found time for a stolen romance while her own life was plagued with fortune hunters.

Christmas was swiftly approaching, and she admitted to herself that it had been terribly lonely while Lily was away. *And James*, her conscience nudged, though she swiftly pushed that thought away.

It didn't matter what she'd once felt for him. It was clear enough that there was no future between them, so why bother? Better to guard her heart and ignore what was never meant to be.

She'd written a few letters to her friends, but she was starting to realise how awful it would be once Lily married Matthew. She would be completely and utterly alone. Letters weren't at all the same. And it wasn't as if she could write to James. Nor did she want to, she reminded herself.

She pretended to study the linen handkerchief in front of her while her mother and aunt were gossiping. Her aunt Amelia had asked her to join them, claiming that she needed something from her, but Evie hardly cared what it was. Her mind was running through the latest profits she'd seen from Aphrodite's Unmentionables. The idea of having garments ready to wear had been well received, and she was already imagining ways to expand it.

But even using that money to help orphanages and the poor didn't ease the emptiness inside her.

In Rose's last letter, her friend had shared the news that she was with child. It should have brought a thrill of happiness within her. Instead, Evie felt the tug of jealousy. Despite her resolve to find contentment in being a spinster, there was a tiny part of her that still wanted a family of her own.

Her aunt was speaking to her, and Evie shrugged off the wayward thoughts. 'What is this about, Aunt Amelia?'

Her aunt's smile brightened, and she set down her pencil from where she'd been sketching. 'Margaret told me that you don't wish to be married, but I've heard your name mentioned along with Lord Davonshire.'

Oh. They were matchmaking again. Evie dismissed the idea. 'He's interested in Lily, not me.' And that didn't matter either, since she knew full well that her friend intended to wed Arnsbury.

'But you liked him?' her aunt pressed. 'I understand he's *quite* handsome.'

Evangeline prayed to the angels above that someone would save her from this inquisition. If anyone enjoyed matchmaking, it was her aunt.

'Oh, there's no doubt of that,' she agreed. 'But although he is very attractive, I could tell his interest was elsewhere.' Her aunt's eyes gleamed, and Evie knew she had to dispel that thought away. 'He never even noticed me,' she finished.

'I see.' Amelia picked up her pencil and began drawing again. 'You wouldn't want someone like him, then.'

Please stop, she prayed silently. But she forced her voice to remain calm and collected. 'No. I'm content to be a spinster. Have there—'

'And what of Lord Penford? Is he still as awful as ever?'

A terrible, unwanted blush spread over her cheeks, and she repeated her prayer for help. God, apparently, wasn't listening.

'Well, he—I don't know if I would say awful,' she hedged. 'But we're not suited at all.' Penford had been quite clear that he didn't intend to marry. She didn't truly understand why. As an earl, he had a duty to wed and sire an heir. But the earl remained steadfast in his refusal. Once again, she was convinced it was because of his travels in India. There were shadows in his eyes, and James didn't really tease anyone any more. The carefree young man he'd been had disappeared.

There were so many mysteries around his journey—but she didn't feel comfortable asking him or Lily about it. If it truly had been that terrible, she didn't want him to relive those days.

He was home again and safe. One day, he might find a reason to smile again, a way to push back the shadows. But in the meantime, it was better to leave him alone. If she dared to get too close, she would only fall in love with him again. And she wasn't about to let her heart shatter a second time.

Her thoughts were interrupted when a knock sounded at the door. 'You have a caller, Miss Sinclair,' the footman announced to Evangeline. 'Lord Penford is here to see you.'

Penford was here? Now, why would the earl come to pay a call?

Her aunt Amelia had a smug expression, and she smiled at her sister. Evie was starting to think that the pair of them had invited the earl. She suppressed a sigh at their blatant attempts at luring Lord Penford.

'Now why would he be here?' Margaret wondered aloud. 'I thought the two of you had parted ways. Clearly, I was wrong.'

'Put your matchmaking thoughts out of your head, Mama,' Evangeline warned. She and Aunt Amelia had plotted this together, hadn't they?

'Matchmaking is such marvellous fun.' Aunt Amelia sighed. 'I've already arranged a wedding for dear Lily Thornton and Cousin Matthew. I could easily find a match for you.'

Never mind that Matthew had already proposed to Lily, far earlier. It had nothing to do with her aunt, though Amelia was glad to take credit. And from the gleam in her eye, she fully intended to find a match for Evie.

No. This was a terrible idea. If they brought the earl into the drawing room, it would be utterly humiliating. Her aunt would ask too many questions, and Penford would believe that Evie had wanted him to pay a call.

'Tell Lord Penford I am not here,' she said. It was better to avoid the call entirely. At least while there were so many people around.

But her aunt wasn't listening at all. 'Show him into the library, Harrison. I will send Evangeline in shortly.'

Were they listening to a single word she said? Clearly not. It seemed she had no choice but to stand her ground. When they ignored her, she saw no choice but to be rude.

'I have nothing to say to that man,' she informed her aunt. 'He is horrid, and I will not be a part of your scheming.'

Lies, lies, lies. James wasn't horrid at all, but Evie saw no choice but to push back. If she didn't, her aunt would have them standing before a minister within a fortnight. A lock of hair fell from her chignon, and she shoved it back into place.

'If you do not see him in the library, I will send for him here,' her mother said gently. 'I know Amelia and I would both like to know why he has come. Perhaps to renew his courtship?'

There never was a courtship, despite her girlish dreams, years ago. It was over and done with, and Evie couldn't imagine how her mother had come up with such an idea. The last time James had paid a call, they had been shooting pistols while they'd discussed an investment opportunity.

Evie tossed her needlework aside and stood. 'That is

the very last reason why he would be here. But if you insist, I will find out and return within one minute.'

She would get rid of Lord Penford, and that would be that. The only problem was that she had to calm the rapid beating of her heart and the surge of anticipation at seeing him again. Because, despite her best efforts to keep him away, he'd been entirely too nice to her. It had barely taken any time at all for her foolish heart to yearn for him again.

And that simply had to stop. She had to firmly dissuade him from any thoughts of friendship.

'Evangeline, your hair is falling from the pins,' her mother warned. 'Take a moment and make yourself presentable.'

She ignored her mother and strode out of the room. Enough of their nonsense. She would find out why he had come and send him away. Better yet, she would drive him away by behaving in the most hostile way she could manage.

Anger and rudeness would become her weapons now. Because if she didn't shove him away by any means possible, she would undoubtedly fall for him again.

You weren't enough for him then, and you aren't now, her brain reminded her.

It was best if she remembered that.

James waited in the library, and within moments Evangeline stormed into the room. She wore a violet day dress with long sleeves and a narrow waist. Every inch of her was covered, but the gown clung to her form, revealing her curves. Her hair was falling from the pins, and her blue eyes glared at him with murder.

Now, why on earth would she be so furious at him? He

hadn't seen her in a month. Before he could greet her, she demanded, 'Why are you here, Penford?'

Well, then. The shrew was back, it seemed.

He withdrew a crumpled note from his coat pocket and held out the message that had asked him to come immediately. At the time he'd received the note, he'd suspected it was not from her, but he wanted to know for certain.

She took the note from him and read through it. 'I did not send this.' She shook her head and added, 'Who would have sent this to you? And why?'

'I don't know.' He leaned back and sat upon her uncle's desk. 'Especially when it was delivered an hour ago, and we've been travelling all day. I thought it best to find out in case something was wrong.'

Beneath her breath, he thought he heard her muttering about meddling, matchmaking aunts. But then she faced him and asked, 'Why would you care?'

The words were a challenge, and he stared back at her. A good question indeed. He probably should have ignored it. But although he had chosen to let her go, it didn't mean he didn't care about her welfare. He wanted her to be safe, and there were plenty of vultures circling her dowry.

Her shoulders lowered a moment later, and she sighed. 'I apologise. That came out before I could stop myself from speaking.'

I do care, he wanted to say but didn't.

It would only cause more tension between them. He'd left London with the intent of creating true distance. And yet, he'd come here straightaway without even questioning why. If there had been even the slightest chance that Evie had needed him, he would come. And he didn't know what that implied.

'You're still angry with me,' he said quietly.

She appeared flustered at his words and tucked another wayward lock of hair behind her ear. 'You've seen for yourself that we are all fine. Just go back home, and we'll leave it at that.' She started to walk away, but he caught her hand in his.

Idiot. He knew better than to do this, but he hadn't been able to stop the urge. Her palm was small within his, her fingers warm. He held her hand a moment as he met her gaze evenly. 'Regardless of what you believe, Evangeline, I am not your enemy.'

Her expression turned vulnerable for a moment before she masked it with a shield of invisible armour. 'I know that, Lord Penford. You may return home, and there's no need to concern yourself with my welfare.'

He wasn't so certain about that. Someone had tried to bring him here, and although it could have been her aunt and mother, he wasn't entirely certain. 'Still, I wonder why anyone sent that note.'

Evangeline pursed her lips in thought, and the gesture reminded him of the warmth of her kiss. Even now, he wanted to touch her waist and draw her close, tasting that mouth again.

He truly needed to do something about those errant thoughts. He missed part of what Evangeline said to him, but she suggested, 'To draw you away from Lily? Perhaps someone wanted you to leave her alone.'

He hadn't thought of that. During their month at Penford, despite the fact that he'd wanted his sister to wait before rushing into marriage, Lily had accepted the marriage proposal from Lord Arnsbury. Perhaps the news of their betrothal had made its way to London. He knew Arnsbury's cousin, Adrian Monroe, had been furious about no longer being the heir after they'd returned from their travels in India.

He'd only met Monroe a time or two, but there was something unsettling about the man.

It was entirely possible that the man might threaten Lily, simply because she was betrothed to Arnsbury. And James would never allow that.

He let out a low curse. 'I believe you may be right. I should go back.' He started to walk towards the door but then turned back. 'I meant what I said. I don't want to be your enemy, Evangeline.'

He still didn't understand why she'd been so angry that he'd come to pay a call. It made little sense, since he'd mistakenly believed that they were past all that. Something had stirred her up again, and he didn't know what it was.

They were on unsteady ground right now, and her eyes held an uncertain emotion as she stared back at him. 'Take care of Lily.'

He nodded, but something kept him from leaving. He was entirely too distracted by the woman standing before him. And he sensed that he wanted far more from her— more than she could give.

Perhaps it was better to keep his distance. For friendship could lead them down a very different path.

Chapter Seven

The Duchess of Worthingstone's winter ball was a grand affair. Sprigs of holly and mistletoe were decked all over the room, and a tall fir tree adorned one corner, gleaming with candles. Evangeline had worn an emerald-green gown, and her maid had tucked pearls into her hair.

She should have worn an ugly gown tonight, but part of her didn't want to look hideous. Lord Penford would be here tonight, and despite all her efforts to create distance between them, something had shifted. He'd said that he didn't want to be her enemy. And after he'd received the note—whoever it was from—he'd come to see her immediately.

It implied that he *did* care about her. And she didn't know how to sort out those feelings or what she wanted to do now.

But somehow, she wanted to look beautiful. It was another gauntlet of sorts, as if to remind Penford that she *could* be a desirable woman, even if he never wanted to court someone like her.

Lord Davonshire was also here tonight. Although Evie had joked with Lily about him being Lord Delicious, something about the man unnerved her. At first, she'd believed it was her own attraction. But then, it was clear that he had no interest in her. It wouldn't surprise her if the man was still trying to win Lily's hand, despite her betrothal to Arnsbury.

Although Davonshire was smiling and behaving as if he were enjoying himself, she noticed him meeting Adrian Monroe's gaze. There was an unspoken conversation happening between them, and her suspicions rose. Did they know each other?

She'd spent very little time with her distant cousin Adrian, but she'd heard from idle gossip that his debts hadn't improved much. Honestly, she was surprised that her aunt Victoria had invited him. Adrian wasn't well liked by anyone in the family because of his arrogance.

She knew she shouldn't care what the men did. Whatever the two men were plotting, it had nothing to do with her.

And yet, her curiosity was piqued. She wanted to know more about why he was here and what he and Lord Davonshire were doing.

As a distraction, she slipped beside the crowd of young ladies, choosing a spot near the fir tree where she could hide herself and eavesdrop. Sometimes, being a wallflower had its advantages.

'Did you hear about Lord Arnsbury?' one of the ladies whispered. 'They say he's a bastard, and Mr Monroe ought to be the earl instead.'

Evangeline frowned and utterly dismissed the rumours. There was no chance of Arnsbury losing his title, especially after his own father had acknowledged Matthew as a legitimate heir. No, this was about publicly undermining him. Adrian was behind it, she was certain. But what did he hope to gain? Was he trying to build an inheritance for himself by insinuating that he was the rightful heir? The very idea was ludicrous.

'*I* heard that they revoked his invitations to every ball except this one,' the other woman said slyly.

'I still don't know why the duke and duchess invited him,' another responded.

Evie had heard enough, and none of it mattered—there wasn't much that anyone could do about idle gossip. All she could do was warn Lily and Lord Arnsbury.

She started to move away from the fir tree, when she overheard the first young woman saying, 'Well, if Mr Monroe is now the heir to an earldom, I think we should be introduced, don't you?'

'I don't know,' the other answered. 'I saw him escorting another young lady. The one from India.'

Something within Evangeline went cold. Though it was entirely possible that this was a coincidence, her skin tingled. Why would Adrian Monroe escort a young woman from India? Who was she, and why was she here?

It seemed entirely too suspicious.

Evie decided she'd had enough of being a wallflower. And more than that, she'd respected James's privacy long enough. If this woman had a connection to his secrets—or even Matthew's—she wanted to know about it. And that meant confronting him right now.

The earl stood beside Lily, but his gaze was searching. She stepped out from behind the fir tree, and he met her glance with his own. He was staring at her as if he wanted to cross the room to her—and yet, he remained in place.

For a moment, she was bewildered at the look in his eyes. It was rather difficult to hold on to her resolve and confront him when he was looking at her like that…as if he found her beautiful.

Don't imagine something that cannot happen, her mind warned.

But she couldn't stop herself from drinking in the sight of him. Lord Penford was still incredibly handsome, and his stare did something to her insides, making her self-conscious.

Just as she was about to turn away, she saw Adrian leaving the room with another man she barely glimpsed. She sent a look towards Penford, hoping he would read her unspoken request. With a nod to him, she hurried towards the doorway, not even knowing what was about to happen. It was likely nothing more than her own curiosity. But she felt an innate need to find out what the men were up to and how it all connected together.

She pressed her back against the wall, straining to listen. Their voices were low, and from this position, she couldn't tell what they were saying. Then she heard the sound of another door closing.

At last, she saw Penford approaching. He'd caught her hint, thankfully.

'Psst—' She tried to catch his attention. Confusion lined his face, but she slipped through the doorway and beckoned for him to follow. If they didn't hurry, she'd never discover what the two men were plotting.

She picked up her skirts, tiptoeing towards another room, but Penford stopped where he was and waited. Didn't he understand how serious this was? She beckoned again, but he only rested his hands on his hips and stared at her.

Of course, *now* he decided to doubt her intentions. Did he think she was trying to get him alone? She rolled her eyes and tiptoed back to him. 'You need to hear this.'

But he wasn't moving at all. Her time was running out, so she lied, 'It affects Lily.'

'Are we eavesdropping, Miss Sinclair?' There was a hint of disbelief in his voice.

'Yes. Now are you coming, or are you intending to abandon your sister in her hour of need?'

At that, his gaze narrowed. *Why* did he have to be difficult now? She took him by the hand and led him to a nearby room.

'Do you even know where you are going?' Penford asked.

'They are inside the library,' she whispered. 'I thought we could go in the adjoining room.'

'They?' He followed her this time, and she silenced him with a finger to his lips. She led him into the music room, closing the door behind them.

Though every part of her knew it was dangerous to be alone with him, her curiosity overcame propriety. The adjoining door was not properly set upon its hinges, and from the crevices along the edge of the doorway, she could clearly hear the conversation of the two men.

When the earl leaned in closer to catch what they were saying, she tried to ignore the sudden flare of interest. But she was fully aware of his large body overshadowing hers and the lean strength of him. For a moment, her thoughts drifted to the vision of what it would be like having a man like this on top of her, his bare skin pressed to hers.

Her skin turned scarlet at the thought, and a tug of need caught her from deep inside. She forced herself to concentrate on the conversation. Some of their plotting made little sense, but then she caught the last part of Monroe's words.

'I have a surprise for my cousin this night,' Monroe

said. 'One that will drive him past the brink of sanity into madness. It has taken a great deal of time and effort, but I have no doubt it will work. Everyone will be shocked at his behaviour, and it will lend credence to my claim that he is incapable of handling the estates due to his mental state. I will be permitted to govern Arnsbury on his behalf.'

She paled at his words, realising this this 'surprise' was very likely tied to the woman from India. Did Matthew or James know her? Or was it merely a coincidence?

'Good,' the other man answered, his voice sounding more relaxed. 'We can then repay our debtors.'

'*I* can repay my debts,' Adrian corrected. He paused as if admiring his own efforts. 'I have been waiting a long time to gain the property that should have been mine.'

There came a slight cough from his companion. 'And what of *my* debts? I thought we were working together.'

'You may pick up the pieces of Lady Lily's broken heart,' Monroe said drily. 'She has a good dowry if you can win her hand. Let *her* pay your debts, for I don't care what happens to her now.'

From behind her, she could feel the tension in James's body at the mention of his sister. He strode towards the door of the music room, but Evangeline put herself in front of the entrance, shaking her head. She didn't want him trying to confront the man—not yet.

He started to push his way past her in the hallway, but Evangeline caught his hand. 'Wait a moment.'

There was a click of the library door opening, and she suddenly realised there was no time. The men would know they'd been eavesdropping unless she did something fast. Anything to make it seem like they weren't spying.

Just as she saw Monroe leave the library, she drew

James's head down and kissed him. Thankfully, he was too stunned to protest. At first, he hadn't responded, and she felt like a complete fool for throwing herself at him.

He doesn't want you, her brain warned.

But she couldn't stop the kiss just yet. At least not until the men left.

Then, without warning, he responded to her gently. His kiss was a reminder of what had once been between them. Evie drank in the sensations, and heat roared through her. She clung to him, as every part of her yielded to him, craving the sensations he'd given her so long ago. And God help her, it was every bit as wonderful as the first time.

'Forgive me,' Lord Davonshire said before the door closed again.

Only then did she gather her senses enough to pull back. 'I'm sorry,' she whispered to Penford, after Davonshire was gone. 'But... I was afraid they would suspect we were eavesdropping. It was the only thing I could think to do that would explain why we were here alone.'

Her cheeks heated with embarrassment that she'd thrown herself at him. From the stoic look on his face, he appeared utterly unmoved by what she'd done. It was as if nothing at all had happened.

When she tried to take a step back, he held her waist with one arm. His gaze was unreadable, and she couldn't tell what he was thinking. 'It has been a long time, Evangeline.'

She didn't miss the pity in his voice. It ruined her pride to realise that he hadn't truly wanted her to kiss him. He'd played along with her deception, and that was all. And now she had to face the fact that nothing had changed in two years.

'I know it,' she answered. She couldn't quite tell what

he was thinking, and right now, she felt unbearably humiliated. 'And I shouldn't have done that at all.'

His gaze remained locked on hers, but he didn't deny it. It was the reminder she didn't want to face—that she still had feelings for James, but he didn't feel the same for her.

James started to lead her back to the ballroom, and she whispered, 'I—I saw the other man,' Evangeline whispered. 'It was Lord Davonshire.'

He frowned and nodded. 'I will protect Lily from them.'

'Will you speak with Lord Arnsbury?' The earl needed to understand the threat and the gossip spreading about him. Though Evie didn't believe a word of it, rumours could cause trouble for Matthew and Lily.

He nodded. 'And I want you to come with me, Evangeline. You can warn Lily in case she won't listen to me.'

There was a waltz playing, and she realised belatedly that Penford intended to dance with her. He led her into the steps, pressing his hand against her spine. Though she knew that dancing was the most logical reason why he might be walking so close to her, she couldn't think of what to say to him now.

I'm sorry for kissing you... What good would that do? Her cheeks were still flushed with humiliation.

'The kiss wasn't that bad, was it?' His deep voice held a hint of amusement, as if he were trying to put her at ease. It was the first time, since his return, that he'd teased her.

But she couldn't joke about this, no matter how hard she tried. Though she had done her best to push aside old feelings, James was her weakness. Perhaps he always would be.

'No.' She closed her eyes for a moment and admitted, 'It was that good.'

The kiss had reminded her that no matter how much time had passed, there was still a spark between them that she couldn't deny. Even if she was the only one who felt that way.

The intensity in his eyes unnerved her, making her wonder if she was wrong. Right now, he looked as if he wanted to claim her mouth a second time, and she didn't know what to think or say. Except that she wanted him.

It was physical attraction, nothing more, Evie told herself. She never should have kissed him, opening that Pandora's box.

'Why didn't you marry someone else while I was away?' James asked. He guided her closer towards Matthew and Lily.

'Not many men would have me,' she admitted. At least, not at first. Not until she had taken command of Aphrodite's Unmentionables and expanded their fortunes. 'Because of my family's…business. And the others were only interested in my money.'

It was still the same, even after two years. No one cared about the woman behind the wealth.

'You are a beautiful woman with a good dowry,' he reminded her. 'It's what every gentleman wants.'

The words came across as mercenary, though he might not have intended them that way. But she felt compelled to remind him of the truth that pained her, even now. It hurt to confess, 'Not even *you* wanted me, Lord Penford.'

James said nothing at first, but she caught a trace of regret in his eyes. A moment later, his attention was drawn to the other side of the room, and his posture went rigid with fury. He let out a low curse beneath his breath.

She couldn't tell why. 'What is it?'

'Go back to your parents,' he ordered. His expression

turned grim, and he continued, 'I know exactly what Adrian is intending. And if Matthew sees that woman…'

She suspected he was referring to the woman from India that she'd heard the other ladies talking about. From Penford's tone, it sounded as if she was connected to his past—and something was very wrong. An unexpected wave of protectiveness slid over her, and she asked, 'What can I do to help?'

She could try to find the woman or search for more answers. Anything, truly.

'I have to stop him.' He glanced around and added, 'Tell a footman to summon Lord Arnsbury's carriage. I need to get Matthew out of here before he sees her.'

'Before he sees who?' She needed to know who the woman was and why her presence was such a threat.

But James offered nothing except to repeat his request. 'Please go and summon the carriage. I will tell you everything later.'

Evangeline did as he asked and ordered Lord Arnsbury's carriage to be brought out. Then, she waited while James went to talk to Matthew, who was holding a glass of lemonade. While he began explaining the conversation they'd overheard, Evie decided to keep a close eye on Lily. She scanned the ballroom, searching for a sign of her friend, and at last, she saw her on the opposite side of the room, speaking to a woman with dark hair. The woman wore a dove-grey gown with two flounces, and a moment later, the two women walked towards the terrace.

She was fairly certain that this was the woman who held a connection to James's travels in India. But why did the woman matter? What was this all about?

'Lord Penford,' she interrupted. 'I think we should go to your sister. I saw Lily on the terrace, and she—'

'Yes, I agree,' Matthew interrupted. But before the two men could take another step, Adrian blocked their path.

Evie suspected it was a deliberate attempt to keep them away, so while the men began to argue, she seized her chance to go after Lily. If nothing else, she could warn her friend. She hurried towards the terrace, eager to reach them.

But just as she passed a narrow alcove, a hand seized her wrist.

'Good evening, Miss Sinclair,' a familiar voice said. Evie tried to wrench her hand away, but Lord Dunwood's grip remained firm. 'I was hoping we could talk.'

The viscount's timing couldn't have been worse. And the last thing she wanted was for him to continue a court-ship that was a waste of their time. It was time to stop being polite and to start being direct.

'Let go of me, or I will scream,' she warned.

'There's no need to cause a scene and ruin your aunt's ball,' he said softly. 'Come into the hallway where we can talk freely.'

She filled her lungs with air, but before she could call out for help, he released her wrist and stepped back. 'I haven't given up on you, Miss Sinclair. And while I admire your spirit, I think it's time you accepted my suit.'

'Are your ears broken?' she demanded. 'I have told you time and again that I shall *never* marry you. Put the idea out of your head.'

His smile unnerved her. 'Now, Miss Sinclair, there's no need to be so unreasonable. A marriage to me will give you the title you so desperately need. You will become Viscountess Dunwood, and my name will open every door to you.' He paused a moment and added, 'It will help diminish the scandal of your family's business.'

Except she was proud of their business. Evie liked having her independence and feeling as if she had a purpose. But she was starting to realise his intent. He was trying to keep her isolated, probably so it would be enough of a scandal that he could force a marriage between them. And then, she realised she was in her own sort of danger.

Her mother was busy talking to her sisters, and she hadn't seen her father in a while. Everyone else in the ballroom was focused on something else, and she needed to get out of the hallway.

'I care nothing for titles.' She started to move past him, but Lord Dunwood blocked her path.

'I haven't finished speaking to you.'

'Well, I *have*.' She gave him a shove, but he caught her by the shoulders and covered her mouth with his hand. She tried to scream, but the sound was muffled as he shoved her inside her uncle's study.

Evangeline glanced around, searching for another way out—but he was standing in front of the only door.

She tried to scream, but he kept his hand firmly gripped upon her mouth. It sounded as if there was a commotion of sorts happening outside the study, and she was afraid it involved Lily and the woman from India. No one would hear her, even if she did manage to scream.

Think. Her uncle might have something she could use as a weapon. Evie no longer cared about what anyone thought—this had gone well past the bounds of propriety, and she was now looking to defend herself by any means possible.

There were large candlesticks on the fireplace mantel that she might be able to use. But then, her gaze shifted towards a pair of duelling pistols on the desk. It appeared that her uncle had been cleaning one of them. It wouldn't be loaded, of course, but perhaps it would deter Lord Dunwood.

She stopped fighting against him, and let her body become slack. Her sudden weight startled the viscount, and she slipped from his grasp. She caught herself at the desk before she could stumble to the ground and moved towards the hearth.

He laughed at her. 'Clever, aren't you? But it really doesn't matter now. Your father has been alerted, and he will find us together here. You'll have no choice but to wed me.'

She made no move but continued talking. 'I always have a choice. Call me ruined, if you will, but my father won't force me to do anything I don't want.'

He took a step backwards towards the door and turned the key in the lock. Then he tucked it inside his waist-coat pocket.

'Then perhaps you *do* need to be ruined, Miss Sinclair. For daring to be so defiant.'

Her heart began pounding, and she realised that he had truly slipped past decency into madness. 'Are you that eager for my dowry that you would attack an innocent woman?'

'For a dowry such as yours, I would stop at nothing,' he said quietly. He unfastened his jacket and set it upon a chair.

Her mind began working rapidly, and the moment he stepped closer, she seized the duelling pistol and aimed it at him. 'Put the key back in the lock.'

'Or you'll do what?' he taunted. 'The pistol isn't loaded.'

'I will pull the trigger,' she promised. 'And we'll find

out, won't we?' It was a terrible bluff, for she didn't believe it was loaded, either. There was no reason for it to
be. She doubted if there were any bullets within the study.
Most likely the pistol was decorative.

'Put the weapon down, Miss Sinclair,' the viscount
ordered.

'Put the key back,' she countered. Then she filled her
lungs with air and called out as loudly as she could. 'Help!
Someone, help me!'

But even if someone did hear, they couldn't get in without breaking the door down. Her skin had gone cold, her
heart still pounding.

No. She refused to stand here and be his victim. She
had to distract him however she could.

But then, he reached for the first button of his trousers.
And she understood that he truly would stop at nothing.

Evie cocked the weapon, and it was then that she saw
the faint traces of gunpowder upon her fingers. Though
it might have been the remnants of an earlier use, she
wasn't entirely certain. Would the duke actually keep a
weapon loaded here? It occurred to her that if the pistol
was truly loaded, she could indeed make her escape. But
she would have only one chance—and that meant taking
a terrible risk.

When the viscount unbuttoned another button of his
trousers, she understood that they were past the point of
reason. Although she didn't truly want to shoot him, she
saw no other choice.

'Put down the pistol, Miss Sinclair,' he commanded
again. 'We both know it's useless to you.'

When he lunged for her, she aimed the weapon at his
feet and squeezed the trigger. To her shock, the gunfire

was exceptionally loud, and Lord Dunwood dropped to the floor bleeding. She'd shot him cleanly in the foot.

'You bitch,' he cursed. 'I'll see you hanged for this.'

He clutched his foot, just as Evie reached into his waist-coat pocket and snatched the key. 'You should be grateful I didn't aim at your chest.' With that, she unlocked the door and hurried from the room.

To her shock, she realised everyone was outside. Had anyone even heard the gunshot? She wasn't certain what was happening, but her father found her and took her by the hand.

'I thought I'd heard a shot,' he said. 'Evie, what in God's name have you done?'

At that, she began sobbing. Her father stepped inside the study and saw Lord Dunwood bleeding and groaning with his trousers unfastened. With that, Cain pocketed the pistol, his expression furious. 'Come on, lass. I'll take you home.'

'What happened to Lily?' she asked. 'Is she—?'

But her question was cut off when she saw the crowd gathered in the garden. She didn't see James or Lily anywhere, and her worry intensified.

'Lily is fine,' her father answered. 'But you cannot stay here, Evie. We have to go now before anyone finds out about this.'

She blindly obeyed him, knowing he was right. A small sliver of relief hit her when she spied James and his sister standing on the far end of the ballroom. Thank God.

Within moments, her father guided her outside and into a waiting carriage. Only after they were well away from her aunt's house did her father speak. 'Did he hurt you, lass?'

'N-no. But he wanted to.' Her voice came out in a quaver. 'He wouldn't believe me when I told him no.'

'Then it's glad I am that you shot him.'

'I'm glad the pistol was loaded,' she admitted. 'I don't know why it was.'

Her father shrugged. 'It doesna really matter. But Dunwood will try to cause a great deal of trouble for you, Evie. I'll talk to your mother, but we may need to leave London for a time.'

'All right,' she agreed. Anything to escape the viscount.

But Cain Sinclair's expression had turned thoughtful as he stared back at the crowd. And she didn't want to imagine what he was planning now.

Or what would happen when the rest of the ton learned that she'd shot Lord Dunwood.

Three days later

James sat in his study, tracing the rim of an empty glass when his footman knocked on the open door.

'What is it?' he asked.

'Mr Cain Sinclair has come to call,' the footman said.

'Send him in.'

He didn't know why Evangeline's father was here, but right now, his head was pounding with a vicious headache. He'd barely slept in the past few days, ever since Lily had been attacked during the winter ball.

Evie had warned him, he remembered. She'd probably saved his sister's life. Lily had been lured to the garden as bait, and she'd been caught in the middle.

Numbness clawed at his gut. He'd instantly recognised Adrian's 'surprise.' Nisha Amat had been one of the inquisitors from the rebel camp in India. Her brother was

Javas, the footman who had accompanied them on their travels and had delivered them into captivity.

He didn't know how Nisha had travelled here this fast—she must have followed them after their escape. Which meant, someone had paid her passage from India to England. And only one man had the motivation to send her this far: Adrian Monroe.

That was what the man had been plotting—James was sure of it. The conversation he and Evie had overheard had brought all the pieces together. He was certain Adrian had orchestrated everything, likely to inherit his cousin's earl-dom. He'd probably hired Javas to ensure that Matthew died. And though Nisha's presence was unexpected, he guessed Adrian had paid her even more, simply to arrive at the ball and drive Matthew back towards the madness he'd been fighting.

Her presence at the ball that night had evoked all the nightmares of captivity. But it wasn't Matthew who had been frozen and unable to act.

It was him.

James had been so stunned when he'd seen her threatening Lily, he'd behaved like a bystander. He'd been so caught up in his own harsh memories, he'd hesitated, not knowing whether there was true danger or not.

And because of his uncertainty, Arnsbury had been injured, trying to protect Lily.

Thank God Matthew had kept her safe. If anyone deserved to marry Lily, it was the man who had guarded her life with his own.

But right now, he could barely feel any emotions at all. No pain. No fear. Only the invisible self-hatred that weighed upon him, reminding him of his failure. He should have acted sooner. Instead, he'd stood back and watched, instead of defending his sister and his best friend.

'You look like hell, Penford,' Cain Sinclair began.

James could only nod. Words would do nothing to blur the nightmares, but he forced himself to shove back the raw emotions and face the man. 'It's been a rough few days.'

'Aye, it has.' Sinclair reached for the bottle of brandy and poured James another glass before he took one for himself. 'And though I ken that you're worried about Arnsbury, I've come to ask for your help with Evangeline.'

'Is she in trouble?' A flare of worry caught him. He hadn't seen Evie since that night and had assumed she'd gone home with her family.

'Aye, she is. It's my hope that you can help her.' The Highlander drained his glass and regarded him. 'Are you aware that Viscount Dunwood attacked Evie that night at the ball?'

An icy rage descended upon him at her father's words. 'No. I hadn't heard.' Fury gathered within him that the viscount had dared to threaten her. He'd warned the man once already, but it was clear that the words had meant nothing to Dunwood.

His hard tone matched the iron glint in Sinclair's eyes. 'Is she all right?'

'Evie shot him in the foot when he tried to accost her,' her father answered. 'The duke apparently left one of his pistols loaded, and she used it against Dunwood.'

'Good.'

He hated the thought of Evie being at that bastard's mercy. And once again, he felt the blame that he hadn't protected her, either. Damn the man for what he'd done.

Her father continued, 'The viscount sent a note this

morning. He intends to have Evie arrested for what she did. But he is willing to forgive her and drop the charges if she marries him. And if I offer her full dowry, of course.'

'She should have shot that bastard in the heart,' James remarked. He stood and regarded her father in silent accord.

'Aye. We're of the same mind on that matter.' Her father gave a nod of approval. 'But since that's no' possible, I'm wanting *you* to wed my Evie instead. Immediately, if possible.'

'I'm sorry, what did you say?' Surely, he hadn't heard Sinclair correctly. Evie had made it quite clear that she intended to remain a spinster and manage the family business. Marriage was the last thing she wanted.

'I intend to protect her from that blackguard,' Sinclair said. 'If she's married to you, then Dunwood canna threaten her.' The Highlander met James's gaze squarely. 'You have a title, and she would become a countess. I'll offer a handsome dowry if you're willing to marry her quickly.'

James had no interest in their family's wealth. But before he refused, he ventured, 'Have you asked Evangeline what she wants?'

Her father's expression grew fierce. 'Evie doesna understand the implications of what Dunwood can do. Even if the charges are dismissed, the gossip would ruin her. It might hurt our business, as well.' He shook his head and shrugged. 'Nay, 'tis better if she has a husband to silence the talk before it starts.'

It was the simplest solution, unfortunately. But Evie didn't truly understand his reasons for avoiding marriage. He'd refused to reveal anything about the past two years to anyone. And he intended for it to stay that way. Better to bury his past sins and silently accept the blame for his father's death and his friend's torment.

He had no interest in sharing his own misdeeds—not when they'd hurt other people. And the thought of marrying someone like Evie, someone who deserved far more than him, wasn't at all fair or right. It was far better if she chose a different husband, one who could give her the life and children she wanted. Not someone like him.

He was fairly confident that she would refuse. The only question was how to grant her the freedom she wanted without causing any trouble.

But if he voiced his reluctance to her father, Sinclair wouldn't understand his reasons. 'I need to speak with her,' he said slowly. 'She deserves a choice.' And she deserved the chance to refuse.

Her father's face softened. 'Aye. And it's why I've asked you to wed her, Lord Penford. Whether she'll admit it or no', my Evie likes you. My wife also approves of the match.'

He didn't want them to get their hopes up, not when he knew it was an impossible situation. 'Where is she now?'

'In your drawing room where I left her.' The quiet admission revealed the truth—her father had not told her why they'd come. Cain crossed his arms and regarded him. 'She thinks she's here to pay a call upon Lily. But we both know your sister isna here.'

'She's with her fiancé,' James agreed. 'At least this afternoon.' He turned back to her father and said, 'When I speak with Evangeline, it must be a conversation between the two of us. And *we* will decide whether or not to wed.'

James wanted that perfectly clear so that her father was prepared for her refusal. Evangeline was a strong-willed young woman and fiercely independent. And when he gave her the choice, he fully believed she would say no. Most of all, he felt confident that they could find another way to help her.

'If Evangeline does not wish to marry, then I will not force her. We will use all our influence to protect her from Dunwood's accusations.'

Sinclair didn't look pleased, but he didn't argue. 'Evie won't want to marry you, I can tell you that now. But she also doesna understand the way the law works. She believes she had a right to defend herself by shooting Dunwood.'

'And I agree with her,' James answered. 'Law or not.' He met Sinclair's gaze and added, 'But as I said before, she and I will discuss this before we make any decisions.'

'Fair enough,' the Highlander said. He paused at the door and said, 'You've always treated my daughter with respect, Penford.'

He said nothing, for he didn't yet know what Evangeline's thoughts would be. At least, not until he saw her. James stood and paced across the distance of his study, uncertain of what to do. And after a few minutes longer, Evangeline entered the room.

Her face had gone utterly white, matching the pale ivory of her gown. 'I came to see Lily. Is she all right?'

He didn't know how to answer that. Instead, he began with, 'We need to talk.'

Her eyes turned the colour of storm clouds. 'Papa told you about Lord Dunwood, didn't he?' She muttered an unladylike curse beneath her breath.

'I'm sorry for what happened,' James began. 'I was distracted when Lily was attacked. I never should have left you alone.' A dark flare of frustration and guilt settled upon his shoulders. He'd been so concerned about his sister, he hadn't thought about Evangeline's welfare.

'It's not your fault. And I protected myself,' she said coolly. 'I don't know why Papa wanted to speak with you, but I don't need your help now. I'll be fine.'

In that, he disagreed. She didn't fully understand the consequences of her actions. If the viscount dared to bring charges against her, the scandal would tear her family apart. Her uncle, the duke, might be able to intervene, but the gossip would destroy her and, by extension, their business.

'Sit down,' he bade her, 'and I'll tell you what your father suggested.'

But she shook her head. 'I can't. After everything that's happened, I just—don't want to think of it now.'

Evie gripped her hands together and paced across the room. It made him wonder if she already suspected what her father wanted. She was behaving as if she needed more time to think. Instead, she asked, 'How are Lily and Matthew?'

'Matthew was wounded during the attack, but he's recovering at home. Lily is with him now.'

'I'm glad.' Evangeline came to sit on the edge of his desk, and he doubted if she was even aware of what she was doing. She was staring off into the distance, her mind preoccupied. But she sat so close to him, he grew aware of the light floral scent of her skin. He remembered how it had felt to brush his mouth against the curve of her neck and the way she had run her hands through his hair.

He couldn't deny that she allured him. But marriage? It wasn't right for either of them.

'We do need to talk about Lord Dunwood,' he began. 'Your father is afraid he'll press charges against you, which is a true possibility.' He poured brandy into his own glass and passed it to her. 'Especially considering the viscount's rage after you shot him.' A smile flicked at his lips. 'Well done, by the way.'

Evie accepted the glass of brandy and took a sip, wincing before she swallowed. 'Lord Dunwood wouldn't listen to reason. And I wasn't going to stand aside and allow him to…force himself upon me.' She shuddered at the words.

The visible reaction only rekindled his anger towards the viscount. The man never should have laid a finger on Evie.

James took the glass from her and drank from it before he passed it back to her. 'He's fortunate that he was only injured. If *I* had been there with your uncle's pistol, Dunwood would be dead.'

She gave a nod and let out a slow breath. 'I suppose so.' After a slight pause, she asked, 'What did Papa want to talk with you about?'

He hesitated a moment before answering, 'He wants me to marry you.'

She blinked a moment, as if she hadn't heard him correctly. 'He what?'

'He believes I should marry you and offer the protection of my title.' He took the remainder of the brandy and finished it in one swallow. 'It would be quite difficult to arrest a countess.'

Evangeline's disbelief transformed into dismay. 'That's a terrible idea. You and I are not suited at all.' But there was a faint undertone in her voice, as if she were trying to convince herself.

'I agree.' Though he hated the idea of hurting her feelings, he couldn't let her build him up into the man she wanted him to be. 'We both know I'll never be the right man for you.'

Her eyes grew luminous with unshed tears, and she

nodded. 'You made that clear enough when you sailed half a world away.'

'You could have any man you desire, Evangeline,' he murmured. 'Just choose one of them instead.' He wanted her to find her own happiness with someone who could give her the life she deserved.

But Evie shook her head. 'They only want my dowry. And the gentlemen who don't care about money only want me to mould myself into their idea of a perfect wife. I can't say the things I want to say or behave the way I want to.' She gripped her elbows and admitted, 'It's better if I just disappear from London society, the way you did. If I stay away long enough, the viscount will forget all about it.'

But James already knew that was impossible. 'Dunwood won't let you go. You've wounded his pride, as well as his foot.'

She stared at the wall. 'Why won't he leave me alone?'

'Greed,' he answered. But more than that, he knew the man wanted to dominate and tame Evangeline. The very thought made James curl his hands into fists. And that was the problem. Every time he tried to do the right thing and let Evie go, he kept imagining her in someone else's arms. And the idea only provoked jealousy he had no right to feel. He forced himself to lock it away.

He took a moment to push back his own anger, and he spoke calmly. 'I could try to use my influence to protect you from the legal consequences. Your uncle could, as well.'

'Then let's do that,' she murmured.

He walked closer to her and said, 'But you should know that a man like Dunwood won't back down. He wants to possess you, body and soul.'

Part of him understood that. He wanted to touch the

soft curve of Evie's cheek that fascinated him. He caught her hand in his and held it a moment. The touch of her fingers suddenly fired up the tempting vision of just how she'd behaved during their first kiss. There was a wild side to Evangeline Sinclair, a wickedness that made him crave more.

But she shook her head and took a step back. 'Tell my father you don't want to marry me.'

'It's what I planned to say. But I wanted to talk to you first.' He released her hand, even as he was fully aware of the temptation of her. It was entirely too easy to lose control around Evangeline. But neither did he want her to face danger or humiliation from being arrested. 'Your father wants this because Lord Dunwood can't force you into marriage if you're already wedded.'

'I don't need to marry anyone.' Her voice was heavy with unshed tears. 'I won't do it.'

'All right,' he said. Yet, he felt compelled to warn her. 'But… Dunwood could cause a great deal of trouble for you, even if he doesn't involve the police. The gossip could harm your business and hurt sales for Aphrodite's Unmentionables.'

At that, she went motionless. 'So many women rely on us for work.'

He gave a nod. 'Then choose a husband who can protect you from Dunwood and be done with it.'

The uneasiness clouded his mood once again, though he knew it was the right thing to do.

She let out a choked sigh. 'I would rather spend a year in Newgate than choose one of them. Why does anything have to change? Why do *I* have to be punished for being attacked? It wasn't my fault.'

She was right; it wasn't fair. And despite his own reasons for avoiding marriage, at least he had no intention of trying to change her. Nor was he in need of her dowry.

In truth, if there was ever a man who could give Evie the freedom she wanted, he suspected he was the only one. And perhaps that was why her father had suggested it.

He turned over the idea in his head as he considered possible solutions. There was a way both of them could get what they wanted.

'You're right,' James agreed. 'You shouldn't have to choose a man you despise, who would make demands of you. But neither can you run away from your problems.'

He knew, too well, that the scandal and gossip could ruin her. Dunwood would do everything in his power to cause trouble, out of revenge for what she'd done.

Her expression narrowed. 'What are you saying, Penford?'

'I'm saying, your father is right. Marriage is the best way to silence the gossip and probably save your family's business.'

She straightened and glared at him. 'Do you honestly think I want to trade my freedom for a life of marital imprisonment with one of those suitors? I'd rather be locked away.'

He didn't tell her that it was a real possibility, if Dunwood convinced the police that she'd harmed him on purpose.

'We need to think of a way out,' he said quietly as he took a seat. 'Give me a moment.'

She pulled up a chair beside him, her head lowered. 'This is awful.'

It was clear now that neither of them wanted marriage. All Evie wanted was her freedom and to be protected from Dunwood. But he knew she was in danger.

There was a solution, but she wouldn't like it. To be truthful, *he* didn't like it, either. But there was a way it could be tolerable to both of them, and they could continue on as they had before.

He reached out and took her hand. 'We're friends, Evie. Aren't we?'

She flinched at his touch but didn't pull away. 'I don't know any more,' she whispered. 'Are we?'

He was entranced by her soft lips and the way she was looking at him now, breathless with anticipation. Once again, he reminded himself to keep his distance.

'What if there's a way to keep things the way they are now?' he suggested quietly. 'Only without the threat of Dunwood or your queue of endless suitors?'

She rested her hands upon his. 'Go on.'

'What if…we *did* marry?' he said. 'But afterwards, we live apart. You could do as you please, and so will I. The marriage itself wouldn't have to mean anything. With my title, the authorities wouldn't dare press charges against you. And we could use my influence in society to protect your family's business.'

The way he saw it, it was the only possible solution. Afterwards, Evie could continue running Aphrodite's Unmentionables in London, while he looked after the estates at Penford. It also meant he could avoid the inevitable questions about marriage. No one needed to know that he had no desire to father an heir. They could believe that Evie was barren. The union would not change their lives in any way.

But from the troubled expression on Evie's face, she didn't agree. She hesitated before admitting, 'I don't want a loveless marriage where I'm left behind and become an object of pity.'

He understood her hesitation, especially after what had happened in the past. Still, he didn't want her under the false impression that this could be real. 'I can offer you my protection and your freedom, Evie. But not a true marriage.'

She pulled her hands away from his and stood. 'I know you don't find me attractive,' she began. 'I'm well aware of that. But rest assured, I—'

'Why would you think I don't find you attractive?' he interrupted. He had always found her beautiful. This had nothing to do with her desirability.

Her face reddened, and she admitted, 'Because you left me behind.'

'I left because I wasn't the sort of husband you needed. Not because I didn't find you beautiful.'

The look on her face showed her doubt. 'You travelled across the world after I threw myself at you. You didn't want me then, and you still don't.'

He hated seeing the hollowed pain of rejection on her face. To prove it, he came up behind her and rested his hand upon her spine. She tensed at his touch but didn't move away. Slowly, he caressed a path up to her nape. Beneath his fingers, he felt the furious beat of her pulse. 'Don't ever believe I didn't want you. Even though I'm still not the man you need.'

She took a step away from him and faced the wall. 'Neither of us wants this, Penford. Why even consider it?'

'You're right. I don't want to marry.' He turned her to look at him. 'But I would consider it if it kept you safe from a man like Dunwood,' he said softly. 'And if we go our separate ways afterwards.'

Her expression held nothing but dismay. 'But...don't

you need an heir? If we have a marriage where we live apart, then that cannot happen.'

'I don't ever intend to sire children, Evie.' Not after the nightmares he'd faced. The thought of fathering a child was unthinkable. It didn't matter what society expected of him. He'd witnessed such atrocities while in captivity, he couldn't imagine being a role model for any child. And he already had another plan in mind.

'If Rose has a son, I'll let my nephew inherit Penford.'

Evie stared back at him, her face pale. 'I don't understand. Do you despise me that much that you wouldn't ever want to have a child with me?'

When she looked at him like that, with heartbreak in her eyes, it reminded him of the night he'd left her. He'd been such a bastard, abandoning her after she'd offered him her heart. He didn't want to hurt her a second time. Evie didn't deserve that. Life had slapped her across the face when she'd never done anything except reach for what she wanted.

'It's not you,' he said softly. 'I don't want children from any woman.'

A tear rolled down her cheek, and he reached out to brush it away. God help him, he still desired her. And he sensed that if he didn't reassure her, she would become bitter and angry—rightfully so.

James leaned down to kiss her, and when he claimed her lips, he tasted the brandy that lingered on her breath. But more than that, he felt the dangerous sense that this woman had slipped past his own defences.

He expected her to shove him away. But instead, she rested her hands on his shoulders. Her lips were soft, and they yielded to him in a way that invited more.

He kissed her harder, trying to rid her from his mind. But it only evoked the memories he'd savoured in the darkness. He knew he had no right to this…and yet, he couldn't bring himself to stop.

He lifted her up to sit on the desk, and the urge to make her remember the passion they'd shared was undeniable. He wasn't aware of anything else but Evie. And nothing in the world could convince him to take his hands off her.

Until he heard the unmistakable sound of the door opening.

'Enough of that, Penford. You can wait until she's spoken her vows first.' Cain Sinclair's words were low, but there was no denying the conviction of them.

Evangeline's face held horror as she looked at her father. 'Papa, no. I did not agree to marry him.'

'You have two days to arrange a special licence,' Sinclair said. 'Or you can be wedded in Scotland.'

He stared back at her father and gave no denial. The man was right. Evie needed his protection, and this marriage would give them both the freedom they needed.

He would protect her from the viscount and allow Evie to continue living her life as she pleased. She could dwell in London or at Penford with his mother, if she wanted to. There were ways to make the marriage an amicable one, even if they remained apart.

James took Evie's hand in his and met her gaze evenly. 'I meant what I said, Evangeline. We can marry and keep separate lives. You would lose nothing at all.'

She didn't speak, but her hand tightened on his in a silent appeal. James simply waited for her answer. It had to be her choice, above all.

For a moment, her expression held bleakness, mingled

with an emotion he couldn't read. Then, at last, she relented and gave a single nod.

Her father appeared satisfied, and James said, 'I'll make the arrangements.'

Chapter Eight

On her wedding day, Evangeline had considered so many reasons why she should refuse to wed Lord Penford. First, he didn't truly want to marry her. He desired her, yes. The kiss had revealed that much. But he didn't want a wife or children.

Which was her second reason for wanting to call it off. She *did* want a child. She wanted a house full of them, especially sons and daughters who would fill the rooms with laughter and messes. The thought of a childless marriage brought a physical ache within her.

She didn't know if she could go through with this.

Why had James agreed to this farce of a marriage? He'd claimed that he wanted to protect her, that she could continue her work and do as she pleased. But how empty that life seemed.

If she had any courage at all, she would defy everyone. Run away and disappear. Her imagination conjured up a vision of taking a carriage and then a ship somewhere far away.

But then, that was a coward's path. So many people relied upon her family for their livelihood. If anything happened to her family's business, they would suffer for it. And she knew James was right. If she married him, the gossip would die down, leaving her business intact. He could reveal to the authorities that Dunwood had tried to attack her, and that she had only defended herself.

Evie waited inside the vicarage beside the small chapel her father had chosen for the wedding. With every minute that passed, her nerves increased. She took a few steps towards the window, questioning what sort of life she would have now. Then outside, she caught a glimpse of a local constable strolling near the chapel. A sudden chill iced through her as she wondered whether the police would try to arrest her. Ever since the night she'd shot the viscount in the foot, her father had tightened security around the house. There were whispers of bribes that he and the duke had given to the local police, but she didn't know how much longer they could delay the charges Lord Dunwood had threatened.

Only yesterday, the viscount had sent her a note:

Your family cannot protect you forever. You will face the consequences of your actions.

She'd burned the note immediately.

Although she didn't want to face the truth, she understood the gravity of her situation. Her father was right; marriage to an earl made it far easier to avoid the charges of assault. And it was far better to choose the Earl of Penford than another suitor who would make unreasonable demands of her. At least they were friends.

Or she thought they were. She didn't know why he'd kissed her. Was it pity, trying to stop her tears? It had seemed like more, though she'd told her treacherous heart to reinforce its defences. She felt so at odds, not knowing how to feel any more.

A knock sounded at the door, and her heart lurched just as she saw her mother coming inside the room. Margaret offered a warm smile and said, 'You look lovely, Evangeline.'

She offered an answering smile of thanks. Her maid had spent hours curling and styling her hair into an elaborate arrangement with curls and flowers. Her gown was made of silk and held the slightest blush of pink. Her shoulders were bare, and the waist of her gown pointed in a deep vee before the skirts formed a bell shape. Around her throat she wore diamonds, and her maid had pinned a soft lace veil to her hair.

'Thank you,' she answered. 'You look pretty, too, Mother.'

Margaret's hair was perfectly combed into an elegant chignon, and she wore a light blue gown. Around her throat, she wore pearls and a matched set of ear bobs. Her mother's eyes glowed with happiness, though for Evie, it wasn't at all a day of joy. More like apprehension and worry about what lay ahead.

'Are they ready for me?' Evie asked.

Margaret nodded. 'Your father is waiting to walk with you, and the vicar is here. But before we go, I wanted to be certain that you are all right. I know this…isn't the sort of wedding you expected or wanted.'

'No, it wasn't.' Before she could stop herself, she blurted out. 'Lord Penford doesn't want children, Mother. And I don't know if I want to marry a man who won't consider it. Because I *do* want babies of my own.'

She expected Margaret to offer excuses or sympathy. Instead, her mother's eyes gleamed. 'Oh, indeed. Well, he'll soon change his mind.' She pointed towards a package wrapped in brown paper that one of the maids had brought earlier. 'Wear that on your wedding night, Evie, and you'll have all the children you could possibly want.'

Evie blinked a moment, suddenly feeling embarrassed. 'I'm…not certain we will have a wedding night, Mother.' Most likely, they would sleep in separate rooms. And the thought was utterly disappointing.

Her mother only laughed. 'Evie, if you are under the same roof, believe me when I say you can have whatever you want.'

She had no idea what her mother was talking about. Although she sort of knew what went on between a woman and a man—especially after the night in the garden with James—she had no idea how to seduce her own husband.

Her mother paused and ventured, 'I'm not certain we ever talked about what you should expect, have we?'

Her cheeks burned, and Evangeline shook her head. This was not a conversation she wanted to have. 'There's no need. As I said, it probably won't even happen.'

'Evie, I don't know what you've heard from others,' her mother continued, 'but believe me when I say, a woman holds a great deal of power in the bedroom. Why do you think women buy the unmentionables we sell? Because *we* can fulfil a man's desires.' She looked her in the eyes and said, 'If he doesn't offer you a wedding night, then wear this and go to him. Tell him exactly what you want, where you want to be touched. And I promise, you'll bring him to his knees.'

Embarrassment flooded through her, though Evie ventured a nod. It was easier to pretend she understood than to argue with her mother. But the truth was, she could never bring any man to his knees. She was awkward and uncertain about herself. It was more likely that James could bring her to *her* knees, from the way the man kissed. It was far better than anything she'd ever imagined.

With that, her mother walked to the door and opened it. 'Shall we go?'

Evie still couldn't believe her mother's advice, but she followed Margaret outside towards the chapel. Her father waited for them, and when her mother passed by, Cain leaned in to kiss her cheek. Margaret's smile was radiant.

Evie thought it was a shame, really, that she had been their only child. A difficult pregnancy had caused her mother problems, but her parents loved her just as much as they loved each other. *Their* sort of marriage was the one she wanted.

Her father offered his arm, and she walked alongside him. Though his bearing was fierce, she caught the gleam of his own tears.

'Be happy, lass,' he muttered gruffly. 'Or I'll shoot him for you.'

Evie managed a smile at that. Her skin rose up with goose bumps, and her stomach twisted into nervous knots as they approached the doors. 'Papa…am I going to be arrested for what I did to Lord Dunwood?'

He stopped in front of the chapel. 'We'll no' let that happen. Your uncle Jonathan and I have delayed the charges, and after you're wedded, Penford will handle the rest.' His expression turned fierce. 'Dunwood willna cause any harm to you. I swear it.'

He gripped her hand in reassurance, and she squeezed it in return. 'Thank you.'

'Are you ready, lass?'

She nodded, and he opened the doors to the chapel. Although it was mid-morning, her mother had arranged for candles to be placed everywhere, gleaming and filling the room with light. Hothouse roses, greenery, and holly decked the church while in the corner, a quartet of musicians played a melody reminiscent of Christmas carols.

There were only a few guests, but her best friend, Lily, was here, wearing a gown of soft green. She had agreed to be Evie's bridesmaid, and the joy in her eyes was infectious.

'I'm so happy for you,' Lily whispered.

Evie gave an answering smile. Although she wished Rose could have been there, there was no time for her friend to arrive from Ireland. But at least she had one close friend here.

A knot caught within Evie's heart when she saw the earl standing beside the vicar. Penford wore all black, his cravat snowy white. His green eyes met hers, and her heart began pounding.

This was what she'd dreamed of, years ago. She'd wanted this man, imagining that he loved her. But that young girl had learned a hard truth, and she reminded herself that this was an arrangement, nothing more. She would guard her heart and remember that this marriage wasn't real.

The earl offered his hand, and she took it. 'You look beautiful, Evangeline.'

Her mouth went dry, but she answered, 'So do you.' Then she blinked when she realised what she'd said. 'I mean, handsome. You look handsome.'

Why in the world was she so nervous? This wasn't a true wedding day, and there was absolutely no reason for nerves. But seeing James standing in front of her was enough to make her imagination roam freely with sinful ideas.

He looked at her as if he wanted to kiss her again. Which made her heart pound even faster.

The vicar began the ceremony, and while he prattled on, Evangeline focused her attention on James. Even now, she was transfixed by his mouth and the strong line of his jaw. She remembered what it was to feel the hard planes of his body pressed close while his mouth explored hers, his tongue sliding inside. A sudden thrill slid over her body as she imagined that mouth on her again, over the secret places that burned for his touch.

But no, that wasn't going to happen.

'Miss Sinclair?' the vicar prompted.

Oh, goodness. She hadn't heard a word of the ceremony. Was it now time for her vows? What was she supposed to say?

'Sorry,' she whispered.

'Wilt thou take this man to be thy husband?' The vicar repeated the rest of the vow, but she was entirely distracted by the warmth of Penford's hand. Despite their gloves, she was conscious of the pressure and heat of his palm. Once again, she envisioned him taking off his glove and tracing his fingers across her bare skin.

The earl smiled at her, and she stammered out, 'I—I will.'

Penford spoke his own wedding vows and then slid a ruby ring with a cluster of diamonds on her finger. She gaped a moment, for she'd only anticipated a single gold ring. Not something so pretty or sparkling.

The vicar finished the ceremony, and pronounced, 'I now present to you the Earl and Countess of Penford. You may kiss your bride.'

Before Evie realised what was happening, the earl kissed her lightly. She didn't even have time to kiss him back before it was over and her mother and father were clapping, along with Lily.

He caught her hand just as she turned. Then he reached over and tucked a wayward curl behind her ear. 'You do look beautiful, Evangeline.'

'Thank you.' She blushed and added, 'I only hope you don't regret being forced into marriage with me. This was never my intent.'

He tucked her hand in his. 'I know. But I also think our marriage will be anything but boring.'

She had a strong suspicion he was right.

After the wedding breakfast, the celebration, and packing all of Evie's belongings and pets, James arranged for a coach to drive them north, towards Penford. The sooner he got her out of London, the better. They would drive for most of the afternoon and early evening before stopping at an inn.

His wife had changed into a blue travelling gown, and inside the coach, Evie had tucked a blanket around her feet. Her dog, Annabelle, snored at her feet with three puppies while her cat, Dasher, had its paws on the window and was staring outside at the snow. James hoped the weather wouldn't cause trouble on their journey, but at least they could leave the city quickly.

It was strange to imagine that he was married now, and he'd certainly never imagined that Evie would be his. What would their life be like now? He'd promised that they would remain friends, even if they would not have a true marriage, and that they would live apart. But he couldn't deny that she still fascinated him.

Her expression held worry while she stared outside, but her beauty was undeniable. Even when Evie had lashed out at him in the past, her blue eyes had been fiery, her cheeks flushed with colour. He rather liked it when she was rebellious. And he preferred her honesty.

'You're staring at me,' she remarked. 'Is something wrong?'

'It's odd to think that we're married now.' He leaned back and rested his feet on the opposite seat beside her.

Her cat jumped up on his lap and nestled against his legs. Evie glared at the animal. 'You've switched your loyalty already, have you? Traitor.' Then she shook her head and sighed. 'You're right, James. It is odd to be married. I always thought I would remain a spinster.'

His expression grew sombre. 'This marriage wasn't really a choice for either of us, was it?'

Evangeline remained silent for a time, and he wondered if he shouldn't have spoken. But it seemed better to have honesty between them. 'Two years ago, it was all I ever wanted. I thought I was in love with you.'

He met her gaze openly. 'You didn't deserve what I did to you.'

At that, she ventured a tired smile. 'I threw myself at you. I should have known better.'

'And I should have sent you away.' He paused a moment and then lifted his foot to the opposite seat again. 'But your kiss changed everything.'

Her smile faded away. 'Don't patronise me, Penford. I didn't know anything about kissing a man. I was desperate to change your mind about leaving for India.'

'My father asked me to go. He told me he wanted to give me the gift of travelling, and he told me to make investments on our behalf.' He paused a moment. 'I didn't know how sick he was.' There was a heaviness in his voice, of a man who wanted to grieve his father's death but continued to hold back the pain. 'I blame myself for what happened to my family. I wasn't supposed to be gone so long.'

She sobered at his words. 'I suppose we both made mistakes. I thought you would offer for me after…that night. It was humiliating when you left.'

'What I did was wrong, and I have no excuse for it. I never meant to hurt you.'

She leaned back and rested her feet on the opposite side, next to his hips, her skirts filling up the space between them. 'But you did. And you probably will again.'

He frowned at that. 'I don't want to, Evangeline. Tell me what we can do to avoid it.'

She paused a moment and said, 'You told me you don't want children. But you never said why. Help me understand your reasons.'

'That's a conversation for a night when I am beyond drunk,' he admitted. 'Not one for our wedding day.'

'Is it that bad?'

He could only nod. He didn't want to admit to her—or anyone really—the horrors that he and Matthew had faced. Even now, the memory evoked fear he didn't want to remember.

'Then we'll save that conversation for another time.' She rubbed Annabelle's ears. 'I assume we will have separate bedrooms?'

'We will,' he agreed. 'And we won't have a wedding night.' More than anything, he needed to initiate boundaries between them. Not only was it the right thing to do, but it was a necessity, for he could hardly keep Evie at arm's-length. She had found a way to get under his skin, tempting him into making bad decisions. Even now, he was entirely distracted by her legs, so close to his.

'I assumed that. Though my mother and aunts gave me a trousseau of undergarments that are...not anything I can imagine wearing.'

His mouth went dry at the thought. 'What were they?'

'Some were red silk, others black. One was actually a lovely emerald green, but none of them are worth wearing. They don't cover anything at all.'

'Lace?' he ventured.

She nodded, her cheeks flushed. 'But I've no use for such things. They're terribly impractical.'

He could think of many uses, and he couldn't stop himself from imagining Evie with her dark hair falling around her shoulders, her body revealed in alluring red silk and lace. James shifted in his seat at the image.

He swallowed hard and continued. 'During Christmas, we will have our own bedrooms with a connecting door so the staff won't get the wrong idea. To the rest of the world, we will be husband and wife—at least until we decide who will live where. But I won't bother you, you needn't worry.'

She let out another breath that sounded suspiciously like a sigh.

'Is something wrong?'

'No, of course not.' She straightened her skirts and glanced out at the snow. 'Will we be able to travel in this weather?'

'We'll get as far as we can,' he answered. 'Penford is a few days' journey north. We'll stop along the way to spend the night.'

'I haven't visited Penford in years,' she admitted. 'What should I know before we arrive?'

'It hasn't changed very much since my childhood. My mother...well, you know she hasn't been well. Her memory is failing, and we thought it best if she stayed there instead of London.'

'Is there a land steward or a caretaker for the estate?'

He gave a nod. 'There is. And I've asked the house-keeper, Mrs Marlock, to give my mother small tasks so she feels useful again. She misses my father and sometimes imagines he's still alive.'

'I suppose that dream is better than the reality of losing him.' Evangeline's voice turned soft. 'We will look after her.'

'So, we will. But if she falls into one of her spells, just let her be. There's nothing we can do to bring her back.'

She relaxed against the coach, and the silence fell between them once more. Evie waited a few minutes and then said, 'I suppose I'm lucky that Lord Dunwood didn't bring any charges against me.'

'Oh, he did,' James answered. 'They were planning to arrest you yesterday.'

She paled and sat up. 'Why didn't you or my father say anything? Are we—are we running from the police?'

He reached out to take her hands. They were freezing, and he detected the faint tremor of fear. 'No. Your father's solicitor and mine are handling the matter.'

'But how? I shot Dunwood.'

'You did,' he agreed, 'and Dunwood wants only one thing—money. We've agreed to pay a fine and settle the matter outside of court.'

'But what about the arrest warrant?'

He squeezed her hands. 'Evie, your uncle is a duke. And your father has enough money to buy three kingdoms. It wasn't difficult to convince Dunwood to withdraw the charges and accept our payment in return.'

Her expression turned to dismayed fury. 'Why should

we have to pay anything at all? He is the one who attacked *me*. Why does he get a reward for doing so?'

'Because life isn't always fair,' he answered. 'And now, he can no longer touch you. We will be hundreds of miles away, and you can remain at Penford for a time until the gossip dies down.'

Her cheeks reddened and she leaned her head against the coach window. 'I rather wish I *had* shot him in the heart.'

James regarded her and answered, 'If he tries to harm you in any way again, rest assured, I will end his miserable life. I promise you that.'

That night, as promised, they stopped at an inn. Though it was late by the time they arrived, Evangeline was grateful that the snow had slowed down. It was freezing outside, and even with her fur-lined cape and muff, she felt the bite of the wind. James rested his hand against her lower back, escorting her inside.

Several of their household servants had travelled in another coach, and they took over the care of the animals while she and James retreated to their private room. Inside, a warm fire burned on the hearth, and she stood beside it while James went to get supper for them.

She eyed the bed, wondering if they would share it. Though she guessed he would offer to sleep on the floor, her mind was spinning with what her mother had told her. Margaret had promised that she could get the sort of marriage she wanted—that is, if she were brave enough to attempt seduction.

Evie didn't know. She was rather afraid James would turn her away. He'd already told her that he didn't want children, so it was unlikely he would change his mind.

Unless she simply tried to tempt him instead of asking.

She wondered what her husband might look like naked, his limbs sprawled upon the bed. Although it had been months, his skin still held the warmth of the Indian summer sun. What would it be like to touch him. Would he allow it?

His mouth had been wicked upon her bare skin that night, his tongue swirling over her nipple. A sudden ache caught between her legs at the memory of his caress. He'd awakened a hunger within her, and now, she questioned whether it would ever be satisfied.

Beneath her gown, she had chosen a corset of white, but it was made of the finest silk and lace. Ribbons adorned the base of her stays, and she couldn't deny that her undergarments were meant to draw attention to her curves. Though it had embarrassed her at first, she was now starting to wonder if there was a good reason to reveal them to her husband—if it meant he might change his mind.

James entered their room, followed by the innkeeper, who carried a large tray of food and wine. 'Put it on the table,' he instructed, and the innkeeper obeyed, accepting a silver coin in return.

Penford poured a cup of mulled wine for her and brought it over. The heat of the mug made her smile. 'Oh, that's wonderful. Thank you.' She tasted the sweetened wine and detected cinnamon and other spices.

James stood across from her at the fire and drank his own wine, but he seemed distracted. Good. She wanted him to reconsider his promise to leave her untouched, though she certainly didn't truly know anything about seduction.

'Are you hungry?' he asked. He moved away from the fire before she could answer and uncovered several plates that contained roasted chicken and potatoes, while another had fresh bread.

She was more nervous than hungry, but she lied, 'Oh, yes.'

He pulled out a chair for her and offered her portions of the food before serving himself. Once again, his mood seemed to shift, and he stopped talking.

Why had it suddenly become awkward between them? Was it because he was questioning the wisdom of sharing a room tonight?

Evie picked at her food, sipping the hot wine entirely too fast. Her husband ate in silence, and while she tried to decide what to do, a lock of her hair fell free of its pin. She decided to remove the flowers and pins from her hair, and as she did, James turned to watch her.

Though he said nothing, she felt the heat of his gaze. And it made her crave his attention.

Slowly, she continued pulling out the pins until her hair fell in a dark wave down to her waist. James was watching her the entire time, but she pretended as if she didn't notice. Instead, she drew her fingers through her hair and went to stand by the fireplace.

'You didn't eat very much,' he remarked. 'Was something wrong?'

Evie glanced at the hearth, staring at the flames licking at the wood. 'No.' Then she amended her words and said, 'Yes. I suppose so.' She turned to look at him and added, 'Why did it suddenly get so uncomfortable between us? Nothing's changed.'

Which was an utter lie. Everything had changed. But she suspected that if she pretended all was well, he might come to believe it.

He pushed his plate aside and went to join her by the

hearth. 'You're right. This shouldn't be difficult at all. We both know nothing is going to happen tonight.'

There will, if I can manage it, she thought to herself.

But instead, she nodded and told him, 'You'll stay on your side of the bed, and I'll stay on mine.'

At that, he cast her a wary look. 'We're not sharing a bed, Evangeline.'

Aren't we?

She feigned mock innocence as she met his gaze with a smile. 'It's not as if you have to worry about anything, Penford. I promise I won't ravish you and steal your virtue.'

Instead, I'll tempt you to steal mine.

A slight grin tipped his mouth at her teasing. 'I don't know, Evie. I am a virgin, after all.'

His words shocked her, and she held back her own reaction. She'd always expected that he'd received his own education like the other London rakes. But instead, she felt a slight thrill at the idea that they would be each other's first lover. 'Are you really?'

He leaned against the fireplace mantel. 'I am. So, you needn't worry that I'll attempt to ravish you, either.'

She didn't know what to think of his confession, for it was the last thing she'd expected. And now that she knew it, she wasn't certain whether her plan of seduction would work. But all she could do was try.

'I would like to change into my nightgown,' she said. 'Could you help me with my buttons?'

'I'll send for your maid.'

'No, don't.' She turned her back to him. 'We're keeping up pretences, remember? And since you've promised not to ravish me, surely you can manage to unbutton my gown and loosen my stays. I can do the rest.'

But she rather hoped he would succumb to his instincts

and surrender to his own desires. She'd made up her mind that she would do what she could to tempt him, and if it didn't work, then she would know that it was a useless effort.

James reached out to her gown and flicked open the top button. 'How many buttons are there?'

'I've no idea. A lot. Which is why I need your help.' She kept her back to him, but as his hands moved over each button, it was an effort not to imagine other places his hands could go. She remembered the way his clever fingers had found secret places, tempting her into sin.

And God help her, she wanted that again.

Evie was conscious of his body so close to hers, and memories flooded through her of the way he'd made her feel. She savoured his touch, wishing he would forget his promise to live a separate life apart from her.

He finally reached her waist, and the gown slipped down, revealing her shift and corset.

Turn around, she commanded herself.

This was the moment she ought to seize. Her heart was pounding rapidly, and before he could untie her stays, she faced him.

'Wait a moment,' she said, pretending she needed to remove the rest of her gown. He started to turn away, but not before he caught a glimpse of her undergarments. His green eyes flared with undisguised interest.

'I'm beginning to see how you made a fortune out of selling ladies' unmentionables,' he remarked.

She couldn't bring herself to speak, but she lifted her wedding gown away and let it fall to the floor. 'Will you help me with my stays now?'

He turned back, and she saw the flare of interest before he shielded it. Gently, he guided her to turn around as he touched her waist. The heat of his hands made her wonder if he was remembering their stolen moment two years ago. Did he desire her in the same way she'd wanted him?

Gently, he untied the stays, loosening them. 'There. That should be enough.'

Not nearly.

Her hands had turned cold, and she didn't know if she had the courage to try to tempt him further.

But before she could turn around again, he walked to the far side of the room. 'I'll let you get into your nightgown while I change.'

He kept his back to her while he removed his jacket and began untying his cravat. Evie lifted her corset away and stepped free of her petticoats, all the while watching him. He stripped away his shirt, and she caught a glimpse of that warm male skin that drew her gaze down to his trousers.

It was an effort to put her nightgown on while she openly ogled her husband. He removed his boots and trousers but kept his drawers on.

With disappointment, she turned back to the fire, pretending as if she hadn't been watching. Her linen nightgown was soft and plain, not nearly as seductive as her corset and shift.

But then, he'd already made it clear that he intended to keep his boundaries tonight.

She heard the rustle of the bedcovers and asked, 'May I turn around?'

'Yes.'

When she saw the bed, he had flipped back the coverlet for her. He was naked from the waist up, and her cheeks flushed at the sight of his muscular chest. She imagined kissing the curve of his pectoral muscles, taking a path lower to his ridged abdomen.

'Goodnight, Evie,' he said, rolling over.

'Goodnight.' She climbed into the bed and shivered at the cool sheets. The room was still rather chilly, in spite of the fire.

More than anything, she wanted a wedding night. Her nerves were raw, her body uncertain about what would happen next. She was so afraid to reach out to him, wishing she could talk him into a very different sort of marriage.

James left you once before, her brain reminded her. *If he wants you, all he has to do is turn over.*

She stared at his muscular back, hoping against hope that he would change his mind. But instead, he continued to face the opposite wall, making it clear that he had no intention of touching her in any way.

And deep inside, it hurt to know it.

The darkness was all he had known for days. His mouth was dry, and James could still feel the heaviness of chains. The earthy scent of the prison surrounded him on all sides. The ache of hunger had dulled, and he suspected that he would die soon.

He struggled to free himself, but the flare of a torch caught his attention. The woman smiled softly at him. Some would call her beautiful from her dark hair and striking eyes. But he knew Nisha for what she was—a viper who delighted in torturing men.

'Tell me what I want to know,' she began. 'Where are the English soldiers?'

'We're not soldiers,' he tried to say, but one of the men struck him across the face with his fist. James tasted blood, and the woman smiled at the sight.

'You lie. Our people are dying in battle, and your men are to blame.'

He tried to deny it again, but another blow caught him across the jaw. 'We only came as travellers.'

'I don't believe you.' Her smile was slow and menacing. 'But you will pay the price for my family's suffering.'

'James!'

He jolted awake and realised he'd pressed Evangeline against the mattress, his forearm across her shoulders.

'I'm so sorry.' He released her immediately and sat up, lowering his head. His heartbeat was racing, and sweat coated his skin. He never should have shared the bed with her. The nightmares were still too frequent.

Evie brought him a cup of water, and he drained it. She refilled it, and this time, he drank more slowly.

'I should have slept on the floor. I never meant to hurt you.'

'You didn't,' she insisted. But after a slight pause, she asked, 'How often do you have these nightmares?'

He didn't truly want to answer, but did it matter? They were never going to share a room. 'Often enough.'

She took the cup back and sat beside him. 'Will you tell me what you dreamed of?'

'I'd rather not.' It was better to lock the memories away and pretend they didn't exist. He took a breath and pushed back the coverlet. It bothered him to realise that he'd confused past and present and had nearly hurt her. 'I'll sleep on the floor.' He took a pillow with him and stretched out before the hearth.

James tried to close his eyes, but sleep wouldn't come. A moment later, he heard the rustling of a blanket, and Evangeline came to sit beside him on the floor.

'What are you doing?' he asked wearily. It was the middle of the night, and he didn't want her to worry about him.

Evie had a blanket wrapped around her, and she faced him. 'You should come back to bed. If you attempt to sleep on the floor, then I'll sleep there, too.'

He blinked at her words. 'Leave me, Evangeline, and go back to sleep.'

'I will not. Do you honestly think I'm so selfish that, after my husband has such a horrible nightmare, I'd abandon him to sleep on the floor? What sort of person do you think I am?'

Honestly, he hadn't thought about it at all, except he didn't want to intrude on her sleep any more than he already had. 'It's late, and I don't want to argue.'

'Then don't argue. Come back to bed, and stop being an obstinate donkey.' She reached out her hand to him. 'There's no sense in behaving like a martyr when we both know you have no desire whatsoever for me. You might as well be sleeping with the dog.'

Is that what she believed? He frowned and rose from the floor, ignoring her hand. 'What do you mean, I have no desire for you?'

'You made that clear enough,' she said. 'There will be no wedding night, and we will not share a room when we arrive at Penford.'

He drew his hand to her waist, wondering if she truly believed he didn't want her. Ever since she'd first undressed in front of him, he'd barely been able to keep his hands off her. The white corset had moulded to her skin, revealing beautiful breasts that he hadn't touched or kissed in two years. Her body was lush and tempting, and he drew a thumb down her jawline.

'You're making it very difficult for me to be a gentleman.'

'Then don't be a gentleman,' she whispered. 'Be a wicked rake instead.' She took his hand and brought it to the curve of her breast. Beneath the soft cotton of her chemise, he felt the erect tip of her nipple, and he couldn't stop himself from caressing it.

'You're a fool if you think I don't want you with every breath in my body,' he murmured. 'Do you think I forgot the way you kissed me? Or the way I pleasured you that night in the garden?'

Her eyes were luminous in the firelight, and he saw the stricken expression on her face. Without warning, she wrapped her arms around his waist and drew her body against his. He couldn't hide the ridge of his erection, and she inhaled as he drew his hands to her backside and pulled her close.

He could feel the tremble of her body and the shock of her fear. Slowly, he led her back to the bed and drew her back beneath the covers.

Then he leaned down and kissed her forehead. 'Goodnight, Evangeline.'

Before he could lose his last thread of honour, he got dressed and went downstairs. He needed to leave before he changed his mind and fully ravished his wife.

Chapter Nine

◇◆◇

They arrived at Penford the day before Christmas Eve. Evie had settled back into the reality that James had meant what he'd said. He didn't intend to consummate their marriage at all. And although it had hurt her feelings to realise it, she'd forced an invisible shield around her heart.

She wasn't good at seduction. Her fumbling attempts to gain James's attention had met with nothing, so why try? It was better if she made the most of the marriage she had instead of the marriage she wanted.

When the coach came to a stop, Evangeline stared out at the snow coating the grounds, feeling as if she'd stepped into an enchanted fairy tale. Although she'd visited the estate once or twice, long ago, it suddenly struck her that she was now Lady of the household—the Countess of Penford.

It had never really occurred to her before that she had married into nobility. Although her mother had been the daughter of a baron, Margaret had settled into their ordinary life with no trouble at all. The only hint of her past was her impeccable manners and her insistence that Evangeline be raised in a ladylike way.

She found herself trying to remember the lessons her mother had drilled into her. What was she supposed to do with a household of servants? She'd never really paid attention, despite Margaret's efforts to teach her. She knew she was supposed to help plan the menus, but what else was there? A sudden rush of nerves flooded through her, and she realised how ill-prepared she was.

James helped her down from the coach, and most of the servants were already there to greet them. She searched for some sign of his mother, Lady Penford, but the dowager was not among the others.

The sea of faces and names blurred as he led her up the stairs and into the estate. There were a few signs of neglect with overgrown hedges and ivy upon the house, but then, James had only been to Penford once since his return from India.

Inside, the house was still a bit draughty, and she pulled her cloak close for warmth. Mrs Marlock, the housekeeper, walked alongside them.

'It's very welcome you are, Lady Penford,' the older woman greeted her. The woman's grey hair was scraped back into a tight bun, and she wore a set of keys upon a chain at her waist, like a chatelaine from the medieval era. 'Would ye be wanting tea or summat to eat?'

'Tea and hot food would be wonderful,' Evie answered. 'If it's not too much trouble.'

The housekeeper straightened. 'Oh, it's ne'er any trouble, my lady. We'll have a wee bit to fill yer bellies, soon enough.' She gave orders to one of the maids and then told another to build up the fire in the drawing room.

'Will the Dowager Lady Penford be able to join us?' Evie asked. She hadn't seen James's mother in over a month.

Mrs Marlock met the earl's gaze, but her expression was unreadable. 'I will let her know that you're here,' she said, 'but she isn't feeling well today.'

'Thank you, Mrs Marlock,' James answered.

The housekeeper excused herself, promising to send up food. Within a few moments, the warmth of the fire began to seep into the room. Evie stood beside it, trying to warm her hands and feet. Soon enough, her dog Annabelle trotted into the drawing room, followed by the puppies, who swarmed their mother as she slumped in front of the fire.

'She's made herself at home, I see,' James remarked.

A moment later, her cat swished into the room. Dasher rubbed against her gown and then flopped beside the dog.

'I suppose they both have.' She smiled a moment. 'Thank you for letting me bring them here. I would have missed them.'

'I remember how much you love your animals.'

'I could fill a barn with them,' she admitted. 'When I was a little girl, I sometimes visited my uncle Jonah in Scotland and rode horses there. He also had a donkey that I adored.'

She grew wistful, remembering. But even as she turned her attention back to her pets, she couldn't help but wonder what her life would become here. 'James, what are my responsibilities at Penford?'

'Whatever you want them to be, I suppose. Do as much or as little as you like.' He walked over to stand by the window. 'I'll stay for a fortnight and then return to London.'

He'd told her that was his plan, to live a separate life from hers. And yet, part of her felt unsettled that he was already planning to leave again. A sadness caught within her.

Am I that undesirable? a voice inside ventured. *Do you really want to leave me behind so soon?*

But then, that was the arrangement, wasn't it? He'd always intended to bring her here for her safety and then return. The problem was her own loneliness. She liked James and enjoyed bantering with him. She didn't want him to go back so soon.

Evie straightened and told herself not to let herself fall back into misery again. There was no reason why she couldn't follow James to London. She had a business to run, after all.

But in the meantime, she wanted a little more time as newlyweds.

'Will you stay a little longer?' she ventured. 'If you leave me behind only a fortnight after we are married, people will talk.'

Before he could answer, Mrs Marlock arrived with a footman who brought in a tray of hot soup, scones with cream and jam, tea, and small ginger biscuits. Evie's stomach rumbled at the sight of the food, and then the footman uncovered another dish, revealing two large slices of cake. Instantly, it brought her back to that ball so long ago, when she'd hidden beneath the desk with cake. A pang caught her heart at the memory of the lonely girl she'd been. But she wasn't about to stand aside and become a lonely wife. She would find a way to fill her life with meaningful work.

'Thank you, Mrs Marlock,' the earl murmured, and a few moments later, they were left alone.

The moment the door closed, Evie poured cups of tea for both of them. She fixed his tea with milk, no sugar, and then made her own.

'You remembered,' he said.

Evie hadn't really thought about it, but it seemed that she'd always known how he drank his tea. She'd seen it often enough when she'd gone to visit with Lily and Rose.

He thanked her and then passed her a plate. 'Cake?' he offered.

But she shook her head. 'No, thank you. Soup will be fine.' Her appetite was fading, and it felt as if their relationship was already shifting away from friendship to something more formal. She didn't want a stilted, arranged marriage.

And maybe it was best to simply discuss this with James.

'I should like to talk about our marriage,' she began, taking a sip of the hot soup. 'The rules, I mean.' She needed to understand whether there was any hope at all for something different between them—even though she was fairly certain that he didn't want her. His actions said as much.

His expression revealed his confusion. 'The rules?'

She nodded. 'You married me to protect me from Viscount Dunwood. And I'm grateful for your help, truly. I do think I'll be safer because of it. But I don't really want to be abandoned and alone.'

At least he seemed to understand what she was saying. 'It's just for a time, Evie. Until the talk dies down.'

'I know. But I'm already away from my family on Christmas. And all my friends are in London, too.' She felt a rise of sadness catching at her heart. 'If you leave, too…' Her words broke off, and she stopped herself, realising how needy she sounded.

He sobered. 'No, you're right. I suppose it's not fair to take you away from everyone else.'

'I would like one week,' she said. 'One week, here at Penford, to pretend to be happily married when we're around the servants and your mother. As my Christmas present.' Before he could impose more rules, she stood from the table and walked towards him. She rested her hand upon his shoulder. 'You needn't worry. It won't be real.'

Though she tried to keep her voice light, he covered her hand with his own. Before she could do anything, he pulled her into his lap, just as Mrs Marlock returned. Evangeline stifled her gasp of startled surprise, but before she could stop herself, a laugh broke forth.

'Och! I came to see if ye were needin' anything else,' the housekeeper said. 'I'll be certain ye're nay disturbed, my lord.' Then she hurried outside the room and closed it again.

The moment she was gone, Evangeline couldn't stop her laugh. 'Did you know she was coming inside?'

A wicked smile slid over his face. 'I might have heard her approaching the room.' She started to stand, but he kept her on his lap. 'Was this what you wanted, Evie? To pretend?'

'I—yes, but—'

He cut off her words when he began nuzzling her neck. A thousand shivers broke over her skin, and she was torn between telling him to stop and wanting him to continue.

'Then we'll pretend.' He reached out for a scone and broke off a piece, feeding it to her.

She hardly tasted it at all, but she was entirely aware that he was teasing her. Trying to make her uncomfortable by kindling desires he had no intention of fulfilling.

'I meant, around the servants and others,' she started to say.

'Did you?' he challenged. From the sudden flare in his eyes, she wondered what was happening. His hands remained at her waist, and she caught her breath at the thought of what he would do next.

Her mother's claim—that she could seduce her husband—suddenly came to mind. It occurred to Evie that she was becoming passive, waiting for James to touch or kiss her. Was that really what she wanted?

Or should she try to take the lead?

This is a terrible idea, her brain warned.

He had already brushed her aside the first time she'd declared her feelings two years ago. Then again on her wedding night. Why should it be any different now?

Yet, it felt like a challenge somehow. He was almost daring her to pretend, to reach for what she wanted.

And two could play this game.

She reached for another piece of the scone from his plate and added clotted cream to it. Slowly, she fed it to James, watching as his eyes darkened. For a moment, she rested her hand against his face, and he caught her hand, keeping it there.

'Are you hungry?' she asked softly. Her voice came out breathless, and from the harsh look in his eyes, she was well aware they weren't speaking of food any more.

'Very,' he answered.

She found herself staring at his mouth, uncertain of what to do. But he held himself back, waiting for her to make the next move. She thought a moment and then glanced over at the tray.

'Oops,' she murmured. 'I forgot the jam.'

But instead of offering him a spoonful of jam with the scone, she dipped her fingertip into the strawberry preserves and brought it to his lips. His mouth closed over her finger, and when he swirled his tongue over it, an echo of sensation ached between her legs.

Her body grew even more responsive while she sat on his lap, for she could feel his rigid erection pressed against her. She could imagine him kissing her, touching her intimately. And Heaven help her, she wanted that.

'I have something you want,' he murmured.

Shocked, she could do nothing but remain motionless as he rearranged her on his lap. The hard length of his arousal rested against her, and she bit her lip when he moved.

Then he reached for a piece of the chocolate cake and brought it to her mouth, feeding it to her. With a wicked smile, he met her gaze, and she understood that he'd fully intended the innuendo, just as she had.

But when she licked his fingertip while staring into his eyes, his smile faded. He gripped her hips, and her body seemed to grow even more heated. His gaze turned hooded, and he drew her face to his.

'Rule one,' he murmured against her lips. 'We will not consummate this marriage.'

I know, she started to say, before he added, 'But there are no rules that prevent us from enjoying one another. If you want.'

She wasn't at all certain what he meant by that. 'Enjoying one another?'

He nipped at her lower lip, sliding his tongue against it, and she couldn't stop herself from kissing him back. His mouth teased hers, lazily kissing her lips while he dragged his hands through her hair.

This was dangerous. It was exactly the sort of touching that she'd surrendered to, two years ago. But she'd asked him to pretend to be married. And he'd given her just that, hadn't he?

Evie yielded to him, opening her mouth against his, and his tongue slid inside. Heat roared through her, and she shifted against the ridge of his desire. He was aching for her as much as she was for him.

Slowly, he pulled back from the kiss, and his eyes were blazing. And suddenly, she questioned what she'd begun between them.

And whether it would end as badly as it had before.

His wife was slowly killing him. She had somehow tempted him beyond all reason, and James knew that if he didn't leave for London soon, he was going to utterly abandon his decision to remain apart from her.

It had taken all his self-control not to drag Evie off to his bedchamber. Instead, he'd muttered an excuse about needing to see to his mother and had left her behind.

He supposed he might as well see Iris, to discover what Mrs Marlock had meant when she'd said that Lady Penford wasn't feeling well. He hadn't seen his mother since their arrival and wondered whether her condition was her memory loss or a true illness.

Either way, he was feeling entirely unsettled when he walked along the hallway that led to a separate wing of Penford. Because there were fewer stairs, his mother and grandmother often stayed in this part of the house.

A maid greeted him as he passed. 'Good evening, Lord Penford.'

'I've come to see my mother,' he told her. 'Is she in her room?'

The maid shook her head, and he could tell she was uncomfortable. 'She's in the parlour, my lord.'

He gave a nod of dismissal and walked inside the small sitting room. The pianoforte was decorated with possibly fifty items, ranging from small porcelain birds and flowers to silver spoons or pieces of coloured glass.

'Hello, Mother,' he greeted her.

Iris looked up and frowned at him. Slowly, she rose

from her chair and moved closer to the hearth. 'I don't know you.'

A slight edge of sadness caught him as he realised what the others meant when they'd said she was unwell. 'It's me. James,' he told her. 'Your son.'

'My son is in India,' she argued back. 'I don't know you.' Her hand closed over a fireplace poker, and he realised that she felt threatened by him.

He was careful not to move but questioned whether he ought to go along with her illusions. 'I am sorry if I disturbed you. I only wanted to see if you were well or if you needed anything.'

'I want you to leave,' she said firmly. 'My husband will be home soon, and if you have not left Penford, he will be most displeased.' She gripped the fireplace poker, and James took a step back.

'My apologies,' he said quietly before he retreated and walked back into the hall. An unsettled feeling caught him, and he decided to step outside on the terrace to gather his thoughts.

The wintry air was cold, and he took a moment to stop and breathe. It was only two days before Christmas, and for a while, he simply watched the falling snow as it coated the hedges and grass. There was a serenity here, a calm he'd not experienced in a long time. Behind him, he heard footsteps approaching and when he turned, he saw Evangeline standing at the doorway.

'I didn't expect to see you here,' he said quietly.

'I was planning to join you and say hello to your mother,' she answered. 'But then I saw you leave. Was it a bad day for her?'

He nodded. 'She didn't know who I was.'

Her face turned sympathetic. 'I'm so sorry. It's hard to

watch someone you love fade away into someone so very different.' She crossed over to him and took his arm in hers. 'Do you want to walk for a little while?'

'It's freezing outside,' he warned.

'Just through the garden,' she suggested.

He escorted her down the snowy pathway and through the arched brick doorway that led into a walled garden. A small stone fountain rested in the centre, and a few fir trees along the perimeter were lined with more snow.

'Tomorrow is Christmas Eve,' she said. 'We should invite your mother to join us for a celebration.'

'She didn't know who I was,' he said quietly. 'I didn't realise it had got that bad.' He had seen her only a month ago, and though she'd had her spells, it had never been like this.

'She might remember both of us in the morning,' Evangeline said. 'We won't know until then.'

He understood that she was trying to be optimistic, but he doubted if anything would change. 'I don't even know what to give her for Christmas,' he admitted. 'I brought a few things from London, but she might not want them any more.'

'Or they might bring her joy,' she countered. 'Give her the gifts anyway.'

He walked alongside his wife, the snow crunching beneath their feet as the darkness descended. The sun had descended, leaving only a sliver of violet sky. Evangeline shivered, and he realised she wasn't wearing a cloak. She'd followed him outside with no regard for the cold. He removed his jacket and put it around her shoulders.

She pulled it close and turned back to him. 'So, what did you ask Father Christmas for this year?' Her voice was teasing as she smiled.

He hadn't truly thought about it. 'I don't need anything.'

He guided her back towards the house, and as they passed by one of the fir trees, Evangeline yelped. Snow had fallen from one of the boughs against her neck, and she swiped at it, jumping from one foot to the other as she tried to brush it off the back of her gown. 'It's freezing!'

A laugh escaped him, and she glared at him. 'Why do you find that funny?'

He had no answer, but he couldn't stop his smile. It was the wrong decision, for a moment later, Evie reached down into the snow and formed a ball.

'Don't you dare,' he warned, reaching for his own snow. A second later, snow exploded against his cheek from a snowball she'd aimed. 'You're going to regret that decision, Evie.'

He made a larger snowball and threw it at her. His wife shrieked as she dodged it. 'Your aim is terrible.'

But his next snowball landed with a splat on her bodice—precisely where he'd aimed it.

'Oh, you will *pay* for that, Penford.' She tried to reach for another handful of snow, but he lifted her into his arms, laughing as she rubbed the snow against his neck. Both of them were soaked, but he no longer cared.

This was the Evangeline he liked, the woman who had a playful side. He could tease her, knowing that she wouldn't cry or complain—she'd get even.

'Our clothes are soaking wet,' he reminded her. She stilled in his embrace, looking away from him, even as her arms remained around his neck.

He carried her up the stairs to the house and past several servants who stared at them. Evie was holding his jacket, and she muttered, 'We're not behaving in a dignified manner. You should put me down.'

'You might have another snowball in your arsenal,' he murmured. 'I wouldn't want to risk it.'

'James,' she chided.

But he carried her up the large staircase and down the hallway. 'Remember, we're pretending to be a happily married couple. Isn't that what you wanted for your Christmas gift?'

'I...suppose.'

He opened her bedroom door and lowered her to stand. Evie tried to straighten her skirts. 'My gown is a mess,' she moaned, as he closed the door. 'It's soaked.'

'You were the one who threw a snowball at me,' he reminded her. 'I was only defending myself.'

She ventured a slight smile. 'You may want to watch your back, Penford. I did promise revenge.'

'You can try.' But he was intrigued by the wickedness in her tone.

'Go and warm yourself by the fire,' he offered, pointing towards his bedchamber.

She stood by the fire, warming her hands. Then she arched her back, fumbling with the buttons of her gown. 'Help me take this off.'

'Do you want me to ring for your maid?' He supposed Evie would want a hot bath and at the very least, a clean nightgown. But she turned to look at him.

'You could,' she acknowledged. 'Or you could help me remove the gown. We could pretend to be a happily wedded couple a little longer.'

Although she kept her words even, he sensed a note of intensity in her voice. It reminded him of the way she'd tempted him earlier, when she'd fed him jam from her fingertip. The memory flooded through his body, reminding him of the temptress Evie could be. He'd been careful enough to keep her at a distance, but every hour only heightened his desire to touch her.

She'd never answered his remark about pleasuring one another, and he didn't know if she was interested or not.

He was fully aware of the wet gown clinging to her generous curves. And, if she agreed to it, there was no reason to deny both of them a chance to explore their desires. The idea of finding out what pleased Evie was a vivid thought he couldn't let go. But he didn't know if she would shy away from him...or embrace the idea.

He walked slowly towards the fire and helped her with the buttons of her gown. 'Is that what you want, Evie? To pretend?' A few patches of snow fell from her bodice as he bared her light rose corset and shift. He'd never seen such finely made undergarments, and they accentuated the curve of her breasts and her slender waist.

Evie stepped out of the gown, removing her bustle, and then her petticoats. Her gaze slid over him, and she appeared nervous, as if she hadn't decided what to do. 'Will you help me with my stays?'

He began unlacing her slowly, drawing out the moment. Evie glanced over her shoulder, and he lowered his mouth to kiss her nape. She gave a slight intake of breath but didn't move.

'Is that what this is?' she whispered. 'Pretending?'

'If you want.' James told himself that there was no harm in touching his own wife or bringing them both fulfilment. Especially when the boundaries were drawn so firmly between them.

From the look in her eyes, he sensed that she was indeed interested in more between them. His conscience warned that it wasn't wise to explore this path...but when he touched the laces of her corset, he wanted so much more from her.

Evie suddenly turned and stared at him, her blue eyes turning intense. And when he moved in closer, she seemed shy as she turned her back to him once again. He rested his hands on her shoulders, his thumbs grazing the soft skin. Right now, he wanted her so badly, it hurt. Slowly, he unlaced her stays, one after another.

When her corset grew slack, she suddenly froze. He saw the moment she went rigid and clutched the rose undergarment to her body. 'James…this isn't real, is it?'

'Do you want it to be?'

She turned to face him, still clutching her undergarments. Her face had gone pale, and her breathing seemed unsteady. 'I don't know what I want.'

Her breathing grew unsteady as she stared back at him with indecision. Then slowly, she let her corset fall to the ground until she wore nothing but a soft chemise. He could see the faint outline of her nipples through the fabric, and the need to touch her, to taste her, went roaring through him.

'I know what I want,' he answered. He lifted his shirt away and discarded it on top of her fallen gown.

Slowly, he slid his hand to the ties of her chemise, which were damp from the snow. She didn't move, but he caught the rise of goose bumps as he moved his hand lower towards her breast. He rested his hand upon her bare skin, just above it. He stared into her eyes, waiting for permission. She closed her eyes and then brought his hand to cup her breast. Beneath his palm, her nipple was swollen and peaked. With his thumb, he stroked her, and she let out a shuddering sigh.

Watching her like this, seeing the emotion on her face,

made him want her even more. His shaft was hard, desperately wanting to be inside her.

Then she reached out to touch his chest, and her cool fingers slid over his pectoral muscles. Her gentle touch was nearly his undoing.

He lowered her chemise to her waist and took her nipple into his mouth. She moaned and drew her fingers to his hair while he swirled his tongue upon her flesh. She was as beautiful now as she'd been two years ago.

With his hands and mouth, he worshipped her. His heart was pounding, but he craved her like nothing he'd wanted before.

Her fingers dug into his shoulders, and she cried out, trembling against him. Her hips pressed close, and he suppressed his groan.

'James,' she breathed. 'Wait.'

God above. He didn't know if he could. Before he listened to her plea, he slid his hand between her legs, cupping the dampness there. She was wet for him, and when he caressed her gently, her body rose to his touch.

Though it was a physical ache to stop, he stilled his fingers. Then he drew his other hand to her nape as he stared down at her. 'Do you want me to stop? Or should I remind you of what it was like that night in the garden?'

Her blue eyes were deep with emotion, her expression vulnerable as he held his warm fingers against her wetness, tempting her towards surrender.

'You left me that night,' she whispered. 'And you're going to leave me again, aren't you?'

He wasn't going to lie to her. It was the arrangement they'd made. This was only temporary between them. Although he'd wanted to touch her and feel her hands upon him, he knew if he stayed with her for any length of time, he wouldn't be able to stop himself from consummating their marriage. Evie tempted him beyond words, making him question everything.

But she deserved honesty. He gave a single nod but never took his gaze from her face. 'It's better if I leave.'

Slowly, she stepped away from him, and her expression turned stricken. Awkwardly, she adjusted her chemise and covered herself. In a thick voice, she admitted, 'I know the agreement we made. And though I do desire you...' She closed her eyes as if the words pained her. 'I don't want to pretend, James. I want it to be real.'

He saw it then—the heartbreak in her eyes. Evie wasn't the sort of woman who could simply enjoy the pleasures of desire without love. He was wrong to even suggest it.

There were no words he could give her, nothing he could offer. He couldn't be the man she wanted him to be—a husband and a father. Not with the dark memories flooding through him of all the people he'd let down over the years. The last thing he wanted was for her to look at him with disappointment.

And so, he took the coward's path and turned away, returning to his own bedchamber.

Evangeline spent most of the morning in the village. Although many of the shops near Penford were closed, she'd convinced several of them to open so she could complete her Christmas shopping. She needed to be away from James, away from Penford. If she allowed herself to remember the humiliation of last night, she would only start crying.

And so, shopping became the distraction she needed.

Last night, she had suddenly understood what James had meant by 'enjoying one another.' His touch had awakened a yearning within her that went so deep, it touched her heart. She had desperately wanted to feel his touch upon her bare skin and become intimate. Earlier, she had mistakenly believed that seducing him would win his heart.

But when he'd undressed her last night, she'd suddenly realised that, to him, it was about physical enjoyment. He'd been quite clear about not consummating their marriage, not wanting to risk a child. Even if they did cross the line between pleasure and seduction, it didn't mean he loved her.

He would never love her.

That revelation had struck her so fiercely, she could no longer hold back her own feelings. Despite her efforts not to care for James, she had already lost her heart to him. It was clear that lovemaking would only shatter her feelings. But when she'd made herself vulnerable, telling him that she wanted their marriage to be real, he'd walked away.

She had barely slept last night, trying not to cry. It was her own fault for hoping their marriage could be more. It was better to avoid temptation, she'd told herself. If she never walked the path, never dared to learn what sorts of breathless pleasure awaited them in their marriage bed, it was the best way to protect herself.

She didn't know if she could bear this marriage, knowing that he still viewed the match as only an arrangement. It didn't seem like they were even friends any more, truthfully. He refused to tell her anything about India, and she was convinced that this was the reason why he held himself apart. Perhaps she needed to gain his trust to understand what had happened to him.

Maybe…maybe they needed to start all over again.

It was Christmas Eve tonight, and she wanted to spend Christmas together and rebuild their friendship.

One of the shops was already open, and she chose a new cravat for James. She started to look for a warm scarf, when suddenly she felt a sense of uneasiness. It was almost as if someone was watching her. But when she turned around, there was no one there.

You're being foolish, she told herself.

But she couldn't shake the feeling.

She turned back to the shopkeeper and asked, 'Was anyone here just now?'

The older man shook his head. 'Nay, my lady. All our customers have gone for the day.' From the impatient tone of his voice, it was clear that he was eager to go home as well. It was only past one o'clock, but she understood his wish to be with his family.

'I'm sorry. I'll just buy these.' She picked up the cravat and one of the scarves, bringing them over. 'Could you wrap them up for me?' Then her gaze fell upon some sugarplums and bon bons. 'And these, as well.'

He nodded, and she walked towards the shop window, gazing outside. Her footman was waiting for her, and she guessed that must have been the presence she'd sensed watching over her. He'd probably wondered how much longer she would be shopping.

'Thank you,' she told the shopkeeper as she gathered her parcels and left. She had also bought gifts for Lady Penford—a soft blue shawl, lavender and rose oils for her bath, and some new handkerchiefs. Although James had brought a few things from London for his mother, she wanted to offer her own gifts.

After she left the shop, she glanced around. Once again, she saw no one there. It had been nothing except her own uneasiness and was nothing to worry about. More likely, it was her insecurities bothering her after last night.

Even now, she was embarrassed by her panic. If she had simply kept her mouth shut, she might have experienced a night like the one in the garden. But instead, she'd stopped him, revealing her feelings once again.

She was an idiot. And now he was going to view her with pity. For she *was* pathetic. He would be kind, and Evie didn't know if she could bear it.

She wanted to go back to the moments of throwing snowballs at him and arguing. Better to say exactly what was on her mind without caution, and that would keep him from treating her as if she were made of glass. She had her pride, after all.

The snow was falling again when she travelled home in the coach. Most of the seats were taken up by packages wrapped in brown paper. It wasn't a long ride, and she suddenly realised how hungry she was. She couldn't wait to enjoy luncheon, and a delicious Christmas meal this evening. Her stomach growled as she wondered what the Cook had prepared.

When they arrived at the estate, her footmen took the gifts and brought them inside. She stopped Mrs Marlock, and the woman bobbed a curtsy. 'Is there aught I can be helping ye with, Lady Penford?'

'If you wouldn't mind, I would like to decorate the house for Christmas. Perhaps there are some servants who might be willing to help?'

'Oh, to be sure.' Mrs Marlock smiled warmly. 'We can hang boughs of greenery and holly, if ye'd like. I'll see to it.'

'Thank you.' Evie untied her bonnet and gave it over to her maid. Then, she walked towards the dining room and suddenly saw the Dowager Lady Penford standing in the hallway.

The older woman appeared so fragile and lost. Evie started to approach, but the footman stopped her. In a soft voice, he murmured. 'It's not a good day, my lady. I can escort the dowager back to her room.'

She brushed him aside. 'No, I would like to share luncheon with her. Please tell Cook that we're ready for our meal.'

With a wave of her hand, she dismissed the others. She took careful steps towards the dowager, who was still standing at the doorway. When Evie grew close, she saw tears on the woman's cheeks.

'Hello,' she said softly.

Lady Penford jerked in surprise and took a step backwards. It was then that Evangeline noticed the matron was wearing a summer gown of lawn, embroidered with lilac thread. It was a wonder she wasn't freezing since she had no cloak or pelisse. From the damp hem of her gown, it appeared that she'd walked outside recently.

'I'm sorry. I didn't mean to frighten you,' Evie said gently.

'Who are you?' the dowager asked. Her voice held fear, and she gripped her skirts as if prepared to flee.

'My name is Evangeline,' Evie answered. She didn't know quite how to explain why she was at Penford, and it seemed entirely too soon to talk about her marriage. Instead, she said, 'I am friends with Rose and Lily.'

'My daughters,' the dowager whispered.

'Yes. They are lovely, aren't they?' Evie was careful not to move towards the woman, not wanting her to feel threatened.

'I miss them,' Lady Penford confessed. 'It's lonely here.'

Evie took a moment to consider what to do next. She could feel the woman's fear radiating out in waves. 'I understand what it is to feel lonely. I wondered...' She paused a moment and glanced towards the dining room. 'Since Rose and Lily are not here, would you be willing to join me for luncheon? I would like to have someone to talk to.'

The dowager shook her head. 'Oh, I couldn't. I've eaten already.'

From her thin appearance, Evie wondered when Lady Penford had last eaten a proper meal. 'Would you keep me company instead? Whilst I eat?'

The older woman hesitated, as if she didn't want to. She appeared as if she'd rather be anywhere but in Evie's presence.

'It's all right if you'd rather not join me,' Evie said. 'I can eat by myself.' She didn't want the woman to feel threatened.

But after she'd spoken, the dowager seemed to make up her mind. 'No, you needn't be alone. Eating a meal by yourself is a wretched thing.'

Evie gave her a warm smile. 'It is, isn't it?' She took a step towards the older woman and asked, 'Will you sit with me, then?'

'I suppose.' The matron took a few tentative steps into the dining room, and Evie nodded a silent order for the footman to bring up the food. While they waited, she asked the dowager, 'Will you tell me about your news of Penford? It's been a while since I saw you last at Rose's wedding.'

The matron's face softened. 'Rose is expecting her first child. I'm to be a grandmother.'

Evie couldn't help but smile. 'That's wonderful. When will the baby be born?'

'In the summer,' she answered.

She didn't press the matron for more but simply sat nearby. A slight movement caught Evie's attention, and she saw her husband standing in the doorway. James's expression grew guarded, but she met his gaze and silently warned him to take care.

He stepped out of the way when the food arrived and remained in the shadows so his mother would not see him. But when the footman offered a bowl of hot soup, Evie remarked, 'It's such a cold day. Are you certain you won't have a little of this soup? It might warm you up after your walk.'

The dowager paused and then shrugged. 'I suppose a little might not be bad.' Within a few moments, they were both eating in companionable silence. The vegetable soup was served with warm bread, and Evie savoured the flavours.

'I understand your son, James, has returned from London,' she ventured. Once again, she caught his gaze from the shadows.

'I'm not certain,' the dowager said. 'I haven't seen him yet.'

'Would you like me to send for him?' Evie suggested. 'He could join us.'

The dowager's eyes filled with tears again. 'I wish George could join us. I miss him so.'

It hurt to see the pain in the matron's expression. A tear slid down her cheek. Evie reached out her hand in silent comfort, but the dowager didn't take it. 'Will you tell me about him?'

Her question seemed to interrupt the tears, and Lady

Penford found a handkerchief to dry her eyes. 'I—no one's ever asked me that before.'

'I would love to hear all about him and how you used to celebrate Christmas with your husband,' Evie urged. And as the woman began to speak, she glanced back at James. An unknown emotion caught within his face before he inclined his head to her and disappeared. He understood that Lady Penford wasn't ready to see him, and he apparently didn't want to upset her more.

But as the woman began to share stories, Evie decided to try to recreate a Christmas from the dowager's past— one that might give her and James a reason to smile again.

Chapter Ten

Later that evening, James found Evangeline in the drawing room, hanging gingerbread biscuits on the fir tree while his mother tied brightly coloured ribbons on the boughs. Although Iris still carried the grief of her husband's death, for the first time in a long while, it seemed that his mother was enjoying herself.

'Hello!' Iris greeted him. 'Are you a friend of Evie's? Or perhaps Rose and Lily's?'

Her question struck him like a fist in his gut. For a moment, he didn't know what to say, but Evangeline saved him by saying, 'This is my husband, James. Could he join us?'

'Why, of course. My son is also named James.'

An ache caught him, but he tried not to react. Iris beamed at him and held out a wooden box. 'There are a few of these to hang on the boughs. I've filled them with sweets for Christmas morning.' She motioned to a small pile of boxes.

One, in particular, caught his eye. It was a box he had painted as a small boy. He remembered his father telling him that if he was a good boy, Father Christmas might place sweets inside it. They had set out several boxes near the hearth, and sure enough, in the morning, he and his sisters had found treats within their boxes.

He reached for the first box, and Evangeline met his gaze with a trace of encouragement. He understood that she wanted his mother to enjoy the evening, so he pushed aside his own feelings and tied the box to one of the boughs.

'Be careful of the candles,' his mother warned. 'Oh, isn't this pretty. I do love this new custom of decorating a fir tree. Prince Albert came up with the idea, and I must say, it is lovely.'

'I agree,' Evie said. Then she thought a moment and asked Iris, 'Do you, by chance, play the piano? Do you know any Christmas carols?'

His mother brightened. 'I haven't played in years. But perhaps I might remember a few songs.' She finished tying another ribbon and went to sit at the piano. For a moment, she closed her eyes and found the keys. A moment later, Iris began playing 'Coventry Carol,' and she attempted to sing. Her voice held a quaver, and it was rather off-key, but James stopped tying boxes and began to listen.

Evie came up beside him and took his hand in hers. He squeezed it hard and pressed his hand against her lower back. Her blue gown was simple in design, but it brought out the vivid colour of her eyes.

'We should sing, James,' she said quietly.

He nodded but couldn't bring himself to start. If he did, he feared he would choke up. But instead, Evie joined his mother and sang loudly.

'Lully Lullay, thou little tiny child. Bye-bye, lully lullay...'

When Evie elbowed him, James joined in at last.

The moment he did, Evie turned in surprise. 'You're a very good baritone, James.'

'He always did have a good singing voice,' Iris remarked. And in that moment, she seemed to remember who he was.

'Sing some more,' Evie said. 'I'll pour the wine.'

As his mother continued to play, he kept singing while his wife brought glasses of wine for all of them. Iris continued playing, and it stunned him that she could remember so many songs. He'd known that his mother could play, but it was as if the music had reached down into a forgotten part of her mind and had brought her back.

She took a sip of wine. 'Oh, my, that's good. I do like your wife, James.'

'I like her, too,' he answered and drank from his own glass. 'And she looks beautiful tonight, don't you think?'

'She does.' Iris nodded over to the corner. 'Why don't you dance with her, and I'll play another song?'

'You don't have to—' Evie started to say, just as James took her hand in his.

'I think that's an excellent idea.' He drew her into a slow waltz, staring into her eyes. He saw a sprig of mistletoe over the doorway and started moving her in that direction.

But instead of playing a slow dance, his mother began a rousing polka. Her hands flew over the keyboard, and there was no choice but to follow the music. Evie started laughing, and so did he.

He took her on a fast-paced dance around the room and spun her in a circle. She nearly stumbled over her feet, and he lifted her up to keep her from falling. And just as the music came to a stop, he brought her beneath the mistletoe and kissed her lightly.

Iris closed the lid of the piano and said, 'I think this is one of the nicest Christmases I've had in a long time.'

'It is,' he agreed.

'We should put out our stockings,' Evie suggested. She handed one to him and one to Iris. They draped them in front of the fireplace mantel, and he then turned back to his mother.

'It's getting late,' Iris said. 'I think I'd like to go to bed now.' She ventured a smile. 'I would like to celebrate Christmas morning with you both. If it's not too much trouble.'

'Not at all.' Evie reached for her hand and squeezed it. 'Thank you for playing the piano. The music was wonderful.'

A maid came to escort the dowager to her room, and James stayed behind with his wife. She looked as if she was about to leave the room, but he stopped her. 'Thank you. I haven't seen my mother this happy in a long time.'

She ventured a smile. 'I enjoyed it, too. I think she's lonely.'

He agreed and led her to stand by the fire. 'Tonight was a wonderful gift for both of us. I'm grateful.' Somehow, Evie had found a way to bring his mother back to the present, even if only for a few hours.

He rested his hand at her waist while they warmed themselves, and he could feel the tension rising within her posture. His wife seemed anxious, which wasn't what he wanted at all. And so, he lifted his hands away.

'Are you afraid of me now,' he ventured, 'after what I did last night?'

'N-no.' But it sounded like an untruth.

'Then why are you nervous?'

She took a breath and turned to face him. 'I shouldn't be. I know that.'

'I would never hurt you,' he said. 'Or make demands.'

She straightened her posture, and it seemed as if she

were trying to make up her mind about something. Finally, she said, 'I am trying to be friends with you. I want to talk openly with you, as we always did. But it feels strange somehow.'

Because of the physical intimacy, he guessed. She walked over to the settee and sat down. 'We *are* friends, Evie. Say whatever is on your mind.'

Her face flushed, but she shrugged. 'All right. You're confusing me about what you want. We both know you never would have married me, had I not been in danger of being arrested. You said you wanted a marriage in name only where we lived separate lives.'

That was true enough. But he felt compelled to point out, 'And you said you wanted to pretend to have a real marriage as your Christmas gift. For one week only.'

She appeared miserable, but she nodded. 'I know what I asked for. And I shouldn't have. Because when you touch me, it makes me want to love you again. It shattered me before, and I don't want to feel that way ever again.'

Her confession seemed to reach within him, evoking both regret and the desire to change. He'd never wanted to hurt Evie, and he understood what she was trying to say. She couldn't separate physical pleasure from her emotions. And though he'd tried, he wasn't certain he could, either. He didn't know what that meant for their future, but she was right. He needed to respect her wishes and be the man she needed him to be.

James moved to sit across from her and tilted her chin up to face him. 'It's all right, Evie. I'll leave you alone.'

She inhaled sharply and took his hand in hers. 'The problem is... I don't want you to leave me alone.'

The yearning in her voice and the need seemed to reach past his boundaries to tempt him. He could kiss her right now. He could lead her upstairs to his bed, and she would yield to him, giving them both the physical release they craved.

But she was right. It was too grave a risk—and he didn't know if he could stop himself from consummating the marriage if she were naked in his bed. He wanted to spend hours exploring her silken skin, learning what gave her pleasure, and surrendering to his own.

With reluctance, he said, 'It's getting late.' He leaned over and kissed her forehead. 'Happy Christmas, Evie.'

'Happy Christmas.' Her voice was tinged with regret, but she said nothing else.

He guided her upstairs and risked a glance back at the stockings they'd set out on the hearth, and added, 'I'll see to it that those are filled.'

But as he walked upstairs with her, he couldn't help but think that he had cast a shadow over their Christmas.

Evangeline waited until after midnight before she crept downstairs and added her own gifts to the Christmas stockings lying on the hearth. James had already put in his own presents, but she added fresh oranges to the stockings and the sweets that she had bought earlier.

For a moment, she sat by the dying fire, feeling like an utter idiot. She ought to go to sleep, but restless feelings kept intruding. Being a countess felt like she was living someone else's life—and she didn't know how to find herself within it.

After a while, she rose from her seat and walked back up the stairs, finding her way in the dark. She opened the door to her bedroom and walked inside. The hearth was glowing with hot coals, and Annabelle and Dasher were sleeping in front of the fire, along with the puppies.

James's room was in the adjoining bedchamber, and she stared at the connecting door, wondering if he was feeling as restless as she was. After a moment, she started to return to bed when she suddenly heard a muffled groan.

It might be nothing, but she walked to the adjoining door and leaned in close to listen.

Was he asleep?

She ought to leave him alone. There was no reason whatsoever to intrude. And yet, when she heard another sound, she carefully turned the knob and opened the door slightly. In the darkness, James seemed to be tossing and turning from another nightmare. Although it wasn't entirely safe, she wanted to help him.

'James,' she whispered. 'Are you awake?'

No response. She crept closer and went to see if he was all right. His body was twisted up in the covers, and she questioned whether she should just leave him.

'Don't,' he mumbled beneath his breath. 'We don't know anything.'

India, she realised. He was still held captive by those memories. He rolled to the centre of the bed, and she sat down on the side. 'It's all right, James,' she murmured. 'It's just a dream.'

When she reached out to touch his face, he caught her hand against his cheek. 'Evie,' he said softly.

'Yes, I'm here.' She kept her voice soothing, hoping the nightmare had ended.

'Come to bed.' He moved over and patted the place beside him.

She couldn't deny that she wanted to lie beside him and feel the warmth of his arms around her. But she knew it was a terrible idea.

More than that, she wasn't entirely certain whether

he was awake. He might not be fully aware of what was happening.

'I just came to see if you were all right,' she said quietly.

His breathing grew steadier, and she was torn between wanting to leave and wanting to lie beside him. She wasn't at all certain what to do.

And yet, wasn't this what she wanted? To lie beside her husband in the hopes that their marriage could become something more?

Don't do it, her brain warned. *He'll only break your heart.*

'Come here,' he repeated. He caught her by the waist and pulled her down next to him. James drew her close against his body and pulled the coverlet over both of them. Was he awake, then? It seemed like it.

His skin was warm, and she froze in place, her mind racing. For a long moment, he simply held her, and Evie finally started to relax. She could sleep in his arms, and that would be all right.

Until he pulled her body against his own and she realised James wasn't wearing any clothing at all. Her cheeks flushed, and she swallowed when his arms came around her. His breath warmed her nape, and he slid one hand upon her calf, rising higher.

Against her spine, she could feel the ridge of his arousal, and her body ached in response. Had he changed his mind about consummating their marriage? She didn't know what he was doing or why, and she questioned whether it was right to stay here.

Don't stay, she warned herself. *This is a terrible idea.*

But then, he began kissing her throat, and all thoughts of heartbreak simply fled. There was only the darkness, the heat, and his hands upon her skin. She wanted her husband to touch her, wanted to remember the same mind-searing pleasure that he'd given her when his mouth had teased her bare breasts.

Although it was undoubtedly a mistake, and she would regret this in the morning, she shifted in his arms and removed the nightgown, dropping it on the floor beside the bed. This time, when he held her, she felt every inch of his glorious skin against hers. And she told her brain to be quiet and worry about the consequences later.

'Evie,' he growled, and he filled his hands with her breasts, caressing the tips with his thumbs. She shifted against him, delighting in the sensation, and he guided himself to rest between her thighs. The thick length of him lay against her, and she reached down to touch him.

He groaned as she closed her hand around his hard, sensitive erection. From behind her, he moved against her wetness, and though she didn't know why he'd changed his mind, she no longer cared. He was moving himself against her, and then, he guided the thick head to her entrance. He remained poised there, while she waited for him to thrust inside.

Instead, he brought his hand around, exploring the delicate skin of her womanhood. He dipped his fingers to the hooded flesh above her, and a jolt of wicked pleasure surged through her. It was everything she'd wanted, and a cry broke forth from her.

Immediately, he stopped.

'No,' she breathed. 'Don't stop.' She hoped he would continue this sweet torment, and God help her, he did.

He circled the sensitive nub, playing with her as she grew even wetter and more aroused. He was still behind her, and he reached around to cup her breast while his other hand explored her flesh.

Her breathing was coming faster, and she no longer cared about anything except having him inside her. She reached back to guide the tip of him partially inside her and was rewarded when he gave a dark hiss.

He groaned as she pressed against him, trying to take more of him. When he started to move his hand away, she guided it back.

'That feels so good,' she whispered. 'Please don't stop touching me.'

He obeyed, and she started to push herself against him, hoping he would embed himself fully.

He gripped her waist and eased her up and down. She was still facing away from him, but he was starting to press a little deeper.

Then, without warning, he thrust inside and was fully sheathed. There was a slight burning pain, but she was so stunned at the sensation, her heart was pounding.

Was that…all he intended to do? She had thought there would be more. But he simply remained motionless within her. From behind, he held her waist and buried his face in her shoulder.

Her breathing was unsteady, but she couldn't help but feel slightly disappointed. Her mother and aunts had led her to believe that lovemaking was a glorious thing.

But, then again, she had never done this before. Perhaps *she* was supposed to do something now? Was it her turn?

She had loved the feeling of his hand caressing her breasts, so she brought her hand to his thigh and touched him. He took her hand in his, and she brought it to her breast. He stroked her, and just then, she felt a delicious ache between her legs.

Evie raised herself up slightly, and it felt so wonderful when he began to move. 'That feels good.'

He started a slow rhythm of moving in and out, and when he continued to caress the tight bud of her breast, it only intensified the sensation. God above, but this was what she had hoped for. From deep inside, she could feel a reckless wave pulsing, and she squeezed him from within her body. Her breathing mimicked his thrusting, but even as she arched against him, there was something elusive, something she was straining for.

She remembered how good it had felt when he'd touched her intimately, and without really understanding what she needed, she brought her own hand between her legs. The moment her fingers brushed against the hooded flesh, a sudden surge of immense pleasure began to rise.

'Evie,' he whispered against her shoulder, and she continued circling her own skin, finding the secret places that moved in counterpoint to his thrusts. She was shaking with need, wanting him so badly, when abruptly, he changed his rhythm and began to go faster.

There. Oh, God, there it was.

Her body erupted in a shuddering tremor of need, and she gripped him as he rode between her legs. A blazing release flooded through her, and she savoured the feelings that erupted within.

At last, James groaned during his thrusting and went still, his body embedded within hers. Her heart wouldn't stop pounding, but she now understood what everyone meant. This was what lovemaking was meant to be. And now that she knew what it was, she felt confident that she could transform their marriage into something far more than an arrangement.

She fell asleep with a smile on her face.

When James awoke on Christmas morning, he was stunned to find his wife naked in his arms. How had this happened? He had few erotic memories of the night before, and from the way Evie's body was curled around him, he suspected that they had, in fact, consummated the marriage.

The moment he thought back to his vivid dreams, he remembered the sweet yielding of her body to his, the way she had arched in her fulfilment. Just like that, he grew aroused, remembering what never should have happened between them.

His body went cold at the thought. Could he have got her pregnant?

He didn't know how it had happened. He remembered dancing with her on Christmas Eve and fragments of last night. He knew the taste of her lips and her bare skin. Raw memories coursed through him as he remembered what it was to be inside Evie.

She was still sleeping, her face buried in a pillow, but her body was very, very naked. The thought evoked an unexpected wave of longing. If he had indeed claimed her body last night, what was to stop him from doing it again? His body went rigid at the thought, even as he pushed the covers aside and reached for his clothing.

No, he wasn't going to do this. He never should have done anything at all, and he couldn't understand how it had happened.

Quietly, he dressed himself and went to stand at the window. Outside, the sky held creases of lavender against the horizon, for it was not yet sunrise. Snow blanketed the ground, and he turned back to look at his wife.

The sight of her caught him with an invisible blow. Evie's long hair was tangled in a dark cloud against the creamy sheets. Her hand was soft in sleep, and he still longed to get back in bed with her.

Instead, he put on his shoes and quietly left his own bedchamber to go downstairs. There were faint sounds of movement coming from the servants' quarters, but he went into the drawing room. He added coal to the fire and stoked the hearth.

Today was Christmas morning. His mind and body drifted between trying to push back the memories of last night and trying to recall how he had taken her virginity. It bothered him that his memories were tangled with nightmares of the past.

What was he supposed to do now? He'd promised her that they would live their lives apart and never consummate the marriage. He'd lasted all but a few days.

James stared down at the Christmas stockings on the hearth, but his thoughts were far too distracted. He didn't want to think of Evie or what she might expect from him now.

Had she…enjoyed their night together? Why had she come to him after they had already agreed to keep their distance? Guilt weighed upon him, even as he was fully aware of how satisfied his body felt. And how much he wanted to go upstairs and awaken her again with his touch.

It was now Christmas Day, and James forced his thoughts back to the present, for his mother might come to join them. Last night, Iris had seemed to enjoy their celebration. He hadn't seen her in such good spirits in a long time. And perhaps that was his fault for leaving his family behind. He reached out to warm his hands by the fire and turned them over, revealing the white scars of the manacles. He'd only been in captivity for a few months, but it had seemed like far longer.

He'd tried to live a normal life, assuming the responsibilities of being the Earl of Penford. And yet, it felt like he was living someone else's life. He had a wife, an estate, and both his sisters had found husbands. His life was in a familiar pattern.

But he felt adrift, lost in the expectations of others.

Evie wanted him to be her husband, and she wanted children, too. She might even be pregnant now. But how could he become a father when his life was such a mess?

He didn't want a child looking up to him, expecting him to be a role model. Despite all his efforts to pretend as if nothing had happened, the nightmares of imprisonment haunted him still.

He was going to disappoint her in every way. And he wished to God that he'd never crossed that line.

Footsteps caught his attention, and he turned to see Evie in the doorway. She wore a dressing gown and stood barefoot. 'Happy Christmas, James.' In her demeanour, he saw an awkward, faltering hope.

His throat went dry at the sight of her, but he managed to nod. Every thought he'd had in his brain simply scattered. 'I— Happy Christmas,' he repeated.

She took a single step closer. 'Are you all right? You left so suddenly.'

He paused, trying to think of how to begin. 'What happened between us last night?'

Colour rose to her cheeks. 'You don't remember?'

He wasn't sure how to answer that. 'I remember pieces of it.'

She fell silent, looking all the world like she wanted to disappear.

'I woke up beside you,' he began, 'but I don't remember how we…' His voice trailed off. 'I know we both went to sleep in our rooms. Did you come to my bed after I was asleep?'

'You were in the middle of a nightmare,' she said. 'I only came to see if you were all right.' She reached for his Christmas stocking and handed it to him. As if the gift would somehow distract him from their conversation.

But he wasn't about to be deterred. 'How did you come to be in my bed?'

When he didn't take his stocking, Evie set it on a chair. She clutched her hands and stared at the wall. 'I don't know quite what to say. I thought you were awake.'

He'd been dreaming for part of it, and later, he'd been unable to stop himself from touching her. That night had been so arousing, even now, the vivid memories made him want her again. He didn't know how to feel about it and was torn between wanting to respect their boundaries and wanting to take her upstairs a second time.

In a heavy voice, he said, 'It was a mistake that won't happen again.'

Evie straightened and faced him. 'I suppose you think that I stripped off my clothing, crawled into your bed, and seduced you. Is that it?'

He didn't know what to think. 'I don't remember how it started.'

Her face flamed scarlet, and she stiffened with anger. 'You were caught in a nightmare. And when I tried to wake you, you told me, "Come here."' She paused and added, 'When you spoke to me, I had no reason to think you were still asleep. I thought you wanted comfort. And the next thing I knew, you were touching me.'

He didn't argue, for he was fully aware that he'd taken advantage of her. 'Was that what you wanted?'

Her expression grew strained, but she didn't deny it. 'You make me sound like I started all this. I promise you, I didn't.'

'This wasn't something I intended to do,' he pointed out. He'd intended to leave her untouched, to protect her heart and maintain their friendship. But now, it seemed that all of that was impossible.

'We're married now,' she pointed out. 'What does it matter?'

Before he could answer, Lady Penford entered the drawing room. She wore her morning gown and gaped at the sight of them. 'Goodness. The both of you should go and get dressed.' Her eyes gleamed at the sight of her Christmas stocking. 'I will wait until you've returned before we open presents.'

Evie turned and hurried away, and James followed slowly. He knew he'd hurt her feelings, but he didn't know how to explain to her the bone-deep fear that he could have got her pregnant. She wouldn't understand.

And from the disappointed expression on her face, he suspected he had ruined her Christmas morning.

He climbed up the stairs towards his own bedchamber, feeling as if he'd kicked a puppy. This wasn't the sort of marriage he'd planned for, but one night had unravelled all of it. He needed to reset the boundaries between them, to make her see that it had been a mistake, nothing more.

The best way to do that was likely physical distance. He would wait a few days until the snow had cleared, and then he would return to London. She would be safe here at Penford with his mother.

He got dressed in silence, but he was fully aware of the tangled sheets of his bed. A flare of need caught him when he saw the adjoining door slightly open. He forced himself to turn away, though he wanted to walk through that door and take her in his arms.

It was better if he left her alone. She'd married a man

incapable of being the husband she needed. And if he dared to reach for more, he would only disappoint her.

Evie couldn't stop her smile when the Dowager Lady Penford opened her first gift. The matron seemed like a small child, eagerly tearing at the brown paper.

When she held up the light blue shawl Evie had bought for her, she beamed. 'It's so soft and warm. I love the colour.'

The dowager then passed Evie an awkwardly wrapped package. 'Here. This is for you.'

Evie untied the strings and found an assortment of coloured stones inside. When she exchanged a glance at James, his expression turned guarded. And yet, she understood that the matron had given her something she believed to be beautiful. It was also entirely possible that no one had given the dowager any pin money to spend.

'They're lovely,' Evie said, tracing the surface of one of the stones. 'I will put them in the garden so everyone can see them.'

The older woman's face held a glimmer of joy. 'I'm glad.'

They exchanged a few more presents, and James gave Evie a set of embroidered handkerchiefs and a large box that contained a frosted cake. Though she thanked him and smiled, the cake brought a pang of emotion she hadn't expected. She was still holding back tenuous feelings from last night.

Never had she thought he wasn't fully awake when she'd come to his bed. She'd believed he had changed his mind and wanted to touch her. Seeing the look of regret on his face this morning was enough to fracture her heart.

You aren't enough for him, her mind taunted her. *He didn't want you then, and he doesn't want you now.*

Though she tried to push away the feelings of insecurity, they plagued her still. Instead, she tried to box them up in her mind and ignore them.

She gave James his presents of a new cravat and shaving soap. He'd thanked her for them, but there was a careful reserve in his demeanour.

How could things have shifted so badly within hours of last night? She'd loved dancing with him while his mother played the piano. It had been an evening of joy and celebration.

But today was, quite possibly, the worst Christmas she'd ever had. Her husband hardly looked at her, and her stomach ached with sadness. Evie wanted to go to her room and sob out the useless feelings of heartbreak.

But then, when they were about to walk to the dining room for breakfast, it was as if a dormant part of herself reawakened. Why should she allow James to ruin her Christmas? Last night, she had done nothing wrong except try to comfort him. Never once had she made demands of him. He had invited her to his bed, and he had taken her innocence—whether he remembered it or not. It wasn't right or fair for him to blame her.

A sudden calm came over her. She wasn't helpless or meek.

She refused to be the same girl as before, pining after a man who didn't want her. Yes, they were married now. But it didn't mean she had to be a quiet, obedient wife. And maybe he needed to realise that. Maybe she needed to stop reacting to her circumstances and instead, reach for the life she wanted.

She had worked tirelessly over two years to build a business of wealth that gave women the opportunity to make their lives better. She ought to do the same for her own life. Even though she still had feelings for James, she could close them away, like shutting a book.

'I have one more gift for you, Evie,' James said, after they had finished eating.

She blinked out of her musings and said, 'You do?' She set her plate aside, wondering what it was.

He nodded and stood from the table. 'This one is outside.'

She couldn't quite understand, but she rose from her seat and followed him. Lady Penford gathered her shawl around her. 'Go on without me. I should like to stay inside and be warm.'

James walked with her to the hallway where he spoke with a servant, who fetched his coat and her cloak and bonnet.

'Shouldn't the servants be celebrating with their families today?' she ventured, after the footman walked away.

'Most of them are. But there are a few who are alone, so I pay them extra, and they celebrate together,' he explained. 'And thank God for it, since I cannot cook.'

He drew the cloak around her, and she fastened her bonnet before they stepped outside. She had no idea what sort of present would be outside, but she followed him down the gravel path towards the stable. A sudden rise of anticipation caught her, and she hoped the gift would be an animal of some kind. A horse, perhaps?

But when they walked inside the stable, he led her to the last stall where she saw a donkey that was slightly shorter than the horses.

'I thought you might like to raise him,' James said. 'You said you liked your uncle's donkey. And I know how much you love your animals.'

'He's adorable,' she murmured, reaching out to rub his head. 'But when did you have time to arrange this?'

'While you were out shopping,' he admitted. 'I've behaved rather like an ass lately, so it seemed apropos.'

A laugh choked in her throat, and without thinking, she embraced him. 'Thank you, James. He's wonderful.'

He stiffened in her arms but hugged her back. She released him immediately and distracted herself with the donkey. He was gentle and sniffed at her as she drew close. He nuzzled his head against her, and James added, 'There was a young family who didn't have enough to eat this Christmas. When they refused my charity, I offered to buy the donkey.' With a crooked smile, he admitted, 'Don't worry I paid them far more than he was worth.'

It was an act of kindness that was the finest gift he could have given her. She scratched the donkey's ears, and he butted his head against her arm. 'You could not have given me anything better.' With a light smile, she added, 'I like the donkey, too.'

There was a warmth in his eyes that unravelled some of her earlier anger. Though she didn't like the way he'd practically accused her of taking advantage of him, the donkey was a step towards forgiveness.

'Have you decided upon a name yet?' he asked.

She considered it for a time. 'I suppose Donkey isn't very creative. I'll have to think.' Her imagination wandered as she considered possible names. Then, at last, she decided upon the perfect name. 'His name will be Hotay.'

'That's an odd name,' James mused. 'Why choose that one?'

'Well, because he's a donkey,' she explained. 'Donkey Ho—'

'Don Quixote,' her husband finished, with an amused

smile. 'I think that name will suit him very well. I hope you like him.'

She stared up into his green eyes. 'I like him very much.'

The sudden intensity in her husband's expression caught her off guard. He reached out to touch her cheek, and his thumb grazed the side of her face.

Evie held herself motionless, waiting for him to lean in and kiss her. The temptation to be within his embrace was so strong, it was a physical ache. But in the end, he let his hand fall away and led her back to the house.

She hid her disappointment and followed behind him, the snow crunching beneath her shoes.

Chapter Eleven

'James, I need to talk to you.'

He glanced up from the ledgers and beckoned for Evie to come in. She wore one of her grey gowns, and in her hand she held a letter. 'What is it?'

She handed it to him without saying anything. He unfolded it and saw the scrawled handwriting.

If you think you can avoid me forever, you're wrong. I know where you are, and your husband cannot protect you. I promise you will pay for what you've done to me unless you send Penford to London with five thousand pounds.
Dunwood

The threat infuriated James, for he would never allow anyone to break apart their carefully crafted life. He and Evie had come to an understanding, and they kept separate rooms with the door locked between them. She slept in her bed, and he, in his. Their marriage was polite, and it was exactly the sort of existence he'd imagined.

Except that he craved his wife every day. And even now, he was entirely too aware of her rose-scented soap and the way her dark hair spilled over one shoulder.

He wasn't about to let the viscount destroy her sense of comfort and safety. He stood from the desk and tossed the letter aside. 'He will not come near you, Evie. I swear it.'

'There's more,' she said quietly. 'My mother wrote that Lord Dunwood has spread stories around London about what I did to him. And now customers are avoiding our family's store. I need to go back.'

'I'll go to London and put a stop to it,' he said.

'And do what? You cannot force people to shop there. Especially if they believe I destroyed a viscount's ability to walk.' She shook her head. 'I don't know what to do.'

He had no intention of remaining at Penford now. Not when Evie was still being threatened. 'I will confront Dunwood and ensure that he recognises the consequences of his own actions.'

'James, I don't think he's…thinking clearly. He's dangerous.'

'If, by that, you mean he's mad, I would agree. And I will not allow him to continue this behaviour. It will stop.'

'If his gossip only hurt my family, that would be one matter,' she said. 'But when he's harming the ability of women to support themselves, I cannot stand back and let that happen.'

The man's behaviour had gone well past the desire for money. Dunwood wanted revenge after Evie had defended herself. And if that meant posing a few threats of his own, James wouldn't hesitate. He suspected Evie's father would be happy to join him.

'I'll leave in the morning,' he promised.

'I'm coming with you,' she insisted. 'I'll do what I can to minimise the damage to Aphrodite's Unmentionables.'

'Absolutely not. You're staying here.'

At that, his wife glared at him. 'Absolutely not.' She

threw the words right back at him and took a step closer. 'That man has caused so much harm. Do you think I intend to hide away at Penford instead of facing him again?'

'You will stay here and remain safe,' he shot back, closing the distance between them. Her blue eyes were flashing with anger, and he refused to back down on this. He would never endanger her.

'Don't ask me to stand aside and let him ruin so many lives, James,' she responded. 'I won't do it.'

'You will.' Because he wasn't about to let her be threatened by Dunwood again. The man wasn't at all sane.

James rested his hands on her waist, meaning to walk past her to leave the library. But when Evie's hands slid up to his chest, he felt the familiar flare of temptation. He should have known better than to touch her again.

'I promised you I would tell you about any threatening notes,' Evie said. 'But I never promised to remain here at Penford. I don't want to be left behind again.'

So that's what this was about. He'd abandoned her once before, and she believed the same thing was happening once more.

She gave him a slight shove, but James held her captive in his embrace. 'You're going nowhere. It's not safe, and you know this.'

'Don't be ridiculous,' she said. But there was a slight hitch in her voice, as if she hated the thought of his departure. 'I'll only follow you if you leave me.'

'You're as stubborn as Hotay,' he said.

'It's not your responsibility to deal with Dunwood.'

'You're wrong.' How could she believe otherwise? He fully intended to put a stop to the viscount's behaviour. 'I am your husband, and it's very much my responsibility.'

'You're my husband in name,' she agreed. 'But we both

know you would never have married me if you'd had another choice. You didn't want someone like me.'

Although she spoke in a matter-of-fact tone, her words carried a weight to them—as if she believed she was unworthy. He didn't know what to say to convince her that this marriage had been of his free will. 'That's not true,' he said quietly. 'I could have let any of the other suitors marry you.'

'But a marriage to me wasn't what you wanted.' A trace of hurt underscored her words. 'And we both have to live with that now.'

'It's not a hardship to be married to you, Evie. We get on well enough.'

'In our separate rooms, living separate lives.' She glanced away from him. 'I know that was the condition of our marriage. But I don't like living this way. We were supposed to remain friends.'

He reached for her hand then and rubbed his thumb over the back of her hand. 'Aren't we still friends?'

She shook her head. 'It doesn't seem so. It's lonely being married to you. I never thought it would be like this.'

He stiffened at that. 'That's not fair, Evie. I was honest with you from the start.'

'You've been anything but honest,' she pushed back. 'You won't tell me any of your reasons why you don't want a real marriage or a family. Or why you don't want children.'

Nor did he want to. It was far easier to push away the terrible memories by refusing to speak of them. He released her hand and regarded her. 'I cannot give you what you want.'

'That's…not entirely true.' Her face turned crimson, but she admitted, 'We did have one night together.' She shrugged. 'But I suppose I wasn't…what you wanted, so—'

She couldn't have been any further from the truth. But he craved her with every moment of every day. Perhaps she needed to be reminded of that.

'I care about you, Evie,' he said. He took her by the hand and led her from the room. 'And I'm only travelling to London to put a stop to Dunwood's threats.'

'Not alone, you're not,' she said. 'And where are we going?'

He led her to the staircase. 'Somewhere more private so every servant doesn't hear this conversation.'

She followed him, her cheeks flushed. 'I'm not going to change my mind about this. I'm not staying behind.'

No, he didn't suppose she would. But right now, he had another way he wanted to convince her to stay. He entered her bedchamber and waited for her to follow. Then he closed the door behind him. 'Sit down, Evie.'

'I am not a dog.'

He moved closer to her and caught her by the waist gently. 'Look at me, Evie. Why don't you want my protection?'

'Because you shouldn't have to fight my battles for me.'

He lowered his mouth to her throat, and she inhaled sharply. Slowly, he kissed a path towards her nape and brought her hips close to his. He was already hard and aching for her.

'And what if I want to fight for you?'

Evie didn't know what had shifted, but the moment James kissed her throat, it was as if her body had awakened. She wanted to run her fingers through his hair and pull his mouth to hers.

His mouth drifted to her lips, and she kissed him back, loosening his own shirt. Eventually, she slid her hands to his bare chest and raised her gaze to his. 'You're not going to change my mind by kissing me.'

'No, I don't suppose I could,' he said. 'Maybe I'm not able to resist you any more.' When his hands moved to the buttons of her gown, she wondered if he was trying to convince her to stay at Penford by showing affection. But if she accused him of it, he would likely stop. And she didn't want him to.

The weeks of loneliness had taken their own toll. This was about more than an argument. She *wanted* to touch her husband and convince him to drop the invisible barriers between them. The thought of years like this, of living a shadow marriage, seemed impossible. Right now, he was tormenting her with each button, slowly dissolving her arguments.

'You've resisted me just fine,' she said, suppressing a shiver when his warm hands grazed her bare shoulders. You haven't touched me in weeks.'

'Which was a torment,' he admitted. 'I only meant to stay at Penford for one week.'

'It snowed a great deal,' she pointed out. 'You had no choice but to stay.'

'Didn't I?' he teased.

She was torn about how to respond, but more than that, she was utterly distracted when he began unlacing her corset. The touch of his hands against her undergarments only kindled her sensitive skin as he lowered her gown to her waist and loosened her stays even more. She moved her hands up the ridges of his abdomen to rest upon his heart.

'I'm not going to change my mind about going to London,' she said. 'Don't try to talk me out of it.'

'I won't let you endanger yourself by coming with me,

Evie,' he said against her skin. 'And I think we should stop arguing now.' He slid her chemise lower and bared one of her breasts. Her nipple was puckered, and he traced it with his thumb. 'There's nothing I want more than to watch you find fulfilment.' To emphasise his words, he lowered his mouth to her breast and swirled his tongue across the tip.

She shuddered at the contact and was dimly aware of him guiding her into a chair. An ache centred within her, and he knelt down, still focused upon touching her. She thought he would remove the rest of her clothing, but instead, he reached beneath her skirts.

'It's been a long time since I touched you,' he said against her mouth. 'And I think it's time we remedied that.'

She didn't know what had changed, but his hand moved against her calf, higher to her thigh. When he reached her drawers, she jolted at the feeling of his fingers against her damp entrance. Against the fabric, he rubbed her, and she dug her fingers into his bare back.

But it was the intensity of his gaze upon her that started to unravel her senses. He was staring at her with a heated gaze, as if he wanted to bare every inch of her.

He moved his hand beneath her drawers, and she gasped when he touched her intimately. She was already wet, and as he explored her, she pulled his head down to hers, kissing him hard. She slid her tongue in his mouth, and he rewarded her by entering her body with his finger. Gently, he rubbed her, and she arched against him as he pleasured her.

'I'm going to lock the door,' he said. 'And you're going to remove that gown. I want you naked on my bed.'

His words held her captive, and her hands were shaking as she started to remove her petticoats and gown. This was what she wanted—to become his wife in all ways.

But her mind warned her that if she did this, she would only lose her heart to him again. And yet, she didn't protest his orders. Instead, she removed her clothes, layer by layer. She didn't know if he would make love to her again, or whether this was only about giving and receiving pleasure.

Right now, she didn't care.

There was only her husband and this moment. She wanted so much more from this marriage. And if that meant setting aside her inhibitions and asking for what she wanted, so be it.

His eyes were heated as she finished undressing. And when she stood naked before him, she walked slowly to the bed.

'Lie down on your back,' he said.

But something made her bristle against his orders. She had never been the obedient sort with James. And although she had tried to settle into this house, meekness had got her nowhere.

Instead, she wanted to seize her own power. And so, she sat on the edge of the bed and stared back at him.

'Not yet.' When he sent her a curious look, she added, 'It's your turn to remove your clothing,' she said. 'After all, it's only fair.'

An amused smile crossed James's face, and he removed his jacket and shirt. His skin was still slightly tanned, and she noticed a scar across his pectoral muscle that she didn't remember seeing in the past.

'Now the rest,' she ordered.

His gaze turned cryptic, and he defied her, walking closer. 'If you want them off, I think you should remove my trousers, Evie.'

His words were a challenge that she hadn't expected. But when he came near, she reached for the buttons. Her hands were shaking as she unfastened them one by one. Beneath her palms, she felt the hard length of him, and an ache echoed between her thighs. She tried to lower his trousers, but she had to free him from his drawers first. His shaft fascinated her, for this was the first time she'd seen him naked up close. She couldn't stop herself from exploring his hard length, and he inhaled sharply when she curled her hand around him.

In response, he reached for her knee and pressed her legs apart. He stood between her thighs while she traced the length of his erection.

'Is this what you wanted, Evie?'

She was afraid to answer. And truthfully, she had no idea what to do now. Did he want her to take the lead? She hesitated and started to guide him to her damp entrance.

Instead, he moved back and pressed her body against the bed. A moment later, he took her breast into his mouth, and she gasped as he teased the erect tip.

'Do you like this?' he asked against her bare skin.

'Y-yes.' Her voice came out in a husky whisper.

'I need to remember what pleased you that night,' he said. With one hand, he circled her nipple, caressing it until she ached to be filled by him.

Then he moved his hand up her thigh, past her damp curls, and slid a finger inside her. The sensation made her moan, for she was already so wet from her own arousal. When she lifted her gaze to his, he slid a second finger inside and began to stroke her. Her body was trembling with need, arching to meet his invasion, and she could feel the pleasure gathering inside like a wild storm.

'I always wanted you, Evie,' he said, his voice rough

with need. 'But I need you to stay here at Penford and re-main safe while I confront Dunwood.'

'No. I won't.'

She had no desire to be a coward, nor was she about to take orders. Instead, she moved her hand to his erec-tion again and matched the rhythm of his hand strokes. His expression grew darker, and when he quickened his pace, so did she. Against the head of him, she felt a slight moisture, and she knew he was close to the edge.

'I'm not going to let you anywhere near that monster.'

He dropped to his knees and moved her legs to his shoulders. She hardly knew what was happening when his mouth came down upon her, feasting upon her intimate flesh. The first stroke of his tongue caused her to gasp as pleasure rippled through her. She was so caught up in the way he was nibbling at her, teasing the bundle of nerves that was so tense, her body moved against his mouth.

She was losing her mind, fighting to keep from scream-ing, and when he suckled at her, a sudden flash of release quaked within, shimmering through her body like a flame bursting into life. The rush of sensation erupted, and she cried out with the force of it.

His own breathing was ragged as he finished her, and she began to move her hand against him. She wanted to give him that same pleasure he'd given her, and she could tell that he was wound up so tightly.

Could she...make him feel the same way?

Without asking, she lowered her legs and moved him to sit upon the bed. She knelt before him and saw the mo-ment his expression grew heated. Slowly, she lowered her mouth to his erection and kissed his shaft. Her husband jolted, and she froze. 'Should I stop?'

'God, no,' he responded. His eyes were closed, and

he appeared to be nearly in pain. She started to kiss him again, teasing him with her tongue, and he moved her hand to curl around the base of him.

She started to find a pace that pleased him, and he was breathing roughly as she continued to pleasure him with her mouth and tongue. His hand tangled in her hair, and she could feel his caged desperation as she took him deeper. He groaned, causing her own body to ache for another release.

But when she sucked against him, he suddenly jerked free of her mouth. He seized her leg, and lifted it over his hip, spreading her apart. He drove himself against the seam of her wetness, and she shattered a second time, her body coming apart as his shaft rubbed against her swollen flesh. A moment later, she felt a warm wetness against her stomach as he found his own release.

His heart was pounding as hard as hers, but she couldn't breathe, couldn't move. This had gone well past pleasuring one another. Hot tears burned in her eyes, but she buried her face in the sheet to hide them.

She didn't know which was worse—being separated from him or being reminded of everything she truly wanted and couldn't have.

James ordered their supper in a tray sent to his room. His shirt hung loosely about him, and he was thoroughly distracted by Evie, who wore only a thin dressing gown.

'Are you as hungry as I am?' she asked, reaching for a slice of warm bread with butter melting upon it.

His attention was fixed upon the curves barely covered by the silk. 'Very.'

'I should order my maid to pack my trunk,' she started to say. He didn't miss the stubbornness in her eyes or the way she raised her chin in defiance. Already he knew that she meant what she'd said. If he left her behind, she would follow within the hour.

James reached for his own bread and ate it, tasting the creamy butter against the crust. Mrs Marlock had given them slices of roast beef and small boiled potatoes, salted with herbs. As he ate, he considered his choices.

He needed to find another way to convince her to stay. And he could only think of one.

'I don't want anything to happen to you, Evie,' he said quietly. 'And I don't trust Dunwood.' Before she could speak, he added, 'I am asking you to stay behind for your own safety. Please.'

When she started to shake her head, he added, 'If you swear to stay at Penford, I'll tell you about India and what happened to us there.'

She stilled at his words. 'That's not fair.'

'It's the only bargain I can offer.' He finished eating and stood. 'If you want to know the truth so badly, I'll tell you. But in return, I'm asking you to wait here until I come back.'

For a long while, she stared at him, considering it. It seemed as if a thousand troubled thoughts were drifting through her mind. '*Will* you come back?' Her voice held a trace of disbelief.

'On my honour,' he answered.

She stood from the table, her own food half-eaten. 'All right. Tell me how you were captured.'

Before he spoke, he poured himself a glass of wine and drank half of it. He needed the liquid courage before determining where to start.

'Our ship landed at Bombay,' he began. 'I think what surprised me most was the intensity of the heat. I've never felt anything like it.' He told her about the open market-places and the stalls filled with spices. 'I tasted fruits I've never even seen before. Mangoes and pomegranates. Sweet bananas that were nothing like the ones I've had here. The food had spices and flavours that were new and delicious. At first, I loved it, and so did Matthew.

'We spent our first few weeks exploring the city. His footman accompanied us—a new one Matthew had hired. Javas claimed he could speak the language, since his mother hailed from Calcutta. It seemed fortuitous, and we were glad to have him with us.'

He poured another glass of wine and glanced over at Evie, whose face remained impassive. But she reached for her own wine glass and took a small sip. 'Go on.'

'I didn't realise, at the time, that the footman was hired by Adrian Monroe to kill Matthew. It was meant to seem like an accident, especially with so many uprisings against the British Army. It was far more dangerous in India than I'd realised it would be. And—' He took a breath, choosing his words carefully. 'I didn't like the way I saw my own people treating the citizens. I saw British soldiers taunting them, and I was ashamed of their behaviour. It wasn't right.'

'What did you do?'

He shook his head. 'There wasn't much we *could* do. We were travellers, and we became a target for thieves. Many times, they attempted to rob us. And I noticed that Javas did nothing to defend us.' Even now, he was torn by the anger at the footman, tangled with the knowledge that the man had had several opportunities to kill them. And yet, he hadn't made an attempt. 'I think Javas might have felt a sense of regret after he got to know us. But he delivered us into enemy hands.'

'How were you captured?' she asked.

'It was December of 1845,' he began. 'Javas claimed that a sailor had told him about how we could make our fortunes in rubies if we went north.' He took another sip of wine. 'We sailed there, only to find that there was fighting between the British and the Sikh. Territorial disputes, mostly, and the maharaja was calling for more troops to fight. Matthew and I realised that it wasn't safe for us to stay. We were trying to leave, but... Javas betrayed us. A young woman claimed she needed our help, and we—' He stopped and shook his head, remembering the first time he had met Nisha Amat. 'We believed her.'

From behind him, he heard the soft footsteps of his wife. Her hand brushed against his shoulder. The silent offer of support was what he needed to get through this.

'The woman was his sister. The same woman you saw that night at the ball.'

Before she could say a word, he forced himself to continue. 'After Javas robbed us of all our possessions, he turned us over to a group of rebels. I don't think we were supposed to come back alive. Which would have made Adrian the new Earl of Arnsbury.'

Evie squeezed his palm and came closer. He held her hand in his for a moment before releasing it.

'We were captured and taken prisoner.' He finished his wine and crossed the room to stare out the window. 'Nisha questioned us about the British Army's movements.'

'But you weren't in the army. Surely, she must have known that.'

'She did. But none of that mattered to her. She and the others hated the British. I think her husband was killed in one of the battles. And, after seeing what the soldiers did to her people, I understand why the rebels wanted to harm us. They were fighting to protect their land and their families. And when Javas gave us into their hands, we were the scapegoats they could use for vengeance.'

Evie came to stand beside him at the window. Outside, the night was clear, the ground frozen with a layer of snow.

'Matthew suffered more than I did,' he confessed. 'I had earlier opportunities to escape, but I was afraid to act. I thought that, if I made a mistake, it would get us both killed. I kept waiting for someone to rescue us.' He expelled a breath. 'But Nisha could have killed both of us from the start. I didn't realise until later that she wanted us to suffer, out of her own rage. We were always meant to die. But slowly.' He took off his shirt and revealed the scars to her. Evie traced the ragged edge that had been carved into his flesh with a knife.

'I'm so sorry this happened to you.' Her expression was stricken, her eyes filled with unshed tears.

But he didn't want her pity. Not now. 'Matthew and I stopped talking after the first month. There was nothing to say any more. I was starting to realise that no one was coming for us.'

'How did you escape?' she asked softly.

James braced himself before revealing the worst of it. 'One night, we heard a little girl crying.' He turned to Evie, and his eyes burned with the force of his emotion. 'I don't know who she was or why she was there. Maybe she was the child of one of the rebels or another prisoner—I never found out. She cried for hours that night, and no one came for her. That was the night I finally stopped waiting to be rescued. Because part of me hoped I could save her.'

'It wasn't your fault,' Evie said, and she took his hand again. He squeezed it, wishing he hadn't been such a coward.

'But it was. I waited too long to escape.' His anger flared with self-hatred. 'I don't know what happened to the girl. If I had got us out sooner, maybe…' His words broke off. He'd never seen or heard the child again. But even now, her cries haunted his nightmares.

Evie's face was pale, but she ventured, 'Is that why you do not wish to have children?'

He gave a nod. 'Children are fragile. And knowing that I couldn't help that girl, it broke something in me. If I ever lost a child of my own…' He shook his head. 'I'd rather be childless than ever experience that sort of grief.'

'You mustn't blame yourself, James,' she said quietly.

'I disagree,' he said. 'It took a child to break me out of my own cowardice. After I heard the girl crying, I was willing to take any risk to get out. By the grace of God and I don't know what kind of luck, I attacked one of my guards and broke free on a night Nisha wasn't there. We barely got out alive, and Matthew couldn't walk. I had to carry him through the streets.'

He poured another glass of wine and drank half of it. 'It wasn't until a few weeks ago that I learned the truth about why we were truly imprisoned. After I saw her again at the ball.'

He turned to look at her, and his face held regret. 'I am sorry you faced Dunwood alone that night. But the moment I saw Nisha, her presence brought all the nightmares back. All the memories of captivity and torture. I knew our imprisonment had nothing to do with the British Army and everything to do with Adrian Monroe's ambitions to inherit the earldom.' He drained the rest of his wine. 'That night, I hesitated again. But Matthew didn't—he immediately went to Lily and protected her.'

'What happened to Nisha?' Evie asked. 'I heard rumours, but—'

'She fell upon her own blade, and Matthew was badly wounded.' He didn't look at his wife but admitted, 'People were hurt because of me. Matthew never would have gone to India, had I not suggested it. So many things could have been avoided, if I'd only acted sooner.'

Evie rested her cheek against his, and he drew her into his arms, taking comfort from her. When he pulled back, he said, 'And that's why I will not stand by again while someone tries to harm you. I'm going to end this threat with Dunwood, once and for all.'

Evie leaned in and brushed a kiss against his mouth. He studied her face, expecting to see disappointment or loathing. But instead, there was empathy. She rested her hand against his cheek and murmured, 'Then I'll stay here while you go to London.'

Chapter Twelve

James left the next day, and it was all Evie could do to keep herself from following him.

She wished she'd never made that agreement when all she wanted to do right now was summon a carriage and go riding after him. But a promise was a promise, even if she didn't like keeping it.

He'd told her the secrets about India that he'd been holding on to for the past two years. She couldn't imagine reliving those moments, and she now understood why he hadn't wanted to tell anyone. But more than that, she recognised the weight of guilt he carried. He blamed himself for not saving Matthew sooner and for waiting to be rescued.

And that was why he was riding to London now—in his own attempt to protect her. In return, all he wanted was for her to remain safe.

Maybe…that meant he was starting to care for her. Their marriage was so fragile, Evie didn't want to risk shattering it. Especially after he'd lowered the boundaries between them, sharing a part of his past that he'd told no one else.

So, after that, she'd had no choice but to stay behind.

Logically, she knew James was right. If there were still any kind of criminal charges against her, despite the bribes they'd paid, it wasn't wise for her to return to London. But she still worried about him. Lord Dunwood wasn't a reasonable man. If anything, he was a greedy, overbearing bastard who had done nothing except relentlessly pursue her. He wouldn't hesitate to threaten James. And she simply didn't know how to help her husband from so far away.

To distract herself from the worry, she'd spent the morning trying to learn about all her responsibilities at Penford. Although she'd hoped to spend time with the dowager, Lady Penford was having a difficult morning, and she'd refused to leave her room.

Which left her utterly alone. Evie wasn't accustomed to idleness, and it occurred to her that she needed to get better acquainted with the local villagers. Many families struggled during the winter, and she wanted to ensure that no one was facing hunger or need.

'Lady Penford,' one of the maids asked. 'Could I do that for you?'

It was then that Evie noticed she'd begun polishing the stair banister with a dusting cloth. 'Sorry, Ann.' She passed the cloth over to the maid. 'I was thinking about the villagers and didn't even notice what I was doing.'

Ann's expression grew curious. 'Is there anything you need, my lady?'

'I don't know the people here,' she admitted. 'I only met a few of them when I was shopping for Christmas gifts. But we've had a great deal of snow since then, and I wondered if anyone was…in need of assistance. Do they need any food for the winter or supplies?'

The maid appeared surprised. 'There are always folk in need. But the church takes care of them, and we look after one another.'

'I do not believe in anyone going hungry,' Evie said.

'It goes against everything I stand for. And if any of the people wish to work, I can try to help.' There was always a need for seamstresses in her family's business.

The maid's uneasy expression revealed that it was the last thing she'd expected her to say. Evie supposed the household staff would expect her to behave like an ordinary countess, someone who embroidered or played the piano. She'd grown so used to her family's servants, who were accustomed to their eccentric ways, that she'd forgotten no one really knew her here.

'I would like to visit the village,' Evie suggested. Her parents had always paid calls on the local villagers when they'd travelled to her father's home in Scotland. She might as well do the same here.

It was the best way to push aside her own troubles, she decided. Visiting others to learn what they needed was a wonderful way to take her mind off her fears, and it might also be a good way to distract the dowager as well. Lady Penford could help her make bundles and baskets of gifts. 'We could bring them supplies,' Evie suggested. 'Grain and food for the winter. Perhaps blankets or wool.'

'It's a good idea, my lady.' The maid quietly picked up the dusting cloth. 'But perhaps you should call upon them first. Get acquainted to find out what they need.'

'You're right,' she agreed. 'Will you ask Cook to prepare some ginger biscuits? I can bring them as gifts during the call. And later, we can load up a wagon with goods to deliver.'

'They may not accept your charity,' Ann warned. 'They do have their pride.'

Evie understood that. 'Perhaps not,' she acceded. 'But we could be discreet. After you speak with Cook, could you arrange for an escort? And I'll need my cloak and a muff.'

She thanked Ann and returned to her writing desk in the drawing room to start making lists of what they might need. Just then, the Dowager Lady Penford walked inside, followed by the housekeeper, Mrs Marlock. Lady Penford's hair was down around her shoulders, and she wore a bright blue ball gown.

For a moment, Evie wondered what to say. Then she complimented Iris. 'That's a lovely colour on you.'

'Most of my gowns are black, grey, and lavender,' Iris admitted. 'I don't know why everything I own is in such wearisome colours. Today, I wanted something more cheerful. George will want to see me in something pretty.'

Evie's smile grew strained, but she didn't try to correct the dowager. 'You do look lovely in blue.' But she realised Iris had been a widow for nearly two years, so it was time enough for her to set her mourning garb aside. 'Perhaps you'd like to go shopping with me today,' she suggested. 'We could pick out some new fabric for gowns.'

But Iris shook her head. 'There are wolves outside,' she warned. 'I saw them prowling, so we must be careful not to leave the house.' Her face was serious, even though her words made little sense.

'Wolves?' Evangeline set down her pen and gave the matron her attention. Though she didn't believe her, she felt she owed it to the dowager to hear her story. 'What do you mean? Tell me what you saw.'

The older woman's eyes held fear when she glanced at the window. 'I saw them outside, lurking.'

The housekeeper took a step inside the room and shook her head gently. Evie suspected that it had been a bad dream. Though she imagined that everyone had already told Lady Penford that there were no wolves, it wouldn't diminish the woman's fear.

'Are you all right?' she asked Iris gently as she stood from the desk.

At that, the dowager's face crumpled, and she rushed forward, reaching for Evie's hands. 'I am, yes. But I worry about you, sweet girl. And the baby.'

A rush of uncertainty flooded through her. 'I'm not—there is no baby.' Her courses had already come once, so she was certain of it. 'You must be thinking of your daughter, Rose.'

The dowager only sent her a sidelong look and said nothing. But the mention of a baby brought an empty ache within Evie. She wanted to believe that one day James might change his mind. Perhaps they could truly be husband and wife after he returned from London. Even if he didn't want a child now, he might consider it later. Something *had* changed between them, and it gave her a reason to hope.

The dowager released her hands and sat down in a chair. Her expression had gone vacant, and she began whispering to herself.

'I thought we might make some gifts to the villagers,' Evie began. 'Do you knit or crochet? We could make mittens or hats, if you like. Or we could bring them blankets and grain for the winter.'

But Lady Penford only continued whispering to herself. Evie overheard the word wolves, and she decided to let the dowager be. She motioned to Mrs Marlock to come forward. 'Bring Lady Penford some tea and breakfast. I'll watch over her.'

She brought her chair beside Lady Penford and asked, 'Have you heard from Rose or Lily?'

'No.' The dowager was twisting her hands together, the worry evident in her eyes. 'Where is James? He should be here.'

'He's gone to London, I'm afraid. But he will return in a few weeks.' Evie tried to keep her voice soothing, but she could already see that Lady Penford would not be deterred.

Instead, her agitation only increased. 'Send someone to fetch him back. The wolves are here. He needs to know.'

'I—all right,' she lied. 'I will send word to him.'

'Good,' the dowager said. 'And promise me you will not leave the estate. The wolves,' she repeated.

Evie nodded, though she couldn't imagine what was upsetting the older woman so much. She walked over to the window and asked, 'Could you...show me the wolves, Lady Penford?'

The older woman sighed. 'I suppose they are in the forest now. But they do come back. I saw one this morning.'

When the food arrived, Evie tried to coax the woman to eat, but the dowager only picked at a slice of toast.

She approached the housekeeper and asked Mrs Marlock in a low voice, 'Have you or any of the others noticed anything around the estate that could be bothering Lady Penford?'

'No, my lady. She does have these spells from time to time,' Mrs Marlock answered. 'There's little harm in them. We've found that when we let her believe what she wants, she's better for it.'

Evie kept her voice low and said, 'I do think I'd like to pay some calls this morning. But I don't want to upset the dowager.'

'We can watch over her here,' Mrs Marlock promised. 'There's no harm in it.'

Evie nodded and then returned to sit across from her

mother-in-law, 'Lady Penford, I will see you later this morning. I need to see to the household.'

The woman barely acknowledged her and continued to murmur to herself about the imaginary wolves.

After she left the room, Evie found Ann waiting for her with a cloak and a warm muff. 'Fred has the cutter waiting for ye, my lady. It'll be faster than a carriage because of the snow.'

Evie cast another look back at the drawing room, feeling sad for Lady Penford. But there was little they could do for the dowager.

'Please take care of her,' she said quietly. 'I'll return within a few hours.'

Evangeline spent the rest of the morning in the village visiting several of the families. She'd brought ginger biscuits for the children and had introduced herself to the tenants. All were respectful, but she sensed that she was keeping them from their work, so she didn't stay too long. But she had noticed which homes were cold during the winter, lacking enough wood or peat for the hearth. She'd also taken note of the children and whether they seemed hungry or well-fed.

At the last cottage, she took her basket with her while the footman escorted her. When the door opened, she saw a young woman holding a screaming baby. Behind her were two other young children, and it didn't seem as if they had eaten any time recently.

The footman wrinkled his nose, but Evie ignored him. 'Good morning. I am Lady Penford. I hope I've not disturbed you. I wanted to meet all the families.'

The woman paled and clutched the baby before she glanced behind her at the other two children. They appeared to be around four years old and two years old, Evie guessed. But she didn't know why the woman seemed so afraid of her.

'Would you and the children like any ginger biscuits?'

The woman still appeared fearful, but she nodded. 'Thank you, Lady Penford.' She bade the children sit down, all the while bouncing the baby in an attempt to soothe it. Even so, her gaze remained searching, as if she expected someone to return at any moment.

Evie gave the children each a ginger biscuit, and the boys devoured it before she'd had a chance to give one to their mother. Tears formed in the young woman's eyes, but she thanked Evie.

'What is your name?' she asked the mother.

'Gertrude,' the woman sniffled. 'I'm sorry about the baby crying, my lady. I've lost my milk, and I've naught to feed her just now.'

Evie murmured to the footman and gave him a coin, ordering Fred to bring back goat's milk for the infant. He obeyed and left them.

'I've sent my footman to fetch milk for the baby,' she explained. 'May I hold her?'

'She won't stop crying,' Gertrude said, breaking into sobs of her own. 'And I've no wish to give her up to another family.'

'I won't let that happen,' Evie said. 'We'll see to it that the baby is fed.' When the woman passed over the infant, yearning caught inside Evie as she patted the baby on the back and lifted it to her shoulder. She noticed a man's hat and cane lying upon the bed, and she asked, 'Where is your husband?'

'Buried in the churchyard,' Gertrude answered. 'Just last spring.' She clenched her hands together and said, 'I promise ye, I'll find a way to pay our rents. I just need to find work.'

A sadness caught Evie when she realised the woman was a widow. 'It's all right,' she said, still walking with the screaming baby. 'Do you sew?'

The woman shook her head. 'Not beyond mending.'

'We'll find something for you at Penford,' Evie promised. 'At least, something to help you get by.' Or until Gertrude could be taught to sew undergarments for Aphrodite's Unmentionables.

A few moments later, the footman returned with goat's milk, and the young mother prepared a bottle. Evie gave the baby back to her, and Gertrude broke down into sobs as she fed the infant. 'Thank you, my lady.'

'Come to Penford in the morning,' she instructed. 'Bring the children with you, and we will see if there is work you can do.'

Gertrude dried her tears and said, 'Thank you, my lady. I am grateful. But—' Her voice broke off and her face appeared pained. 'I am so sorry for the trouble I've caused you. I never meant to—' Her words broke off and she shook her head as the emotion overtook her.

It was a strange apology, but Evie dismissed it. 'It's no trouble at all.' She left another basket with the family with food from her own luncheon.

But after she departed, she felt a sense of exhaustion and sadness, mingled with purpose. She was glad she'd come to visit, but it bothered her that the young mother was struggling to feed her children.

As she climbed into the cutter, she glanced behind her. For a moment, she thought she saw a horse and rider disappearing into the trees. There were more footsteps in the snow, but that could easily have been her own servant when he'd gone to fetch the goat's milk.

She told herself she was being foolish for no reason. There was no reason for her own uneasiness. Perhaps, she was just feeling alone.

Evie raised her hood against the chill as the cutter moved through the snow, drawn by their horses. The wintry air was frigid, but there was a beauty in the stillness. For a moment, she drank in her surroundings, realising that Penford was truly a place where she could be happy. Not only was it peaceful, but she could find a way to take care of the people in the same way she'd helped women in London. She had more money than she could ever hope to spend, but her wealth meant so much more when it gave her the power to change the lives of so many, lifting them out of poverty. Her father had taught her that.

They continued driving back to the estate, and aside from their own tracks, the snow appeared undisturbed, a fresh layer having fallen early this morning. As they pulled closer to Penford, she thought of Lady Penford's claim that wolves were surrounding the house. What was the reason for the dowager's fears? Had it been nightmares? Or perhaps it was the fact that James had left for London. The more she thought of it, the more Evie realised that this could be the source of Lady Penford's terror. She hoped to reassure the dowager and help her have a better evening.

Her footman Fred drew the cutter to a stop and helped her out. Just as Evie was about to walk towards the house, she heard a loud braying noise coming from the stables.

She paused a moment and decided to see how her donkey was. It was unusual for him to make such noise, although Hotay was starting to show his personality and make mischief. Fred started to unhitch the horses from the cutter while Evie walked inside.

Hotay was practically screeching, and she called out, 'It's all right, Hotay.'

In the darkness, it took a moment for her eyes to adjust, but it was then that she saw a man standing on the far side of the stable near Hotay. It wasn't one of her servants, and her heart began pounding at the sight of him.

When he turned around, Lord Dunwood smiled. 'Hello, Evangeline.'

Chapter Thirteen

From the moment he'd left Penford, James felt uneasy.
He couldn't quite put his finger on it, but he'd taken the
note Dunwood had sent and studied the letter. Although
he supposed it was only idle threats, there was something
that unnerved him.

They had travelled south in the morning, but with every
mile, his sense of unrest deepened. Though logically he
knew Evie was safe, he wanted to turn around and return
to her. One moment, he thought he could distance himself and lead his own life. Then the next, he couldn't stop
thinking about her.

He remembered the smell of her skin, the hint of soap
and rose. Even now, he remembered her pressed close to
him, her soft curves against the hard planes of his body.
Her innocent touch had only kindled a fierce need.

Last night, he had told her about his nightmares of
India, revealing the truth he'd hidden for so long. He
hadn't known what she would say or believe about him.
He'd lived with his own self-hatred for so long, it seemed
that she should feel the same way, too. And why not? He
deserved the shame he'd earned.

He'd allowed himself to become complacent, to wait
for someone else to rescue them. And only the little girl's

torment had spurred him to act. It sickened him that he'd been so passive, he'd allowed this to happen. A part of him believed that Evie would view him with the same disappointment.

Instead, she'd held him, offering her own compassion. He'd slept through the night beside her without waking, for the first time in as long as he could remember. Rather than being horrified at his story, she had been steadfast. And somehow, it had lightened the guilt that he'd carried.

He studied the threat from Dunwood again, still wondering what it was that seemed strange about the note. It wasn't the words themselves—they were only empty threats and promises.

Part of him wondered if he was overreacting by taking this long journey to London. But the more he thought of it, the more he recognised that he couldn't stand aside and pretend as if Evie wasn't in danger. He couldn't ignore the parallels of his captivity in India. He hadn't acted then until it was nearly too late, and Matthew had suffered for it. James had no intention of making the same mistake with his wife.

He needed Dunwood to understand that any threats towards Evie would be answered swiftly and with severe consequences. And if that meant travelling for days, so be it.

But when he studied the letter, he suddenly noticed the postmark. The letter hadn't been posted from London.

Though he didn't recognise the marking, it occurred to him that there had been enough time for Dunwood to travel north. Perhaps the note wasn't a demand for money, but a means of luring him away from Penford. Although it was improbable, James couldn't dispel the possibility that the man might travel to the estate. And if he did, Evie was alone and unguarded.

James rapped on the door of his coach and alerted his coachman to stop. He opened the door and went to speak with the driver. Holding out the letter, he asked, 'Do you know where this was postmarked from?'

The driver studied the stamp. 'It looks like Barnsley, my lord.'

A chill caught him, for Barnsley was just over a day's ride from Penford. An inner sense warned him that Evie could be in danger. He'd mistakenly believed that the worst of the danger was in London—but this letter seemed to prove otherwise.

What if Dunwood had already travelled north to gain the element of surprise?

'We need to go back,' he told the coachman. He couldn't risk Evie being attacked a second time. Not if he could do something to stop it.

Dunwood's pride had been wounded, and he'd been injured by the gunfire. Although an initial bribe had convinced him to drop the charges against Evie, if he was still sending threats, then he clearly wanted to punish her. And James refused to let that happen.

A sudden clarity flooded through him. Evie was his wife, the woman he'd vowed to honour and cherish. She had filled his life with a brightness and a feisty spirit of joy that he loved. Being apart from her left a physical ache and a need to see her again.

He was in love with her.

The sudden realisation made him even more eager to reach her side. He didn't know how they would sort through their future, but he wanted those years with her.

The moments of dancing on Christmas Eve or throwing snow at one another.

Or sinking deeply into her body and experiencing a glimpse of heaven.

He stared at the written note from Dunwood and made a silent promise of his own. If the viscount dared to threaten her again, he would see to it that the man lost everything.

Terror sliced through Evie at the sight of Lord Dunwood. 'What are you doing here?'

The viscount's smile deepened as he limped a step forward. He leaned on a cane for balance. 'I've told you that already in my note. I came to ensure that you pay the consequences for your actions. I lost two toes because of your gunfire. Do you honestly believe that one bribe would atone for that?' As he came forward again, she took a few steps backwards. 'No, indeed. I intend to make you suffer the way I did.'

'You travelled all this way…for vengeance?' She could hardly believe it. The man had truly fallen into madness.

A chill slid over her with the fear that he intended to kill her. And James wasn't here to protect her. Her heart faltered at the realisation that she was utterly at this man's mercy. No one would save her, except herself.

Evie spun around, intending to run back to the house, but another man caught her. She had never seen him before, and she guessed he was Lord Dunwood's servant.

She let out a scream, but the servant clamped his hand over her mouth, cutting off the sound.

Lord Dunwood appeared utterly unconcerned. 'Bind her hands, John, and bring her back to the cutter.'

Evie fought against them, trying to break free. She bit her captor's hand, and John cursed before he struck her across her ear with his other fist. She saw stars and sagged a moment, dizziness washing over her. A moment later, he tied her wrists together with rope, shoving a dirty handkerchief into her mouth as a gag.

How could this be happening? Where were the servants? Where was Fred?

Her question was answered a moment later when John and the viscount forced her out of the stable. Her footman lay in the snow, blood pooling around his head while a shovel rested against the stable wall.

Dear God, what had they done to Fred? And what did they plan to do with her now?

The men hauled her towards the cutter, and Evie struggled against them. She tried to scream again, but the sound was muffled by the handkerchief. With a last, desperate look at the house, she hoped someone would notice what was happening. And yet, no one came out of the house. Why? She couldn't understand it.

John shoved her into the cutter, and Lord Dunwood gripped her hard around the waist while his servant hitched the horses back up. She fought, twisting against him, but his strength overpowered her.

'Don't expect anyone to search for you,' the viscount said coolly. 'The servants are rather occupied at the moment. The dowager has had one of her spells, you see.'

Evie stilled, terrified that he had somehow harmed Lady Penford. It was then that she realised the matron had tried to warn her. She'd asked Evie to stay indoors to avoid the 'wolves.'

No doubt Iris had meant Lord Dunwood and his servant, who were most definitely predatory.

Still, Evie found it hard to believe that none of the servants had seen her. Surely, one of them would find the footman soon enough and try to follow them. But, as the cutter pulled past the stable, Evie realised that John had already dragged Fred's prone figure into the shelter and kicked snow on top of the blood.

Her head ached, and the world seemed to spin as the cutter departed. But they followed the same tracks towards the village, which made her wonder where they were taking her.

Her mind was racing, fighting to come up with the right plan. She had no weapons, except her wits—and she already knew she lacked the physical strength to defend herself from the men. Lord Dunwood tried to pull her on to his lap, and she elbowed him hard.

He only tightened his grip on her and leaned in against her ear. 'You can fight me all you want, Evangeline. I'll only enjoy it more.'

Evie stopped her struggling then, realising the viscount's intent. The last thing she needed was an injury that would prevent her from running away. She held back her sobs, knowing she would have to wait for the right opportunity to break free. But instead of driving towards the village, the cutter pulled away in a different direction.

She wanted to cry out for help, but the gag in her mouth prevented her from making any noise at all. They continued travelling, nearly a mile away, until she saw what appeared to be an abandoned church. The years had not been kind to the structure, and the stones were crumbling from the foundation. Even the roof was falling apart.

Was he truly taking her here to…assault her? It was far enough away from the village that no one would hear her, which was likely why they'd chosen the spot.

Evie swallowed back her fear, forcing herself to concentrate on her escape. Her father had taught her how to shoot, but neither man had a pistol, it seemed. Or even a knife.

She would have to make her escape soon, and her best hope was to run into the forest. Lord Dunwood couldn't keep up because of his limp, and the cutter couldn't go through the trees. Which left her to defend herself against one man.

She had to find a way to get them to lower their guard. And that meant playacting to make them believe she was weak.

It didn't take long to conjure up tears. She lowered her shoulders and began sobbing. Her tears seemed to satisfy the viscount, and he relaxed his hold on her.

'You see, now, what mistakes you've made,' Dunwood said quietly. 'And while I intend to punish you for your misdeeds, I am a forgiving man.' He let the reins go slack. 'But do not, for a moment, believe that you will ever be permitted to misbehave again. I do not tolerate defiance in a wife.'

Was he still under the delusion that she was unmarried? Her confusion must have shown in her face, and he shrugged. 'It isn't difficult to make you a widow. There are any number of brigands in London who will gladly kill the earl.'

'I will never marry you!' she muttered against her gag.

'What was that?' he asked. 'Now that we're away from the village, I would like to hear your apology.'

Lord Dunwood took out the gag, and it took Evie a moment to choose her words. If she lashed out at the viscount, he would only force the handkerchief back into her mouth. And she needed her ability to scream for help.

'Why—?' She coughed a moment, trying to force out

the words. 'Why would you still want me, Lord Dunwood? Surely, there were other women who wanted to marry you.' She kept her tone even, playing into his vanity.

'But none had a dowry such as yours,' he pointed out. '*You* were the one being stubborn and wilful. Your father should have beaten your pride out of you, years ago.'

'What do you want from me?' she managed, even as she was staring at the forest straight ahead.

Just a little farther, she told herself. She had to choose her escape plan carefully.

'I want what I deserve,' he answered. 'And if you are an obedient wife, you will be cared for and protected.' He smiled slightly. 'I shall enjoy taming you. I enjoy your spirit, and I look forward to breaking it.'

The cutter slowed as they travelled towards the abandoned church. Now was her best opportunity to flee. Evangeline slammed the back of her head into Lord Dunwood's face, and pain blasted through her skull, even as she freed herself from his grasp.

The viscount let out a growl, but she had already leaped out of the cutter and was running through the snow towards the woods. Her hands were still bound, but it didn't affect her feet. She raced uphill, struggling with her skirts as she reached the tree-line. Behind her, she heard John cursing as he followed her.

Almost to the top, she told herself as she struggled through the crunching snow. *Don't stop.*

But when she reached the apex, the snow had turned to ice. Her footing slipped, and she slid down the hill and screamed as loudly as she could before she was caught by Dunwood's guard. She hoped that somehow, someone might have heard her.

John struck her across the face, and she tasted blood.

This time, her tears were real when she realised that her hopes of escape were falling apart. She stared back towards the empty horizon but could see no one at all.

Help me, she prayed silently. *Help me find a way out of this.*

The viscount was already limping towards the church, and John carried her, this time holding her so tightly, she could scarcely breathe. She tried again to scream, but no sound came out.

She twisted and fought, trying desperately to break free. And then, a moment later, she heard the unmistakable braying of a donkey. What on earth?

The men began laughing, and in the distance, Evie caught a glimpse of Lady Penford riding Hotay downhill. The matron wore the blue ball gown, her cloak, and a bonnet, riding the donkey as if she were a white knight on horseback. Hotay was trotting swiftly through the snow, his head raised as if he were a proud Arabian stallion.

It was both wonderful and terrifying. She couldn't believe that Lady Penford had left the estate alone, much less with Hotay. And yet, she was so afraid that the men would hurt the dowager. She didn't want any harm to come to the older woman.

'I see that Lady Penford has come to rescue you,' Lord Dunwood said. 'How quaint.'

'Leave her alone,' Evie pleaded. 'She's—'

'Addled in the head is what she is,' John finished. 'Perhaps we'll put her out of her misery.'

The men dragged her inside the ruins of the church, seemingly unconcerned about the dowager. Evie could only pray that Lady Penford had brought some of the other servants with her. Or better, if they pursued her.

Lord Dunwood removed his jacket and pointed towards a wooden pew. 'Put her there.'

She began to fight harder, twisting and turning in the man's grasp, but Dunwood held her fast. 'Remember what I said, Evangeline. If you continue to fight, I will only punish you more.' His eyes gleamed with interest, and her blood chilled.

Evie screamed as loudly as she could, in the hopes that a servant might hear her. The viscount struck her jaw, and pain exploded in her cheek. He shoved another handkerchief into her mouth, making it impossible to scream.

Only a moment later, she heard the harsh braying of Hotay from outside. Lady Penford came riding inside, brandishing a candlestick.

In a cool voice, she demanded, 'Take your hands off my daughter-in-law.'

James couldn't find his wife or mother anywhere at Penford. One of his footmen, Fred, was in the hallway downstairs, clutching his bleeding head.

'Where are they?' James demanded.

'My lord, I'm so sorry. I didn't see where they took her,' Fred apologised. 'The countess is gone.'

'I'm so sorry,' Mrs Marlock apologised. 'Lady Penford was beside herself, screaming about wolves. We were trying to calm her down. When Jenkins told us that the countess had been taken, we tried to search the grounds. Lady Penford went riding off before we could stop her. We were just about to go after her.'

James levelled a stare at the housekeeper. 'I want every able-bodied man to help me find them. And they must be armed.' He hurried into the study and gathered two duelling pistols, loading both with ammunition. Then he took a decorative sword from the wall and handed it to another footman who was waiting. 'Take this.'

It infuriated him that no one had pursued the women yet. It was only when he found the stablemaster waiting outside with several saddled horses that his anger calmed slightly.

'My lord.' The servant offered him a gelding, and several other footmen chose their mounts. 'The donkey is gone, but we think Lady Penford took it.'

James mounted his horse, grateful that the snow revealed the tracks of both the cutter and the donkey. Though he hated the thought of both his wife and mother in danger, he was glad that Iris had followed. It made it somewhat easier to track them.

A little farther where the trail diverted, he saw his mother's glove in the snow, a vibrant red marker of the path she'd taken.

Let them be all right, he prayed. *Let me be there in time to save them.*

The cutter had taken a different path from the village, and they tracked it nearly a mile away. James rode as fast as he could, trailed by his men. His heart was pounding, and he leaned against his horse, unsure of what he would find. Clearly, the viscount was beyond reason if the man would travel this far, just for vengeance—or worse.

But he would defend his wife at all costs. The thought of her being in danger sent a chill through him. His defiant, courageous Evie didn't deserve this. When he thought of everything she'd endured, it sobered him to realise that he was quite willing to kill the viscount for what he'd done. And he didn't even care what that meant for his own future.

In the distance, James saw the abandoned church, and he urged his horse to go faster. The glare of sunlight on the snow was blinding, but he kept his head down and focused on what lay ahead.

As soon as he reached the entrance to the church, he swung down from his horse and cocked the pistols, prepared for anything. Three footmen trailed him, just as heavily armed.

James stormed into the church and saw a stocky man he didn't recognise, holding Evie down. She was still trying to fight back, and blood was flowing from her temple. Behind them, on another church bench, his mother lay unconscious.

A blend of rage and fear pulsed through him when he saw the viscount's shirt hanging out. James levelled his pistol at the man. 'Let go of my wife.'

'Or what? You'll murder me?' Dunwood taunted. He lifted Evie up and used her as a shield. 'Careful with that pistol, Penford. You might shoot your wife instead.'

The moment Evie saw him, she began sobbing. Whether it was fear or relief, he didn't know, but he reassured her, 'It's all right. I'm here.'

Lord Dunwood nodded to the other man. 'Take care of the earl.'

The other footmen joined James, and one of them lifted his sword at the stocky man. 'Don't come any closer, or I'll gladly skewer you.'

'You wouldn't know which end to use,' Evie's captor replied with a leer.

And unfortunately, he was right. The moment the footman swung the sword, the larger man dodged the blow and caught the servant by the neck, squeezing tightly. Before he could harm the footman, James seized the weapon and stabbed the man. For a moment, the assailant appeared confused as blood welled up, and he staggered backwards. Then he slumped to the ground.

'It's a good thing I *do* know which end to use,' James remarked, handing the sword back to his footman, who was clutching his throat and gasping. He kept the pistol trained on the viscount and moved forward. 'Let her go.'

Lord Dunwood only smiled. 'You wouldn't dare shoot me.'

'You've been threatening my wife for months now. I won't hesitate.' And he meant what he said. He was furious with the viscount for daring to harm Evie. He only needed one chance to end this, once and for all.

But Dunwood only shifted Evie's position and kept his arm across her throat. 'If you want her to live, you'll lower that pistol.'

James had no intention of doing so—and yet, he was aware that he couldn't pull the trigger with Evie in place. 'If *you* want to live, you'll let my wife go,' he countered. 'This is your last and only warning.'

A slight movement caught James's attention, but he didn't dare move or let himself get distracted. He met Evie's gaze and nodded to her. Though he knew she was tired and suffering, he needed her to fight. 'Evie Sinclair is no man's prisoner,' he insisted. 'She is a strong countess in her own right.'

After he spoke, he gave a nod, and his wife began to struggle harder. While the viscount clutched her by the throat, Evie stomped both of her feet down on his injured foot. Dunwood lurched, cursing at her, but she ducked low, leaving James with a clear shot.

But just as he pulled the trigger, he saw his mother rise

up from behind the viscount, swinging her candlestick at Dunwood's head.

Blood covered her gown, and Iris crumpled backwards.

Oh, God. He'd missed.

Chapter Fourteen

The weight of Dunwood's body dragged Evie down, and though she tried to pry herself free, her hands came away slick with blood. The viscount fell to the ground, clutching his chest.

Her husband rushed forward, but James halted beside her, his attention caught by the dowager, who was also on the ground, covered in blood.

'Is she all right?' Evie asked, horrified to realise that James had pulled the trigger, not knowing if he'd struck both of them.

'My pride is wounded,' came the elderly woman's voice. 'I lost my balance, and my ball gown is a mess. I'll never be able to wear it again.'

Evie started to laugh through her tears, and they both reached out to help her up. Lady Penford winced at the sight of the blood. 'The blood's not mine, don't worry yourselves. After I took a swing at that blackguard's head, I fell.'

'Thank God,' James said. 'I thought I'd shot you.'

The dowager reached out and hugged him. 'I'm fine, you needn't fear.' But then, she turned serious and eyed the footmen. 'You will be our witnesses, if needed. And when the constable asks you what happened, you are going to tell him that it was *I* who pulled the trigger and shot Lord Dunwood to defend my daughter-in-law.'

Understanding dawned within Evie. If the dowager took responsibility, she would not suffer in the same way. Everyone already believed she was mad.

'I will tell the police that Lord Dunwood tried to strangle me,' Evie said. 'You both came to my defence.'

James pulled her into his arms then, and she laid her head against his chest. Despite her tears, she'd never been happier to be in his arms. 'Thank you for coming back.'

'I never should have left,' James remarked. 'The moment I realised the letter wasn't sent from London, we returned.'

Evie was dimly aware of James giving instructions to the footmen to send for the constable, but right now, she could only be grateful that none of them had been harmed. And Lord Dunwood would never come after her again.

Her hands were shaking as she held on to her husband, even a few hours later, after they had spoken to the constable and the undertaker had removed the bodies. They brought Hotay back to his stall, and James gave the donkey an extra bucket of feed for the animal's heroism.

'I was so happy and scared when I saw your mother riding him,' Evie said. 'She truly tried to save me.'

'I never knew a donkey could go that fast,' James confessed. 'It made it easier to track where they'd taken you.'

Once they reached the house, Lady Penford was already walking up the stairs, accompanied by a maid fussing over her.

Evie still felt shaken, and James turned to her. 'I've ordered hot baths for both of you. I'll give you privacy,' he promised.

'No, I... I want you to stay with me,' she pleaded.

He hesitated a moment but nodded. 'I'll be upstairs shortly.'

The servants were already bringing up buckets of hot water, and Evie was grateful for it. She was still covered in the viscount's blood, and she fully planned to burn her clothing. She never wanted to wear it again, for the gown was utterly ruined.

After she was inside her room, her maid helped her undress. Evie sank into the tub of water, washing herself with soap. She dismissed the maid, wanting time to be alone.

Even after she scrubbed herself, over and over, she couldn't stop thinking of the way the men had tried to hurt her. It was a nightmare that kept trying to interfere with her feelings of safety.

And perhaps that was what it had been like for James. It was hard to pretend as if nothing had happened, returning to the rest of her life. If her husband hadn't come back, she didn't want to think of what the viscount would have done to her. Lord Dunwood's cruelty was beyond anything she'd ever imagined.

It would take time to drive away the fears and the harsh memories. But she told herself she could get through this. James *had* rescued her when she'd needed him most, just as Iris had come to help. A warmth slid through her, and she tried to hold fast to that memory instead.

A soft knock sounded at the door, and she heard James ask, 'May I come in?'

'Y-yes.' She drew up her knees, and the door opened quietly.

He closed the door behind him and asked, 'How are you?'

She didn't know how to answer that. Although she

knew she should answer, 'Fine,' it wasn't really true. Her body and mind were still racing, and she couldn't quite calm down.

'I think I understand how you felt when you returned from India,' she admitted. 'I try not to think of what happened to me—but it will take time for this memory to fade.'

He held back and asked, 'What can I do to help?'

Evie met his gaze and took a moment to breathe. 'Will you hold me?' She wanted his arms around her, but more than that, she wanted to feel safe again.

He walked forward slowly and reached for a towel on the chair. She twisted the water from her hair, and when he stood before her, she rose from the bath and took the towel from him. After she wrapped it around herself, he lifted her out of the tub and brought her to stand by the warm fire. Then he pulled her into his arms and simply held her close.

'Thank you,' she murmured.

The water dripped from her, but she was so grateful to be in his arms again, she said nothing else.

'There were many nights when I woke up and didn't know where I was,' he confessed. 'Sometimes, I could hardly breathe.'

She understood that more fully now. But more than that, she hated the idea of allowing this fear to command her life. She wanted it gone, driven out of her memories.

'James,' she whispered. 'Will you kiss me?'

He cupped her nape and leaned in, capturing her mouth. The warmth of his lips and the strength of his body were what she needed most right now. She wound her arms around his neck, and the towel slipped slightly. His tongue slid against hers, and she welcomed him inside, letting herself fall beneath his spell.

'You are the only man I've ever wanted,' she said against his mouth. 'And forgive me if I need you to push away every last memory of him. Please.'

'You don't ever have to beg me, Evie,' he said, removing his jacket. 'After I realised you were in danger, I could think of nothing more than coming back to protect you.' He cupped her face between his hands. 'I was an idiot to think I wanted a marriage in name only. When the truth is, I want everything.'

Tears caught up in her eyes again, spilling over with happiness. 'I love you, James. And I want a real marriage, too.'

She helped him remove his shirt and traced the edges of his body. The soft touch of her fingers drove him towards his own madness. His body was hard and aching for her, and he needed to feel her body, skin to skin.

'I love you, too,' he answered. 'I can't ever imagine living apart from you. Not any more.'

When she rested her hands upon his thundering heart, she let the towel drop, baring her naked body. He started to pull her close, but she reached for the buttons of his trousers.

And God help him, he couldn't strip his clothes off fast enough. He needed her close to him, needed to taste every inch of that beautiful skin.

When he stood naked before her, she came into his arms, and he lifted her up while she wrapped those long legs around him. It was all he could do not to take her now, pressing himself inside her up against the wall. But he wanted to savour this moment. Although it was not their first time of lovemaking, he intended to brand every second of it into their memories until she could remember nothing else.

He brought her back to her bed and laid her down upon it. Her dark hair was wet against her skin, and he leaned down to kiss the droplets away.

'It's cold,' she said, shuddering. He moved upon her body, shielding her from the air, until she sighed. 'That's better.'

It was, except that she had opened her legs slightly, and his erection was cradled between her thighs. She shifted against him slightly, and a searing flare of desire caught him, making him aware of her wetness.

He needed a distraction right now, something to take his mind off how easy it would be to simply guide himself inside. And so, he bent down and took her nipple into his mouth, savouring it with his tongue. As he'd hoped, she gave a slight cry and arched against him. While he tasted her sweetness, he caressed her other breast, arousing her nipple as he tormented her with his mouth.

'I need you so much,' she said. Reaching down, she took his shaft in her palm, squeezing it gently and easing him to her entrance.

'I want to make this good for you,' he said, his voice holding by a thread.

Her blue eyes met his. 'It's always good between us, James. But please, don't make me wait. Not now.'

And he understood, then, her need for haste. Slowly, he eased himself inside with gentle, shallow strokes. She sighed, meeting his thrusts as he went deeper each time.

It was, quite possibly, the most incredible sensation he'd ever felt. Being connected to his wife like this, watching her eyes flare with need that mirrored his own simply disintegrated every last barrier between them. He could no more deny her than he could deny his own needs.

He could feel her clenching him deep inside, and the exquisite pleasure made his breathing unsteady.

She drew her knees up to give him deeper access, and when he finally embedded himself fully, she met his body with her own, making love to him just as he did to her. She had always been his equal, challenging him. Pushing him to be more than what he was.

And he loved this woman, from her ridiculously coloured ball gowns, to the way she argued with him. He quickened his pace, seizing her bottom as he thrust and withdrew. He kept up his pace, and she guided his head back to her breast in a silent demand. He could feel her straining against him as her breath came in quick gasps, and his own need was barrelling fast.

But he wanted her to experience the pleasure first. He slowed down, keeping a steady rhythm of penetration until he felt her trembling and arching, her face pained with need. With one more stroke, she broke apart, half sobbing as he pushed her over the edge of release. He could feel her body welcoming him, the inner walls spasming against him. He drove within her a few more times until he allowed his own pleasure to erupt and spilled himself inside her.

His body reverberated against hers, giving as much as she could take. And when he lay spent against her, the scent of her hair was a welcome sensation as he collapsed upon her.

'I love you,' he said again, kissing her.

'I love you, too.' She reached out to touch his face and stroked his cheek. Emotion held her in its grip, and she ventured, 'We could have a child from this. Is that…all right?'

A knot clenched in his throat, but he understood that their marriage was far more important than the nightmares of the past. And with her, he could overcome all of it. 'I want to make you happy, Evie. That matters more than anything else. If it's a child you want, then we will keep trying.'

She smiled at him, and he leaned in to kiss her again. 'I'm not very good at this,' he said. 'It will take time for me to learn everything you desire.'

Evie's smile turned wicked. 'Then, I suppose we'll just have to practise.'

Epilogue

Eighteen years later

'I do not want to go to a ball, Mother,' her daughter Mari moaned. 'Why is it necessary?'

Evie smiled and opened up a trunk of her older ball gowns. 'It's a family Christmas tradition. My mother forced me to go, years ago, even though I didn't want to. And I ended up marrying your father because of it.'

The ball was being hosted by the Earl and Countess of Arnsbury, in honour of their eldest daughter, Catherine. They had been married nearly as long as James and herself, and no one had ever questioned Matthew's claim to the earldom again. Arnsbury had banished his cousin Adrian to America, after he'd bought up all the man's debts, and thankfully, they had never seen him since.

James chose that moment to enter the room, a bemused smile upon his face. Though his brown hair was now tinged with grey, he was still as handsome as ever.

'Your mother was, and still is, the most beautiful woman in London,' he remarked. 'And as I recall, she had some rather memorable gowns. You might wish to borrow one of them, Mari. I quite fell in love with her when I saw her in them.'

'Now, which one was your favourite?' Evie teased. 'The one the colour of mouse fur or the one the colour of horse dung?'

Her husband winked at her, and she smiled slowly with a promise for later. When she turned back to the dresses, she held up a brown one, and Mari's face held horror as James laughed. 'Both were indeed eye-catching.'

'You are not serious.' Mari stared at them. 'I would never wear a gown like that. Why would you, Mother?'

'Your mother could have worn anything, and she captivated my full attention,' James said.

'I see no reason for me to attend a Christmas ball,' Mari said to Evie. 'I don't even like to dance.'

'But there will be cake,' Evie countered.

'That's not a reason to go.' Her daughter sighed and pleaded, 'Don't ask me to do this, Mother. I don't know why you ever agreed to the invitation.'

'When I was your age, I attended family balls because it was expected of me,' Evie said. 'And you will do the same.'

'But it will be awful,' Mari moaned.

'It won't be. You'll see your friends, and you might meet someone. It's how I fell in love with your father.' She tried to reassure her daughter, but Mari would have none of it.

'We're not the same,' Mari insisted. 'I'm not going to find a husband.'

'You might be surprised,' Evie countered. 'Contrary to what your father says, there was a time when he was adamantly opposed to marriage.'

'You changed my mind,' he said, leaning down to steal a kiss.

'Will you both stop?' Mari pleaded. 'It's bad enough

that the two of you still kiss each other around all of us. It's not respectable.'

Evie saw the glint in her husband's eyes, along with the promise that they could be quite disrespectful later on. She smiled at him as she put the ball gown away, for she fully intended to make good on that promise.

'I used to be a wallflower, you know,' she told her daughter. 'Before I became the worst sort of shrew.'

'You're lying,' Mari accused. 'You could never be a shrew. You're entirely too nice to everyone.'

'Oh, I assure you, I was,' Evie answered. 'I had a dreadful reputation.'

'The worst,' James teased, offering his hand as she turned around.

'Indeed.' But it was clear that their daughter didn't believe a word of it. Evie continued, 'Truly, Mari, all I want is for you to be yourself. And if a gentleman doesn't like who you are, let him be. He's unworthy of you.'

'And if he dares to take liberties, your mother will shoot him,' James said. 'She *is* an excellent shot, after all.'

Their daughter gave a groan of disbelief and left the room. After she was gone, Evie turned back into her husband's arms. 'Just think, James. We only have to endure this four more times.'

He leaned in to kiss her. 'Five daughters and two sons. I never imagined we would have such a family. But I'm glad of it.'

'So am I.' She embraced him hard, so grateful for all the years of happiness they'd shared together.

And all the years still yet to come.

* * * * *

If you enjoyed this story,
why not read Michelle Willingham's
The Legendary Warriors miniseries?

The Iron Warrior Returns
The Untamed Warrior's Bride
Her Warrior's Redemption

And let yourself get swept up in her captivating
Untamed Highlanders duology

The Highlander and the Governess
The Highlander and the Wallflower

Harlequin® Reader Service

Enjoyed your book?

Try the perfect subscription for Romance readers and get more great books like this delivered right to your door.

See why over 10+ million readers have tried Harlequin Reader Service.

Start with a Free Welcome Collection with free books and a gift—valued over $20.

Choose any series in print or ebook. See website for details and order today:

TryReaderService.com/subscriptions